Would Napier and his cronies slip through their fingers?

When a fugitive had billions at his fingertips, the odds against justice being served leaped from daunting to astronomical. But the odds-makers, like Napier himself, had reckoned without Mack Bolan.

Brognola knew from personal experience that the Executioner wouldn't quit—ever. He'd stalk Napier around the world and back again, to do the job at any cost. Katzenelenbogen's death aside, it was Bolan's style, the way he made war. No quarter. No refuge. No mercy.

If Napier thought his nemesis would tire, get bored, or find another cause, he had misjudged the Executioner. The hunt was on and there was no turning back.

Brognola almost felt sorry for Bolan's quarry. Almost. Hell was coming. And if Napier stopped to listen, he would hear the flames.

D0913536

Don Pendleton's **Mack Bolan**®

Retaliation

A GOLD EAGLE BOOK FROM
WORLDWIDE®

TORONTO • NEW YORK • LONDON
AMSTERDAM • PARIS • SYDNEY • HAMBURG
STOCKHOLM • ATHENS • TOKYO • MILAN
MADRID • WARSAW • BUDAPEST • AUCKLAND

First edition November 2003

ISBN 0-373-61493-4

Special thanks and acknowledgment to
Mike Newton for his contribution to this work.

RETALIATION

Against naked force the only possible defense is naked force. The aggressor makes the rules for such a war; the defenders have no alternative but matching destruction with more destruction, slaughter with greater slaughter.

—Franklin D. Roosevelt
August 21, 1941

Our enemies have given us no choice. We're matching force with force, terror with terror.

—Mack Bolan

To our frontline soldiers in the war on terror.
God keep.

CHAPTER ONE

The Syrian frontier

Mack Bolan watched the desert landscape sweeping past beneath him, bathed in moonlight, seemingly close enough to touch. Ten minutes had elapsed since the Sikorsky Super Stallion helicopter crossed the border into Syria from Israel. There was no line in the sand to be observed by day or night, but Jack Grimaldi had announced it from the cockpit with two simple words: "We're in."

In danger, that would be.

In trouble so deep there might be no saving any of them if the operation blew up in their faces.

In the shit, David McCarter might have said, if he'd been talking rather than intently double-checking gear and guns.

But were they in time?

Bolan couldn't answer that one until the chopper set them down and they covered the last two miles to their target on foot—and what would happen then? They were three against fifty or sixty, minimum, and Grimaldi had sworn to stay out of it unless he got the killing signal. Only then would he return with mini-guns and rockets to mop up the target, and by then it would most likely be too late.

Alive or dead, they would've failed.

"Seven minutes," Grimaldi announced.

Ten minutes since they'd crossed the border, running under radar, and seven more to reach their drop point. The Sikorsky's cruising speed averaged 173 miles per hour, which meant they were making good time. It would be all for nothing, though, the flight and what came afterward, unless they found Ammar Samman where the rat had predicted he'd be.

The rat hadn't wanted to give up his info at first. Another rat had given up *his* name for money, but the low man on the food chain was a fighter, committed to the cause he served. It had taken two days and part of a third to convince him that discretion was the better part of valor. Rebecca Mindel's people handled the interrogation, hammering away at one question and only one until the young man broke. It was distasteful business but they had the answer now, for what it might be worth.

Mindel's people had recommended a surgical air strike. An F-4 Phantom in the night, perhaps, with fuel-air bombs to fry the life from every breathing thing and fuse the very desert sand into a sea of molten glass. Bolan had argued long and hard against scorched earth this time, because it would've left him in the dark and let the men behind the front-line enemy escape to plot another day.

And that was unacceptable.

He had a score to settle with the men he sought, wherever they had gone to ground. It was a blood debt, granted, but it went beyond revenge. Payback was only part of it, and not the greatest part at that.

Bolan had reason to believe their grand design was operational despite setbacks, still more or less on track. Revenge was pointless if he couldn't stop them cold, before they cleared the finish line. Unless he killed the *plan,* it made no difference what happened to the men.

And to locate them, Bolan needed Ammar Samman.

"One minute!" Grimaldi said.

"Final check," Bolan replied, going over his gear from habit more than from necessity. The AKS assault rifle was ready, cocked and locked. Likewise, the Beretta 93-R semiauto pistol on his right hip, tied down in a gunfighter's style. The rest of Bolan's gear was ammunition and grenades, canteens and basic medical supplies. He carried nothing in the way of food, because he didn't plan on being down that long.

If he was on the ground more than three hours, chances were that he'd be dead and snacks would be superfluous.

"It's time!" Grimaldi announced, and they could feel the chopper settling, vertical descent bringing Bolan's stomach into his throat the same way it had on his first combat drop. Some things never changed.

He let McCarter lead the way, Mindel close behind him. Bolan lingered for a last word with their pilot, while the chopper hovered six feet off the ground, riding a swirl of dust.

"Remember what we talked about," the soldier stated.

"I know, I know," Grimaldi said. "Wait for the squeal."

"Whichever way it goes."

"Whichever way. I hear you."

Bolan slapped his old friend on the shoulder and bailed out, dropping into a crouch and scuttling through the sandstorm with his eyelids narrowed to slits. When the Sikorsky lifted off and banked away, it felt as if the rotor wash might suck him after it, but gravity hung on and Bolan cleared the settling pall of sand.

"This way?" McCarter asked him, pointing off to the northeast.

Bolan spent several precious seconds with his compass. "That way," he confirmed.

The three of them began to run.

TWO MILES AND SOMETHING to their target from the drop, McCarter thought. It was an easy run by moonlight, over flat and fairly solid ground. The drill instructors who had tried their best to break him years before, when he was still a green recruit with SAS, would call it nothing but an easy lap around the track. Soldiers were driven to the limits of endurance in training for precisely that reason, so that they could run for miles on hostile ground and still reach their destinations ready to kill or to die, whatever the mission might demand.

Killing tonight, McCarter told himself. We'll let the other bastards die.

He didn't check his speed to let Rebecca Mindel keep up, and there was no need for it. After all they'd been through the past two weeks, her stamina was taken for granted, fueled by anger and a strong desire for revenge.

McCarter shared her feelings in that respect, wanting a chance to spill some blood on behalf of her uncle—his friend—but the mission took priority over vengeance. Sublimating rage, he reckoned Katz would understand.

The Briton counted footfalls, judging every stride to be another yard behind him, closer to the target. Marking off the distance helped, along with regulated breathing. It gave him a sense of progress toward his goal, when all about him looked the same as far as he could see. Soon the enemy should be within his reach.

But would they find the man they sought?

McCarter had memorized photos of Ammar Samman, trusting that he could recognize the man on sight under most conditions short of pitch darkness. He had studied the face not to smash it, however. This time he was hoping to bring its owner back alive.

For a while, anyway.

McCarter ran with simple grace, feeling the bandoleers of ammunition slap his ribs with every step. Their weight was comforting. Surveillance estimated sixty shooters in the Arab camp at any given time, and sometimes twice that many doubled up in crowded tents. No matter. With the gear he carried, if they didn't drop him first, McCarter could kill each mother's son among them three to six times each. Bolan and Mindel helping out meant they were into bloody righteous overkill.

And if that wasn't enough to do the job, he'd fight the bastards hand-to-hand.

But one of them was meant to live, at least until he talked. Whether Samman was in the camp this night or not, they needed one live tongue wagging to send them on their way.

Desert nights were cold, whether a trekker found himself shivering on the Sahara, the Gobi, the Kalahari or the alkali wastes of Death Valley. It was a cosmic joke of nature that desert wildlife had to hide from the relentless heat by day, then search for sunbaked stones to keep them warm by night. Cold or not, McCarter was sweating by the time he finished the first half a mile, and with the best part of a second well behind him now, he hoped the men he'd come to surprise wouldn't smell him coming.

That thought led him to an image of Rebecca Mindel, running on his left, but McCarter dismissed the thought before it could take root and distract him. She was a woman, certainly, but they were fellow soldiers at the moment, and she had her grief besides. Altogether, it was the worst possible time and place for a distraction.

Hold on, he thought. *We're almost there.*

REBECCA MINDEL SEIZED the opportunity to catch her breath. She would've run all night, if need be, but that form of exercise had never been her favorite. The gear she carried weighed nearly one-quarter of her body weight, slim as she was, but no complaint escaped her lips. She was intent on listening, absorbing what she had to know and what she had to do.

To stay alive.

To make it right.

They had one target in the camp. The other sixty or one hundred men were rifle fodder, but the trick was this: if they missed Ammar Samman somehow, they'd have to choose another of his men to milk for information, and they couldn't know which of them was the best choice. It thus became a challenge, and she hoped she wouldn't let the others down.

She owed this to her uncle, more than anything, although he'd never know what happened here tonight. Mindel had no settled opinions on the afterlife, but she didn't believe the dead kept watch on those they left behind. If that were true, she'd have been paralyzed for fear of doing anything at all.

The camp was spread before them in a natural declivity that hid the tents and single-story buildings from a casual observer passing relatively close to the east or west. It didn't spare the camp from aerial surveillance, though, nor did the camou netting stretched overhead between poles prevent infrared cameras from noting signs of human habitation underneath. Sun-warmed equipment, generators, cooking fires and body heat—all registered and were recorded on the fly.

A missile or a "smart" bomb could've easily found the camp and leveled it, but this mission demanded the personal touch. Mindel was lucky, after everything, that she had been allowed to come along. Her superiors had initially protested, citing her uncle's death as a distraction and unsettling influence, but they'd finally conceded that her established working relationship with David McCarter and Mike Blanski made it impractical to insert a new player so late in the game. They would trust her to a point, but if she faltered...

They were splitting up again, the plan determined well before they boarded the Sikorsky for their moonlight run across the border. It was triply dangerous that way, but also more efficient. Ammar Samman wasn't quite the proverbial needle in a haystack, but they still had better odds of spotting him and taking him alive if they divided forces and fanned out around the camp.

Above all else, Mindel wanted to do it right, locate the men responsible for her uncle Yakov's death and punish them, defeat their plan for wiping Israel off the map.

Estranged as she had been from her religion for the past decade or more, Mindel found time to offer up a silent prayer. She didn't know if anyone was listening, but reckoned it could do no harm.

Blanski briefly ran down the plan again, his voice a whisper in the night. Mindel would take the southwest corner of the camp, nearest to where they stood. Blanski and McCarter would circle away toward the east and northwest sectors, respectively. They synchronized watches, agreed to step off at precisely 2:15 a.m. From that point, it was every soldier for him-

or herself until one of them found Samman and radioed the others to confirm it. Failing that—as fail they might—it would be the big American's call to disengage and call their pilot for a pickup that might save their lives.

Or not.

Mindel watched Blanski and McCarter move away in darkness, quickly lost to sight. They used the night effectively, accustomed to its moods and shadows even here, on unfamiliar ground. Despite the hostile odds, Mindel was grateful not to be among their enemies this night. There would be blood before sunrise, and plenty of it, or she missed her educated guess.

More blood.

When would it ever be enough?

When all of them were dead, she thought, and felt no trace of pity for her enemies.

It had become a race war in the Middle East, the last thing any Jew desired, but what choice was there when the enemy made up the rules? She had a choice tonight: to play the cards as they were dealt, or die.

She chose to live if possible, and failing that to take as many of the bastards with her as she could.

A moment later it was time, and she moved in, a gliding shadow bearing death among her enemies.

KALIQ FARRAN WAS happy he'd been left in charge. It was a sign of trust that Ammar Samman permitted him to serve as acting captain when Samman was called away to deal with pressing matters elsewhere.

It was perilous but promising, perhaps a taste of rank and new responsibilities to come.

Granted, Farran would've preferred to be promoted under better circumstances. He'd been stricken, as they all had, by the news of Wasim Jabbar's death in Israel. Farran had known no other leader since he first joined Allah's Lance at age nineteen. He had been on the verge of weeping when he heard about the massacre, but rage quickly replaced his grief. There would be vengeance soon, when Samman returned from—

What was that?

Farran was startled from his cot by scuffling sounds outside, behind the two-man tent he occupied alone. Frozen in place, the dirt floor gritty underneath bare feet, he listened, waiting for the sound to be repeated. When it wasn't, he debated whether it was best to check or simply pass the matter off as insignificant.

It might be nothing, he decided, but a vigilant commander wouldn't let it go. The price of negligence was too high, and the cause had lost too many men already in the past ten days.

Farran dressed swiftly, silently. He scooped up his pistol belt and buckled it around his waist, pleased with the 9 mm Tokagypt pistol's solid weight against his hip.

Outside his tent, the night was cool and fragrant with wood smoke. Farran circled his tent, seeking the source of that elusive sound, suspecting that he was on a fool's errand. Trouble now meant he would have to deal with it, and for all his pride of leadership, Kaliq Farran lacked confidence. He had gone raiding into

Israel half a dozen times, had shot and bombed his share of unarmed Jews, but when it came to combat with a seasoned enemy, he knew himself to be on shaky ground.

Farran's eyes were still adjusting to the night when he stumbled, tripped over something in his path and fell sprawling on his face in the dirt. Mindful of watchers in the shadows, he sprang instantly erect and dusted off his stinging palms.

"By Allah's beard!"

The young man now had a clear view of what he'd tripped on. It was a body, stretched out prone as he had been a moment earlier. He whipped out his pistol, grimacing as raw flesh met cold steel. He felt slightly absurd but kept the silent form covered as he advanced, ready to fire at once if it appeared to be a trap.

"You there!" he whispered. "Get up!"

The figure didn't answer, didn't stir. Farran crouched to its left, noting the khaki uniform before he reached out with his free hand, prodding at the body.

Nothing. Not a flinch or whimper from the man whose face was still concealed.

Farran probed for a pulse, recoiling as his fingertips sank half an inch into the dead man's open throat. His fingertips were crimson in the faint moonlight, dripping. That meant the wound was fresh, the killer doubtless still close by.

Farran bolted to his feet, nearly losing his balance as he spun full circle, sweeping the night with his pistol. No one sprang upon him from the darkness, but he still didn't feel safe. One of his men was dead, the blood still fresh and warm, his throat slashed by unknown hands.

He didn't know the dead man's name, but if he was in uniform at this hour of the morning, he had to be one of the sentries on duty. That meant he should be armed, but a second glance revealed no weapon anywhere in sight. And that, in turn, meant that the man who'd stabbed him now had a Kalashnikov assault rifle.

Farran made another full turn, scanning shadows, clutching his pistol in a two-handed grip to keep it from trembling. He was about to raise the alarm when someone beat him to it, squeezing off a burst of automatic fire that shattered the camp's brooding silence.

Too late to take the lead, Farran left the corpse where it lay and sprinted toward the sound of gunfire, on the north side of the compound. As he ran, breathless, he somehow found his voice and shouted to his men, "Wake up! Attack! The enemy is here! Wake up and bring your guns!"

McCARTER HADN'T PLANNED on firing, but the two young Palestinians had given him no choice. It was a bloody piece of bad luck, running into them that way, and both men armed. If they'd been closer, possibly he could have clubbed down one or both of them, but they were twenty feet or more away, both staring at him, breaking off their conversation as they recognized a stranger by his outfit and the war paint on his face.

Surprise might slow them, but not enough to let McCarter survive a one-man banzai charge against their rifles. In the circumstances, there was only one thing he could do, and having recognized that fact, he didn't hesitate.

The stream of bullets from his AKS cut through both men before they had a chance to raise their weapons. One of them got off a short burst of his own, but it was wasted on the dirt—or maybe on his own right foot, the way he flinched and slumped in that direction as he fell. Both guards were dead or damn close to it by the time they hit the sand.

Shouting began immediately, as he'd known it would, and in another beat McCarter heard the reinforcements coming at a dead run, sentries breaking toward the sound of gunfire while their sleeping comrades scrambled out of sleeping bags and tents to join the fight. The one thing that would surely get him killed in record time was staying where he was.

McCarter moved.

There was no system to it, only instinct backed by years of field experience and training. One second he was rooted like a statue where he stood, the rifle warm in his hands; the next, he was away and heading through the shadows on his way to somewhere else— if not safety, perhaps the next-best thing.

He was hunting, with no idea of where his human quarry was or if the man he sought was even in the camp at all. It was a gamble, information possibly mistaken, maybe obsolete, but it was still the only game in town.

McCarter met two gunners bolting from a tent, lurching erect with automatic rifles in their hands. He scanned their faces swiftly, saw that neither one of them was Ammar Samman and killed them where they stood. They fell together in a heap, one's outflung arm taking the near end of the tent down with him as he dropped.

Another Arab barred his way, aiming a weapon, and McCarter fired on instinct, no time for reflection. Afterward, standing above the young man, watching as his life bubbled from blowholes in a scrawny chest, McCarter was relieved to find he didn't recognize the face.

Another dying stranger, nothing more.

He was surrounded now, if they got organized and worked out where he was... Spraying a camp with automatic fire was one thing, but the danger cranked up to another level when it came to going in and bringing out one of the enemy alive. The Briton wished they could've sat back on the rim and blazed away, or let Grimaldi hose the camp with fire from several hundred feet above, but he would play the cards as they were dealt.

Even if it turned out to be a dead man's hand.

He owed Katz that much. The extra bit of effort that would make or break an operation, send them on their way to other killing fields or leave them facedown in the sand.

Two more, and neither of them saw Samman. McCarter gutted them with short bursts from his AKS and left them thrashing on the ground as he passed them by. There was no time for mercy now, no place for hesitation.

It was do-or-die, and he could feel the bloody reaper breathing down his neck.

BOLAN BUTTSTROKED the sentry with his rifle, felt his jaw go as the AK's pistol grip made contact, following through with force enough to put the young man down and keep him there. Two more were rushing toward him through the darkness, firing as they came, and Bolan ducked aside, going to ground behind an empty tent.

It wasn't cover in the strictest sense, as canvas wouldn't stop a .22 slug, much less military rounds from a Kalashnikov assault rifle, but all he needed was a moment of confusion. Time enough to make the play he'd worked out in his mind at lightning speed, even as he began the move.

He rolled the full length of the tent, hearing the hot rounds tear it up behind him, concentrating on the angle he would need when he came out the other side. He'd have a second, maybe two, before they recognized their danger and swung right around to bring him under fire.

Call it two heartbeats, maybe three at the outside.

They weren't expecting Bolan at the west end of the tent, maybe believing they'd already cut him down. One of the shooters blinked and spun to face him as he rose from cover, barking something at his friend in Arabic, but it was already too late. The Executioner raked them left to right and back again, watching the points of impact blossom crimson in the firelight.

He was up and moving even as they fell, not trusting luck to cover him. Bolan had no idea how many shooters still remained alive in camp, but every one was a potential deadly enemy. Until he found their leader or someone to put him on the leader's track, the only tactic that made sense was pushing forward, dropping any riflemen who crossed his path.

Gunfire was audible from every quarter of the compound now. Bolan knew much of it was members of the opposition firing at one another or at shadows. If Mindel or McCarter had been singled out and cornered, he'd expect the shooting to be concentrated, more deliberate. Instead, wherever Bolan looked he could see young men running about in various stages of undress, muzzle-flashes from their weapons blistering the night. It covered the soldier's passage through the camp, but it also made his work more dangerous, since stray rounds killed as quickly and efficiently as any sniper's well-aimed bullet.

Bolan had covered half the distance from his entry point to Mindel's when he met a different kind of soldier. Moving through the chaos of the compound, brandishing a side arm while he shouted orders Bolan couldn't understand, this one was trying to rally the troops before they killed one another, grabbing a straggler here and there, dragging them into line behind him. He had picked up half a dozen in this manner, calming them enough to quell their random firing, moving on a course that would cross Bolan's in another forty yards or so.

It wasn't Ammar Samman—too young, too lean—but Bolan guessed he would have some idea where Samman could be found. First, though, he had to be disarmed and stripped of his supporters, so that they could talk in private without interruption.

Bolan pulled the magazine from his AKS—not empty, but depleted—and replaced it with a fresh one, veering off to meet the little party as it neared him. Sheer ferocity was all he had to power through a confrontation where the numbers were against him. Guts and the precision of a master sniper who had made tough shots before, when everything he had was riding on the line.

He came against the party from its left, dropping the leader's men with 3-and 4-round bursts that toppled them like cutout targets in a shooting gallery. A couple of the troops were fast enough to turn on him, one even squeezing off a short burst of his own before he died, but it was wasted effort. None of them had ever faced an adversary like the Executioner, or would again.

The leader of the slaughtered squad was stunned. He gaped and tried to raise his pistol, but Bolan was on him before he could make target acquisition. The AKS slashed down across his wrist and snapped it, numbing fingers on impact, dropping his weapon to the ground. The guy was brave enough to go for it left-handed, staring in the face of death, but Bolan caught him on the backswing, opening his right cheek to the bone with the rifle's blade sight.

The Arab staggered, blood streaming from his wounded face and soaking through the khaki shirt he wore. Bolan reached out and caught him by the throat, slippery now, and jammed the autorifle's muzzle underneath his chin.

"English?" he asked.

"I speak."

"Ammar Samman," Bolan grated. "Where is he?"

"Not here," his captive gasped.

"You want to live, make me believe it."

Wide eyes locked on Bolan's, dark drowning pools of terror. "Yesterday he went."

"Went where?"

There was a flicker in the eyes this time, a warning of the lie to come. "I don't know where."

"We'll see about that," Bolan said, already reaching for the transmitter clipped to his belt.

GRIMALDI THOUGHT it was the killing squeal, at first. They had two signals prearranged, on different frequencies. One meant the probe had gone to hell and he was wanted back there on the double, bringing fire from heaven to incinerate the enemy. The other meant his recent passengers were ready to dust off and hurry back to Israel.

This was the pickup signal, though. Grimaldi saw that when he double-checked the frequency and felt his dread morph into pure excitement, jumping nerve synapses as if he were holding live wires in his hands.

Strangely, it had a calming influence, as if danger thrilled and relaxed him all at the same time.

Grimaldi powered the Sikorsky, its six-blade main rotor a howling blur of motion, thirty-six-foot blades holding the chopper fifty feet above the desert floor. At that altitude, the Stony Man pilot pulled a screen of dust and grit along behind him, as if laying down a smoke screen. In daylight, his adversaries would've seen him coming. But this night, with running lights switched off, the snarl of his twin GE turboshaft engines was all they'd have for warning.

And from what he saw at one mile out, that wouldn't be enough.

Deprived of sound effects, the camp looked like a nest of fireflies gone berserk. The camou netting had been torn in places, shot to hell more like, but even where it held together he could see the muzzle-flashes winking, knew that every shooter still alive down there was burning rounds on something, whether they had targets in their sights or not. That made it rough for anybody coming out, but Grimaldi had faith in Bolan and McCarter. If the woman was on par with either one of them, he guessed she'd do all right.

At half a mile he keyed the jungle penetrator's automatic winch, unreeling the steel cable with an object on the end that vaguely resembled an anchor or grappling hook. Its three flanges were seats, though, the probe designed specifically to be lowered through jungle canopy for extraction of personnel waiting below. Five hundred feet of cable waited on the spool, but Grimaldi wasn't deep-sea fishing this time. Ten per-

cent of that would do it, once he found his comrades
waiting for their lift.

· There, just ahead of him and slightly off course to
the south! A plume of white smoke wafted from a
marker and he spotted them a few yards farther out.
He counted four figures and wondered how they meant
to work the pickup, but his first concern was focused
closer to the camp, where armed guerrillas were
emerging from the gully, streaming from underneath
the camou net like fire ants searching for the enemy
who'd kicked their nest.

Grimaldi hovered, reeling out the jungle penetrator's cable, while he lined up on the hostile pointmen
with his GE M-134 Miniguns. Electronic sighting did
the work and Grimaldi manned the triggers, each six-
barreled weapon spewing 7.62 mm rounds at a cata-
clysmic rate of six thousand per minute.

Living flesh could never hope to stand before that
storm of fire and metal, each round traveling downrange at 2,850 feet per second. Grimaldi's targets
weren't merely toppled; they were shredded and dis-
membered, painted on the slug-swept sand in shades
of brown and crimson. Those who quailed and turned
to run were cut down anyway, too slow in reconsid-
ering their options. After fifteen seconds of ungodly
carnage, when the last ranks broke and fled, Grimaldi
swallowed hard and let them go.

He held the chopper steady for another moment,
feeling weight on the line as he reeled in the probe,
waiting to see if the shaken survivors would counter-
attack. No shots were fired his way, and no one raised

a head above the rim of sandy earth to test his marksmanship. A moment later, glancing back, he saw McCarter and the woman scramble through the open side door, reaching back for someone still outside. They dragged a weakly struggling figure through the portal, followed instantly by Bolan, rifle slung across his back.

"Somebody call a cab?" Grimaldi asked, flashing a smile.

"We're done," Bolan replied, "for now."

"Home base?" Grimaldi asked.

"No rush about it. We need to have a few words with our new friend here before we land."

CHAPTER TWO

Bolan couldn't be sure what would happen to their prisoner on touchdown, since captured terrorists had an uncertain life expectancy in Israeli custody. Liaison was another problem, even with Rebecca Mindel on the team. He took for granted that they'd lose custody of their prisoner on arrival at the Tel Aviv air base, and there was no guarantee that anything he told Mossad's interrogators would make its way back to Bolan's ears.

It was a one-shot deal, and with Grimaldi holding the Sikorsky to a steady cruising speed, Bolan knew they were swiftly running out of time.

He sat directly opposite the hostage, watching the Arab nurse his fractured wrist. They hadn't bound his hands, small mercy, and his feet were likewise free. Where could he go, unarmed, with Mindel and McCarter flanking him?

"When we touch down," Bolan informed the man, "you'll be delivered to Mossad. You know who they are?"

"Butchers of my people," the prisoner said defiantly.

"I don't know what they have in mind for you," Bolan replied, "but there's a chance it might go easier if I could tell them you cooperated."

The hostage smiled at him, a pained expression, but he seemed to find some cause for mirth in Bolan's words. "You think me so important?" he inquired. "Perhaps I am entrusted with some knowledge that will help you to destroy my comrades?"

"I don't give a damn about your friends right now," Bolan told him, veering only slightly from the truth. "I'm looking for the men who use your people to further their own agenda. An American, a Greek and a Chinese."

The captive's face went blank. "Your trip is wasted, then," he said. "I know of no such men."

"I didn't think you would. That's why I need to speak with Ammar Samman."

"You lie!" the prisoner retorted. "You would kill Ammar, as you or others like you murdered Wasim Jabbar!"

The hostage was closer to the truth than he realized but Bolan let it pass. "You trust Samman?"

"Of course!" The Arab's tone was scornful now.

"I guess you'd be surprised to learn he's sold out Allah's Lance and everything you're fighting for to fatten up his new Swiss bank account?"

"More lies!"

"We're wasting time on this one," McCarter said. "Let me throw him out."

The captive tried to edge away from McCarter, on

his left, but the move brought him closer to Rebecca
Mindel, and she jabbed a sharp elbow into his ribs.

Bolan pretended to consider the suggestion, frowning as he said, "We radioed ahead that we were bringing in a prisoner. How would we cover losing him?"

"An accident," McCarter replied.

"Or better yet," Mindel put in, "a suicide. His sort
all think they're guaranteed a place in paradise if they
get killed in Allah's service."

"I don't know," Bolan said, playing good cop.

"Here's a thought, then," McCarter suggested.
"We could strap him to the probe and do a little sand
fishing. I've got a tenner says he can't run fast enough
to keep up with the whirlybird."

"I never bet on a sure thing," Bolan replied, watching the Arab's worried eyes.

"No money, then," McCarter said. "Just for the
sport, or for a round of drinks. I'll say our pilot's good
enough to drag him ten miles, anyway, before his legs
drop off."

"Does that include his feet?" Mindel asked.

"Feet, who knows?" McCarter shrugged. "His
boots aren't even laced, much less top quality. I'll give
you three miles on the feet."

"What would we use to strap him on the probe?"
Bolan asked.

"Duct tape ought to do it," McCarter replied.
"Bound to be some tucked away in here somewhere."

"Okay. You've got a bet."

The captive didn't panic until Bolan reached across
to grab the jungle probe and lifted it across the deck,

setting it between his feet. McCarter rose and took a short walk aft, returning moments later as predicted, with a roll of silver duct tape.

"Never fails," the former SAS commando said, smiling. Then, to their prisoner, "You need help getting on?"

"You can't do this!" the Arab blurted out.

"Why not? Mossad will likely shoot you anyway. We're saving them the trouble."

"Think of all those virgins waiting for you in the garden," Mindel told him, winking. "Milk and honey. You're a lucky man."

"You can't do this!" the prisoner insisted stubbornly.

"It's done," Bolan replied. "You've got your principles, and we're fresh out of time."

"I'll help you," McCarter said as he gripped the Arab's broken wrist. The heavy roll of duct tape dangled from his other hand.

"You're making a mistake!" the captive wailed.

"Won't be the first time," Bolan said. "I'll live with it."

McCarter tossed the roll of tape to Bolan, gripping the prisoner's right arm in both hands now, while Mindel took his left. Together, they grappled the struggling Arab to his knees and edged him toward the slim yellow shaft of the jungle probe. Their prisoner fought back as best he could, but he was overmatched. Bolan peeled off a long strip of tape, drawing it out with a sound like canvas ripping, and held it ready to receive the captive's jerking hands.

"No, please!" the young man blurted out, before adhesive met his flesh. "I'll lead you to Amman!"

"We're not recruiting guides," Bolan said. "Tell us where he is and let it go at that."

"The Bekaa Valley," he responded, his shoulders slumping as he spoke.

"That's not exactly pinning down coordinates," McCarter said.

"I only visited the camp one time," their hostage said. His voice hitched in his chest, as if he were about to weep. "Give me a map. I'll show you where it is."

"One map of Lebanon," said Bolan, "coming up."

THREE SOLDIERS WERE waiting when the helicopter landed, with a sergeant in command. The prisoner rushed toward them, shaking off McCarter's grip, and did his best to hide behind them as they stood together on the helipad. The sergeant glanced at Mindel, frowning. She gave nothing back to him except her cultivated poker face.

The sergeant handed her a set of keys that fit a gray Volvo sedan. Their weapons were stowed in the trunk, except for side arms, and the other combat gear was piled on top. Mindel didn't ask Bolan or McCarter if either wanted to drive.

The safehouse with a small attached garage was situated two miles from the air base where they left their prisoner. The helicopter pilot, known to her simply as Jack, rode in the back seat with McCarter, the big American seated to her left, unflinching as she drove too fast and jumped the traffic signals, careless of po-

lice. When they were parked in the garage and cut off
by its metal door from prying eyes, she let herself
relax, but not entirely, even then.

They were settled at a table in the kitchen, under
bright fluorescent lights, before McCarter broke the
silence. "So," he said, "the bloody Bekaa Valley. I
call that pretty rich."

"You've been there?" Mindel asked him.

"Haven't you?"

She shook her head, rejecting the impulse to be embarrassed. "No. It's not the sort of place Mossad sends
female agents."

"I can see that," McCarter said. "Though you'd
pass all right, I reckon, in a chador."

"Not my style," Mindel assured him.

"We can put wardrobe on hold," Bolan said, interrupting them as he spread out the map their prisoner
had marked. "We need to know the ground, first
thing."

Mindel was already conversant with the basic geography. Lebanon was Israel's northern neighbor, half
the size of her homeland at four thousand square
miles. More than half the nation's 3.6 million people
lived in Beirut, on the Mediterranean coast. Two
mountain ranges ran north to south, cupping the fertile
and treacherous Bekaa Valley between them. The Li-
tani River traveled south through the valley, then
veered west to feed the sea below Beirut.

The Bekaa was notorious for many reasons. As a
launching pad for terrorist raids against Israel, it
hosted training camps for a variety of militant groups:

the Syrian-backed Kurdistan Workers' Party, Hezbollah, Hamas, the Palestine Liberation Front and two mutually hostile factions of the Popular Front for the Liberation of Palestine—to name only the most prominent or notorious. Shiite Muslims under tutelage of Iranian intelligence units also used the Bekaa as a base for counterfeiting, producing ''supernotes,'' American hundred-dollar bills so sophisticated that detection outside a crime laboratory was virtually impossible. In any given year, Mossad estimated, the Bekaa Valley's craftsmen produced twice as many C-notes as the U.S. Treasury, shipping their product to Europe in wholesale lots for infiltration of the tourist trade. And politics aside, the fertile Bekaa was a perfect place for cultivating poppies, refining their sap into opium base and then heroin, an illicit traffic protected by state-of-the-art weapons and security devices.

Taken altogether, the Bekaa Valley was a good place to avoid and an easy place in which to die.

The site their prisoner had marked was midway up the valley, ten or twelve miles west of the Syrian border, some forty miles by air from Israel's northern frontier. An overland approach from Syria compounded danger of betrayal, meaning they would have to make another airborne run, and this time there would be no safe place for their craft to linger, waiting while they did their work.

''You think he told it straight?'' McCarter asked.

''I think he told us what he knew,'' Bolan replied. ''That doesn't mean it's accurate. Samman could have moved on by now, if he was ever in the Bekaa to begin with.''

"So, you want to let it pass?"

The tall American glanced up from studying the map and shook his head. "We can't do that. I'm thinking maybe it's a one-man job."

"Except you don't speak Arabic," Mindel reminded him. "That means I'll have to go along, at least."

"And leave me out?" McCarter wore a thin, off-kilter smile. "I don't much like the sound of that, after I booked the special tour and all."

"You both know what you're getting into?" Bolan asked rhetorically.

"Nobody knows exactly, with the Bekaa," McCarter replied. "That's the beauty of the place. Just when you think you've got it hacked, it turns around and hacks on *you*."

"Sounds like we need to brush up, then," Bolan replied. "Why don't you start?"

"THE BEKAA'S unpredictable," McCarter said, "except in one respect—if anything can possibly go wrong, it will. You want to work out who's in charge of any given sector at a given time, haul out a Ouija board or throw darts at a list of suspects. It's as close to anarchy as anything I've seen, outside Colombia, of course."

"You make it sound like the Wild West," Mindel remarked.

"I wasn't in the Wild West," McCarter said, "but

I've been in the Bekaa Valley a time or two. It almost got me killed. I won't say it's the worst action I've seen, but it was damn well bad enough.''

"No law enforcement as we recognize the term,'' Bolan stated.

"It's more accurate to say no *law*,'' McCarter said. "There's no dearth of official uniforms, per se—too many, sometimes, if you're working on the covert side. The Lebanese army isn't good for much, but it makes the occasional sweep, mostly collecting payoffs for its officers and muscling any operators who won't come across on schedule. Then you've got the *South Lebanese Army* to make things interesting.'' He half turned toward Mindel. "You'd know that lot, I think.''

"Not personally,'' she replied, distant.

"Of course not. My mistake. The SLA was left behind when Israel pulled up stakes in 1985, and they've been a sort of early-warning system for Tel Aviv ever since. It has de facto control over eight or nine percent of the countryside, below Beirut. In practice, small units probe northward whenever they can, sometimes as far as the Bekaa, looking for contact with hostiles. And since anyone they meet up there is hostile, they shoot first and pass on the questions entirely.''

"We'll be on our own,'' Bolan observed.

"With every man, woman and child against us,'' McCarter confirmed. "America and Britain may still have a few friends in Beirut, but you'll play hell finding any in the Bekaa. As for an Israeli representing the Mossad…'' He left the comment unfinished, smiling ruefully at Mindel and shaking his head.

"I'll take my chances," she told him.

"We all will, up there," McCarter said. "Even in mufti there'll be no mingling with the locals, not with a woman as our only interpreter. We'll be sounding alarms all the way, if we're spotted."

"A quick in-and-out, then," Bolan stated.

"In theory," McCarter replied. "Still, that means we have to cover half the length of the country undetected and make the insertion without jumping into an ambush. That done, we need to hit our mark on the first try. If this—" he waved a hand over the map "—is anything but spot-on accurate, we won't have any means of judging where we ought to go or how to get there. We'll be stuck waiting for pickup, and damn lucky just to get out empty-handed, with our skins intact. We've barely got a first chance. There won't be a second."

Bolan frowned at him. "What happened to positive thinking?"

"All right," McCarter said. "I'm *positive* we won't have any second chance to do it right."

"It's down to trust, then," Mindel commented. "I could reach out and have my people squeeze the prisoner, see if he tries to change his story."

"That won't prove he lied the first time," Bolan answered, "only that he'll say whatever is required of him to hold the pain at bay."

"What, then?" she asked.

"I'd vote to go with what we have," Bolan replied. "I've seen men scared to death, and he was right there on the edge. I don't believe he lied."

"But was he right?" McCarter asked.

"You know the only way to answer that one," Bolan said.

"Go in and have a look."

"That's it."

McCarter turned to Mindel once again. "It would be nice to know we had some backup from your people if it starts to fall apart," he said.

"I have approval for logistical support. They'll fit us out with costumes and disguises, weapons, anything we need in that respect, but there's an end to it. Your friend and the Sikorsky are our lifeline. If we lose them, we'll be on our own. Deniability will be preserved."

"That's bloody marvelous," McCarter said. "No stain on Israel's honor, then, I take it. God forbid you'd cross a border without asking for permission first."

"You understand the situation, just as I do," Mindel said. "We've crossed that border countless times."

"My point exactly," McCarter retorted.

"But this mission is strictly covert," she challenged. "You were aware of that, I think. There's been no overt act against my country, and Mossad won't tip its hand to Global Petroleum on our behalf. The powers that be would rather start from scratch with a new team and do it right, if we go down."

"It's always nice to be expendable," McCarter said.

"That's nothing new," Bolan reminded him. "We've all been there."

"And done that, thank you very much," the Briton

added. "It doesn't stop one hoping for a change of pace."

"Maybe next time."

"If there is one."

"We either play the cards we're dealt, or else we fold," Bolan replied.

McCarter thought of Yakov Katzenelenbogen and the sacrifice he'd made to bring them this far. "Right," he said. "I'm in. But you should know that if I get my head shot off, I won't be pleased."

That brought a smile to Bolan's face. "Can't fault you there. Before we pin the details down, I'd better make a call."

HAL BROGNOLA WAS was reading a report on illegal arms traffic and the Russian Mafia when his telephone rang. There were two on his desk, placed side-by-side, but only the private line rang through without a heads-up from his personal assistant in the outer office. Marking his place in the Eyes Only folder and steeling himself for bad news, Brognola snared the receiver on its second ring and brought it to his ear.

"Brognola."

"Striker," the familiar voice said. "Are we scrambled?"

"Just a second."

Brognola reached out again and thumbed down a button on the telephone's chunky base. A green light winked twice at him, then shone steadily. The red bulb next to it remained inert, telling Brognola that the line was clear of taps.

"All set," he said. "What's happening?"

"We missed Samman, but we've got a new line on him from the guy he left in charge."

"Reliable?" Brognola asked.

"We won't know that until we're on the ground."

"And where would that ground be, again?"

"The Bekaa Valley," Bolan said.

Jesus. Brognola felt his stomach tighten, had to consciously relax his jaw to keep his teeth from grinding. There were certain godforsaken places on the planet where he wouldn't care to send an enemy, much less his oldest living friend. Calcutta's slums. Colombia's Guajira district. Sarajevo. The Bekaa Valley ranked high on any list he could think of.

"Are you there?" Bolan asked.

"Sorry. Tell me what you need."

"Just Jack, for now. I think we've got logistics covered."

"Backup?" That would be a touchy one, Brognola guessed.

"We're on our own, beyond material assistance," Bolan said. "Mossad doesn't want to get caught with its hand in the cookie jar this time."

"Terrific."

"Anyway, I thought you'd better have a line on where we're going, just in case."

Brognola snared a ballpoint pen and notepad from the top drawer of his desk. "Okay. Let's have it."

Bolan rattled off coordinates, waiting for the big Fed to read them back. "How firm is that?" Brognola asked, when Bolan had confirmed the longitude and latitude.

"I think the source was playing straight," Bolan replied. "Whether he knew his sphincter from a subway tunnel is another story. As I said, we won't know till we're on the ground and in the thick of it."

"It doesn't get much thicker than the Bekaa," Brognola reminded him.

"We're taking every possible precaution."

"Short of staying home," Brognola said.

"I don't mind passing on it, if you've got locations on our targets. Napier? Mak? Andrastus?"

"Nothing yet," Brognola said, disgusted.

"So, we're going in. If we can find Samman, smart money says he should be able to give up one of the three, at least. From there, we just connect the dots."

Brognola didn't waste his breath telling the warrior to be careful. Bolan knew the risks of every move he made, but danger seldom put him off. He'd risked his life for less important missions in the past. This time, the fate of nations could be riding on the line—Israel's, at least—and there was still the vengeance factor, settling up the score for Yakov Katzenelenbogen's recent death. Bolan had known the old Phoenix warrior for years, had fought beside him more than once, and David McCarter had been Katz's companion on deadly missions without number. There was no good reason to suppose that either one of them would let the matter rest without more blood.

No damn reason at all.

"What can I do to help?" Brognola asked.

"It wouldn't hurt if you could spare Jack for a few more days," Bolan replied.

"He's yours. Anything else?"

"I think we're covered, hardware-wise. If we can find Samman and pin him down, we'll need transport ASAP, to keep the ball in play."

"I'll reach out now and see what I can do."

"Appreciate it," Bolan said. "That's all I can think of right now."

"Okay. I'm around if you need me."

"We'll be in touch soon," Bolan said and then broke the connection.

I hope so, the big Fed thought.

It was bad, going into the Bekaa with no idea if your target would even be present. There were too many ways to die in that free-fire zone as it was, each new uncertainty only serving to make the risk greater, the peril that much worse. Bolan and McCarter were pros, of course; they knew what they were doing and how best to get it done in any given situation. But skill wasn't the only factor in a killing game. There was chance to be considered—or call it luck. Hell, call it Fate if that helped the bitter pill go down.

It all came out the same anyway, in the end.

And it meant there were factors no amount of planning could predict or control. No degree of training or experience made the least bit of difference when a soldier's proverbial number came up.

Brognola stopped that train of thought before it pulled out of the station, but it still left a sour smell in the room. Bolan had pushed his luck for so long now, each time he took on another mission it was like playing Russian roulette. So far, the hammer had always fallen on an empty chamber.

Brognola snared the other telephone and gave his assistant a name at the Pentagon. She'd have the number in her Rolodex or somewhere close at hand. It helped keep him from picturing disasters in his head, if he was busy, and he still had promises to keep.

If anything went wrong for Bolan and McCarter in the Bekaa Valley, it wouldn't spring from any omission or oversight on Brognola's part.

He swore that to himself and hoped that it was good enough to let him sleep at night.

"THE PROBLEM ISN'T getting in," Jack Grimaldi said as he scanned the large-scale map of Lebanon. "It isn't even getting out. The problem's getting *back* in, if you need the transport in a hurry."

"You can do it, though," McCarter stated, not really asking him.

"Give it the college try and then some," the Stony Man pilot replied. "It helps that they don't have an air force in the normal sense. Scout planes and that, but nothing in the way of modern fighters."

"Radar?" Bolan queried.

"Where it hasn't been knocked out," Grimaldi said. "They want that early warning if Israeli jets come over, not that it does them much good."

He felt the woman watching him but didn't flinch from it. He'd meant no criticism, but if she was bound to take offense, to hell with her. He'd known her less than one full day and she was easy on the eyes, but he was there for Bolan and McCarter, not to snuggle with Mossad.

"Stingers," McCarter said. "That's what you'll need to watch."

"They might have Grails or Gremlins, too," Grimaldi added, referring to the Russian SA-7 shoulder-launched surface-to-air missile and its big brother, the SA-14. With the American-made FIM-92 Stinger, any one of those weapons could bring his next flight to a sudden, fiery end in the Lebanese sky.

Grimaldi glanced up from the map and found the others watching him. He smiled and said, "No worries. The Sikorsky's got a flare-cartridge dispenser to confuse heat-seekers. And they'd have to know I'm coming anyway, to get a fix in time."

That wasn't strictly true, Grimaldi knew. If any of the paramilitary groups whose territory he'd be crossing had lookouts posted, armed with any kind of decent SAM technology, the sound of his approaching helicopter would provide all the warning they needed to shoulder a firing tube and activate the sighting mechanism. He could vary his route between the first penetration and withdrawal, but after that he'd be running short of options in a country the size of Lebanon. Granted, it wasn't a postage stamp like Liechtenstein, but if Bolan and the others needed him for pickup in a hurry, there'd be no time for elaborate evasive maneuvers or swinging miles out of his way around the target zone.

He'd have to keep his fingers crossed and maybe say a little prayer or two, for what it might be worth.

And he would fly like a bat out of hell.

"You'll have to get out right after the drop," Bolan said.

"That's affirmative," Grimaldi answered. There was no place in Lebanon for him to safely hover, much less land the whirlybird and wait for his colleagues to complete their mission. It galled him to leave them that way, but variations on the theme had been Grimaldi's lot since he had volunteered for Bolan's war, back in the day when it was Bolan going one-on-one against the Mafia. He'd always found the big guy waiting for him, more or less intact, when he returned, running on guts and sheer audacity.

So far.

"I'd like to get the chopper fitted with some rocket pods before we do this thing," he told Mindel. "Can do?"

"It's not a problem," she assured him.

"Good. The quad-mount Hellfires are my first choice, but I'll take what I can get. Something with punch, for air-to-ground engagement."

"I'll see to it."

"Leave the Miniguns in place and top the ammo off," he added.

"Right."

"Aside from that," Grimaldi said, "it comes down to you three. I can get you in, fall back and hold on station till you need a lift. I've got the easy job."

All present knew that wasn't strictly true. They also

knew, without saying so, that if Grimaldi took a missile up his tailpipe on the flight back to Israel after the drop, they'd never know it. Not in time to help themselves, at any rate. They'd go about their mission, maybe even pull it off, but there'd be no pickup when it was time for them to go.

And that, barring some kind of miracle, would mean they were as good as dead.

There'd be no hiking out of Lebanon, not from the Bekaa Valley, eighty miles north of the nearest Israeli frontier. Syria was closer, a mere stroll by comparison, but they'd find no help there, only more peril. Escaping on foot with a prisoner in tow was unthinkable.

Grimaldi was plainly and simply their only way out.

They were trusting him with their lives and the fate of their mission.

And he didn't mean to let them down.

"Okay," Grimaldi said. "Just so we're clear on everything, let's just go over it once more."

BOLAN STOLE some time for himself when the meeting broke up. There was no more to say at that point.

The mission had begun as a rescue effort, ten days earlier. Yakov Katzenelenbogen, lately retired from Phoenix Force to ride a desk at Stony Man Farm in Virginia, had been visiting family in Israel when he recognized some faces on a busy street and tagged along to see what they were doing in the heart of Tel Aviv. His curiosity had put Katz in a cage, confined and tortured by a group of mercenary terrorists intent on learning what he knew about their latest plot. His disappearance had made waves back in the States, Brognola sending out two of his best to find Katz and retrieve him if they could.

They'd managed that, all right, but rescue hadn't been the end of it. Katz knew enough to put them on the track of a conspiracy involving wealthy men from the United States, Greece and the People's Republic of China. More to the point, while Bolan and McCarter were hunting, Katz had slipped away from his niece on the eve of a transatlantic flight and went to do some hunting of his own. When the smoke cleared, Katz was dead, with lots of company, but Bolan and McCarter were no closer to their quarry than they had been on day one.

He had three names and faces to fit them. Arnold Napier was the jet-setting CEO of Global Petroleum, rarely at home in the United States these days. Christos Andrastus was the Greek shipping magnate whose fleet carried much of Global's crude. Lin Yuan Mak was a Chinese trade official based in Hong Kong, scheming with the others to arrange a shift of power in the Middle East and thereby earn his nation access to the region's vast oil reserves.

All three of them, it seemed, had disappeared.

Running them down required information he didn't possess at the moment, and that in turn led them to Ammar Samman, assuming they could ever track *him* down. The lead in Lebanon was promising, but they would have to play it out to know if it was just a lethal waste of time.

A waste of life.

Bolan thought of Katz and all the others who had died since Brognola handed him the ill-fated rescue mission. Going in, he hadn't known what it would become, but he would've taken the job anyway. There was no refusing when friends were in peril, no letting the killers walk because Bolan had failed to prevent Katz's death. The mission had evolved from that point.

It wasn't simply payback anymore, although he had a debt to settle with the enemy that wouldn't be expunged as long as any of the principals were still alive. There was a great deal more at stake than sweet revenge.

Justice was part of it, but only part.

Peace was an issue, though the region where he found himself had known no peace for generations, going back three-quarters of a century or more.

More than either of those concepts, it had to do with keeping the predators in line, jerking the leash and calling for a reckoning.

It was what Bolan did best of all, addressing savages in the only language they truly understood. Negotiation was a futile exercise, because a predator by nature wanted it all. He—or she—was never satisfied with one score, one victory, regardless of its size.

Sometimes they got what they were asking for.

Sometimes they got Mack Bolan.

The first round had been too expensive for Bolan to think in terms of victory just yet, but neither would he countenance defeat. A soldier who dwelled overlong on losing had already given up his edge. Defeatism was a disease, and no combatant was immune. Each warrior had to guard against it constantly and pledge that if the battle went against him, he would take as many of the opposition with him as he could.

Surviving in the Bekaa Valley wasn't easy, but it could be done. Finding their quarry wouldn't be a milk run, but they had a fix on him and carried the advantage of surprise.

The rest of it came down to guts and skill, a willingness to do what had to be done and live with it for long years afterward, holding regret at bay with knowledge that some deeds were necessary.

Bolan had come to terms with that mind-set in his youth, and it served him well now. McCarter knew what had to be done and wouldn't hesitate.

As for Rebecca Mindel, she had done her part so far without complaint. The trial ahead would test her further. She would either pass the test, or she would die.

Bolan was hoping she'd survive.

There was no time for him to start a Berlitz course in Arabic.

CHAPTER THREE

Jakarta

Arnold Napier sat before his computer, rereading the e-mail from Damascus. It was cryptic, not so much coded as a string of euphemisms seeming innocent to a casual observer, but the tale it told produced a sour feeling in his stomach. It read:

> Surprise developments. Our field reps have met with surprise opposition from new competitors. We assume but cannot document a link to previous transactions in the area. A number of the sales force have retired. The foreman was on holiday and missed an opportunity. Your call on whether disciplinary measures are appropriate. Standing by.

The e-mail wasn't signed, but Napier recognized Worthington's style. The Global Petroleum representative in Damascus always phrased his messages as if he were dictating a telegram to Western Union. It surprised Napier, sometimes, that Worthington ended his sentences with periods instead of typing "Stop."

For all that, the message required no code book to decipher it. The "field reps" in Syria were soldiers of Allah's Lance, the Palestinian guerrilla army Napier had recruited as part of his plan to destabilize Israel and thereby earn the gold-plated gratitude of certain oil-rich Arab states. "Surprise opposition" meant another in the series of attacks that had already decimated Allah's Lance and killed its leader, Wasim Jabbar. "Retirement" of the "sales force" meant that a substantial number of guerrillas had been killed or gravely wounded. The missing "foreman" was Jabbar's heir apparent and Napier's new toady, Ammar Samman. His "holiday" would be a bid to save himself by leaving the grunts to fend for themselves.

Napier was on the verge of answering, fingers poised over the keyboard, prepared to order Samman's execution in bland, oblique terms, when he caught himself and leaned back in his chair. He swiveled toward the eastward-facing window, thankful it was tinted as the tropic sun reflected from hundreds of windows in the office tower across the street.

He could seal Samman's fate with a word, but what would it accomplish? Allah's Lance might have some life left in it yet, and even if the group was finished, Napier knew he had to be cautious of appearances when dealing in the Arab world. Without the Lance, he'd need another army to perfect his plan, and allies might be hard to come by if word got around that he was prone to killing those who let him down.

A wiser course of action, he decided, was to simply let Samman fend for himself, wherever he had gone to ground. If the heir to Allah's Lance could rally his forces and destroy their still unidentified opponents, the lethal shadows who had dogged Napier's tracks and tormented him for the past ten days, it would be self-defeating to eliminate him. By the same token, if those faceless enemies were too much for Samman, they would most likely do Napier's work for him, relieving him of any guilt among other Palestinian militants.

That decided, he tapped out a short message in response: "No action necessary at this time. Keep me informed." He read it twice, hit Send and waited for the task to be completed, then switched off his computer.

Jared Wagner hadn't moved a muscle while Napier read and answered his e-mail, planted in a seat directly opposite the massive teakwood desk, sitting ramrod straight in his chair. He was too nervous to relax, painfully aware that his predecessor had been shot to bloody ribbons less than sixty hours earlier. He didn't know—need never know, in fact—that those bullets had been fired by Napier's men, on Napier's orders.

Why disturb the young man's mind with trivia?

"Bad news from Syria," Napier informed his new vice president. "Cigar?"

"No, thank you, sir."

Napier chose a Havana from the humidor and lit it

with his gold-plated desk lighter, careful to hold the flame an inch below the cigar's square-cut tip. He kept Wagner waiting, stretching it out, until the tobacco was burning smoothly and he'd managed two long draws.

"Another strike against our Palestinian associates in Syria," he said at last. "I'd hoped this might be settled, but it seems we've still got trouble on our hands."

The hope had been a faint one, granted. Napier knew enough of violent men to understand they seldom just gave up and walked away, especially when they were winning.

So much blood already, and he still didn't know what the bastards wanted.

"I'm sorry to hear that, sir," Wagner said.

"Don't be sorry," Napier challenged. "Help me end it."

"Yes, sir. If I can."

"First thing, we need to warn our friends. It wouldn't do to have them think we've kept them in the dark."

"No, sir."

"I'll let you handle that," Napier said. "Jump in at the deep end, as it were."

"Yes, sir." There was less confidence behind the words this time. Wagner had lost a bit of color in his face at the prospect of dealing with Mak and Andrastus directly.

"They'll have questions, naturally. Don't feel

obliged to answer them. We're waiting for details ourselves, that sort of thing. You know the drill.''

"Of course.''

"I'm unavailable, but I'll get back to them as soon as possible, tomorrow or the next day unless something breaks, meanwhile.''

"I understand.''

"I don't anticipate Mak giving you a problem, but Andrastus sometimes likes to throw his weight around. Don't argue with him, don't be rude, but hold the line. You've told him what we know so far.''

"Which is?'' Wagner asked.

"Just the bare-bones basics,'' Napier said. "More trouble with the Palestinians. We don't know who's responsible, so far. Could be Israelis or some rival faction. They'll find out when we do.''

"Yes, sir.''

"In the meantime, there's no reason to believe they're personally at risk. Both have security in place. They don't need our advice on how to watch their backs.''

"Shall I get started on that now, then?'' Wagner asked.

"You may as well, in case I'm wrong.''

"Wrong, sir?''

"About the threat assessment,'' Napier said. He took another pull on his cigar, enjoying it, and smiled. "I'm not wrong often, Jared, but it happens. And I'd hate to see one of our partners get his ass shot off because I told him not to worry.''

Wagner lost the bit of color he'd regained. Napier

watched him swallow some ill-advised comment, his Adam's apple wobbling up and down. "No, sir," the young man said. "We can't have that."

"Damn right, we can't. You go take care of it, all right?"

"Yes, sir."

Napier maintained the smile until he was alone, then let it go. His natural optimism had taken a beating over the past ten days, and this morning's news from Syria was another sucker punch, landing where it hurt the most. He could've badly used a victory just now, but the Arabs had let him down.

Again.

It wasn't their fault altogether, but Napier needed someone to blame at the moment, and who better for the role than a troupe of self-styled holy warriors who'd gotten their asses handed to them time after time, beaten bloody by a team of hostiles they couldn't even identify, much less pin down and destroy. It was embarrassing, a travesty, but Napier reckoned it was small potatoes for a people whose military history included being run out of their own homeland by poorly armed invaders and crushed in six days flat when they sent the massed armies of three nations against tiny Israel in 1967. Defeat was almost a religion with some Palestinian "armies."

He couldn't fault them for their nature, but it would have been a treat to see them kick some ass for once, instead of getting pounded like a slab of beef.

Maybe, he thought, they needed a little help.

THE PROBLEM with being promoted over someone's dead body, Jared Wagner decided, was that it meant he could go the same way. In some jobs, when you got the ax, you *really* got the fucking ax.

Or bullet, as the case may be.

He wasn't privy to the gruesome details, granted, but from what Wagner had heard around the office—and it wasn't much—his predecessor in the VP slot he occupied had soaked up something like a hundred bullets, maybe two hundred, and went to his reward in a closed casket, no viewing allowed. Wagner had only known Sterling Holbrook casually, wouldn't miss him to speak of, but he didn't relish going out the same way.

Not by a long shot, pun most certainly intended.

He was apprehensive about calling Lin Mak and Christos Andrastus, but he would do as he was told. He was playing in the big leagues now, and there was no slack cut for squeamish members of the team. Napier would shelter him from any flack, he thought, unless...

The rumor troubled him from the moment he'd first heard it whispered. Never mind by whom. The source was less important than the gist in this case. And the gist was that smiling Arnie Napier might have sacrificed his loyal number two in the heat of the moment, angling for a personal advantage in a deadly game.

Truth be told, that notion bothered Wagner less than the idea that Napier had failed and the game was still going on. It was his turn to play now, and he couldn't help wondering how best to avoid Holbrook's fatal mistakes. He'd have to keep a sharp eye on personal security until the problem was resolved and avoid giving anyone a clear shot at his back, "friends" included.

On second thought, make that "friends" *especially.*

Wagner was proud of his promotion, looking forward to the pay raise and a chance to work with real movers and shakers, legality be damned, but he wouldn't sacrifice himself for Global Petroleum or Arnold Napier.

No damn way at all.

He'd made it this far in the cutthroat world of multinational business by striking a happy medium between loyalty and self-preservation. Now, when the term meant more than simply hanging on to a job, the costs of letting down his guard were all the more obvious.

All the more lethal.

Wagner had the contact numbers for Lin Mak and Christos Andrastus memorized. It had been his first order of business, upon assuming Sterling Holbrook's duties. They were cutout numbers, naturally, set up to reach their principals anywhere on Earth without giving their locations away. That was fine with Wagner, since he didn't want to know where they were. The less he knew on that score, in fact, the safer he might be over the next few days or weeks.

His office was a loaner, vacated on short notice by a dark-skinned man who bobbed his head and faked a smile on his way out the door. Wagner hadn't bothered to read his name on the door and couldn't care less what the stranger was thinking. He needed a desk and telephone for the duration of their stay in Jakarta—however long that proved to be—and no one argued with the new vice president of international development.

The newly acquired bodyguards were stationed outside his borrowed office. Wagner knew them as Lyle and Cage, last names irrelevant and of no interest to him whatsoever. They were tall men, muscular beneath their richly conservative suits, bulked up as much with hardware as with muscle. He didn't know what they were carrying—guns had never been one of his hobbies—but he trusted Napier's word that they would kill or die for him as needed. Wagner expected nothing less from a pair of professional bullet catchers.

Lyle, sporting a blond bad-boy ponytail, nodded to Wagner as he passed. Wagner tilted his chin in reply but kept his face deadpan. He didn't court familiarity with subordinates—unless, of course, the subordinate in question was an attractive female, in which case he had charm to spare. As for these two, it couldn't hurt to be civil when his life might depend on them, but he refused to support the illusion of friendship.

What was the point of promotion, if he couldn't look down on those left behind?

The borrowed office didn't suit him, but it hardly mattered. Settled at the desk, door closed, he didn't miss the view of London that his normal office windows offered. Here, with no windows at all to distract him, he could concentrate on his assignment. Reaching out to God knew where and touching base with Napier's partners.

His partners now.

It struck Jared Wagner, not for the first time, that he was playing in a vastly different league. Running the London office was one thing, a sort of rear-echelon command where shuffling paper and stroking egos was the order of the day. He'd now received the equivalent of a battlefield promotion, propelled toward the literal firing line by forces beyond his control. Wagner was as close to real danger now as he had ever been in his life.

And it had never once crossed his mind to resign.

You're stalling now, he told himself, frowning at the thought. There was no room for hesitation in his new position. The vice president in charge of international development for Global Petroleum would be decisive, confident, aggressive—even if he didn't know what the hell he was doing.

He picked up the telephone receiver, keyed 9 for an outside line and listened to the dial tone humming in his ear. Wagner tapped out the number from memory, reaching out, halfway around the globe, to give one of the world's richest men more bad news.

Aboard the Aristotle, *Strait of Boniacio*

CHRISTOS ANDRASTUS had chosen his small yacht— the *Aristotle,* a mere hundred-footer—for the sense of privacy and intimacy it afforded him. He owned two others, larger, which he preferred for parties and cor-

porate functions. The *Aristotle,* named for his old
friend and one-time competitor Onassis, was reserved
for occasions when Andrastus wanted to get away
from the world and his life, roughing it with only a
dozen TV-VCR-DVD combinations, one modest satellite dish, one sauna and a positively claustrophobic
dining room that seated only twenty-five.

This time, he'd even left the whores at home.

Their place had been taken by gunmen, standing aloof from the yacht's working crew, no task on
their plate beyond making sure that Andrastus kept
breathing. If they failed in that task, it was well understood, the corporation he commanded would stop
payment on their checks and send better, more efficient men to hunt them down.

Lounging on the yacht's foredeck, watching Corsica
slide past to starboard, Sardinia to port, Andrastus felt
no immediate threat to his life. He had enemies, of
course, and bloody ruthless men among them, but
those he feared most at the moment were far away,
hunting one of his partners in the blighted Middle
East.

Or were they?

The uncertainty dogged him, soured his mood and
put a frown on his deeply tanned face. Andrastus
viewed everyone with suspicion as a matter of course,
but the sensation troubling him now was something
else, something more.

He had begun to think one of his teammates in the
bold new game might want him dead.

There was nothing to support that notion yet. Indeed, for all he knew it might be nothing but an idle fantasy. Still, much had happened in the past two weeks that made him wonder, made him doubt.

Of the two candidates, Lin Mak and Arnold Napier, he mistrusted the American more. Chinese were cagey, sly in business, but Andrastus thought Lin Mak had far too much to lose by tipping the boat, as it were. Arnold Napier, on the other hand, was devious to a fault, entirely capable of manufacturing a threat and using it to help consolidate his power in their small consortium.

But would he do it? Was it worth the risk?

Napier had to know the consequence of betrayal at this rarified level, when the stakes were nothing short of monumental. There would be no reprimand and no recrimination, certainly no litigation to resolve disputes. Betrayal meant death, carried out by professionals and without recourse to appeal.

Andrastus took another slow sip of ouzo to calm himself, enjoying the licorice flavor on his tongue. It was early days yet, to imagine himself at war with Napier and the marshaled forces of Global Petroleum. It might be a war to remember, but why borrow trouble when there was always enough to go around anyway?

He would be ready if and when the trouble came, but it wasn't time to consider a preemptive strike.

Not yet.

If he had evidence…

Andrastus heard the squeak of deck shoes coming up behind him. A shadow fell across his face, Theron looming above him, offering a giant hand in which the white cell phone looked like a toy.

"A call for you, sir," Theron said. "The oilman."

Andrastus took the phone and waited for his valet to withdraw. Satisfied with his solitude, he brought the phone to his ear and said, "Good afternoon, Arnold."

"Excuse me, sir," an unfamiliar voice replied. "My name is Jared Wagner. I'm the new VP for international development at Global Petroleum. I'm calling on behalf of Mr. Napier. At his instruction, actually."

Andrastus frowned at that, considering whether the handoff to a mere vice president was insulting enough to make it an issue between them. "I suppose it's too much trouble now to make the call himself," he said.

"No, sir." It was a young man's voice, not fully confident. "There's been a problem that demanded his attention elsewhere. I was asked to let you know and offer Mr. Napier's most sincere apologies."

The boy was lying now, Andrastus knew. Napier apologized for nothing, ever. It implied that he was fallible, and that would simply never do.

"Apology accepted," the Greek replied. His turn to lie. "What is the problem that bedevils him?"

"More of the same, sir, I'm sorry to say. There's been another, um, incident with our Palestinian associates."

"Indeed?"

Andrastus didn't like the Arabs, didn't trust them. They were necessary for a job like this, and while his own success was bound to theirs, he couldn't find it in his stony heart to mourn whatever injury they suffered for the cause.

"Last night in Syria," Wagner went on. "We just found out and don't have all the details yet, but Mr. Napier wanted you to know first thing."

"Steps will be taken, I assume?"

"They're in the works, sir."

"And will I be privileged to know what steps those are?"

"As soon as it's been finalized, sir. I assume you'll be among the first to know," Wagner replied.

Among the first. Andrastus felt his frown twitch toward an outright scowl. "Does your employer recommend any particular precautions at this time?"

"No, sir. We think the danger's localized. Containable."

"But not contained."

"We're making every effort, sir."

"Of course you are. I understand. What of Samman?"

"I understand he missed the show, sir."

"We should all be thankful for small favors, I suppose."

"Yes, sir. If you have any need to get in touch with me—"

"I doubt that very much, young man. If your employer needs to speak with *me* for any reason, I believe he knows my number. Yes?"

"I'm sure he does, sir. If I may just say—"

Andrastus switched off his cell phone before Napier's vice president for international development could pucker up and kiss his backside. There were times when he enjoyed obsequiousness, even needed it, but not this day. Just now, he needed time to think without some upstart droning on and on, tireless as some mechanical rabbit with everlasting batteries.

He was safe for the moment, vulnerable only to air strikes or submarines, and willing to assume that Napier's nameless enemies—his now, by extrapolation—possessed neither the requisite technology nor knowledge of his whereabouts. While the foe was preoccupied twelve hundred miles to the east, mopping up ragtag Arab "soldiers," Andrastus had time to review his priorities and triple-check his security precautions.

If trouble overtook him, on sea or land, he wouldn't be caught napping. One benefit of being grossly, extraordinarily wealthy was that virtually nothing lay beyond his reach. He had access to fighting men and weapons, armored vehicles, aircraft, luxurious hideouts—the world was literally at his fingertips.

Christos Andrastus meant to use it well, and to remain alive no matter how his adversaries schemed to bring him down. Good men had tried it in the past, but they hadn't been good enough. Nor, he was certain, would this lot prove equal to the job.

Andrastus wished he knew their names, though, or at least where they had come from, whom they served. It would've made things so much easier in terms of dealing with the threat.

Still, there were ways to get things done. At one time or another, Andrastus had mastered them all. He would survive because it was his nature. And the men who schemed against him would be sorry, screaming out the final hours of their lives.

Andrastus sipped his ouzo in the sunshine.

And he smiled.

Macao

LIN MAK WAS SIPPING coffee laced with bourbon when his secretary knocked, then entered without waiting for a summons. Mak greeted the twenty-five-year-old man with a raised eyebrow, wishing for perhaps the thousandth time that the Communist Party could be somewhat less efficient in erasing gender-traditional work roles. It would have pleased Mak greatly to have a twenty-five-year-old woman at his daily beck and call, but instead he had Zhou Peng.

"A phone call, sir," Peng said, as straitlaced as ever. He looked as if an honest smile would cause his face to shatter.

Not a bad idea, Mak thought. "Who is it?"

Peng made a show of consulting the notepad he carried in his left hand. "A Mr. Wagner, sir, from Global Petroleum."

Mak frowned at the name. "I'll take it."

"Line three, sir."

Mak was reaching for the telephone but hesitated, glowering at Peng in the doorway. "Is there something else?" he demanded.

"No, sir."

"Then close the door as you leave."

Idiot.

Mak waited for the door to shut, then lifted the receiver to his ear and pressed the only lighted button on the telephone. Line three, of course, as if he couldn't see that for himself.

"Hello."

"Mr. Mak?" The voice was strange; Mak was certain he'd never heard it before.

"Sir, my name's Jared Wagner. Mr. Napier asked me to call you on his behalf. I'm his new vice president for international development."

A euphemism, Mak decided, as when spies attached to foreign embassies were labeled cultural attachés. The man on the other end of the line would be what Americans called a "gofer," though doubtless well paid for his efforts.

"I see." Mak kept his tone neutral. He'd been expecting bad news from the moment he learned the call's source. Now, understanding that Napier couldn't bring himself to break that news personally, Mak guessed it would be even worse than he'd anticipated.

"Sir," Wagner said, "I'm afraid we've had another spot of difficulty with the Palestinians."

No great surprise in that, Mak thought. The more he heard of them, the more he was convinced that all Middle Eastern revolutionaries were incompetent or demented, with the worst a mixture of both.

"What is it this time?" he inquired.

"They've taken more casualties," his caller said. "In Syria this time."

Mak's mind leaped ahead, projecting results and repercussions. If their Arab strike force was disabled, it would set the project back at least six months, perhaps a year or more. If their security was breached above the local level, it could be the end of everything they'd planned and worked for over the past eighteen months. And if they couldn't identify the enemy—identify and eliminate the enemy—then it could be the end of everything.

The end, perhaps, of Lin Yuan Mak.

"What's the assessment of exposure at this time?" he asked.

"We think the problem is contained," Wagner replied, "but that's a judgment call. We haven't managed to isolate the opposition yet, so nothing's definite. With luck, they'll focus strictly on the Palestinians and not pursue it any further."

With luck. Mak scowled. Another idiot.

"I would have expected your employer to deliver this news personally," Mak said. He made no effort to conceal his displeasure at being forced to deal with flunkies, at arm's length.

"No slight intended, sir," the young man said. "I'm taking over for Sterling Holbrook—"

The late Sterling Holbrook, Mak silently corrected him.

"—and Mr. Napier thought it wouldn't hurt for us to get acquainted, as it were. He's following the situation closely, as we speak, and I was asked to reassure you that he'll be in touch as soon as possible."

"I don't need reassurance," Mak replied stiffly, "nor am I much concerned with simple courtesy. It would displease me greatly, though, to think that Mr.

Napier has abandoned his responsibilities to save himself."

"Believe me, sir, nothing is further from the truth. He has a firm, continuing commitment to the project. It's his first and last priority."

The young man was an accomplished liar. Mak gave him credit for that, without crediting all that he said. It was Arnold Napier's nature to protect himself at any cost—he called it looking out for number one—and Mak expected nothing less from a wealthy man of influence. He had honed those skills himself, through years of political intrigue and party infighting, carving a niche and defending it against all comers, accumulating and consolidating power in a system where paranoia ruled and every man was suspect.

Lin Mak hadn't survived this long by fully trusting anyone but himself, and he trusted Arnold Napier only within narrow limits. Napier and Global Petroleum had influence in realms where Mak could never reach. By the same token, the ultimate success of their joint venture hinged upon *him* and his contacts in Beijing. Without him, the scheme was a dead letter.

Unless other arrangements had been made.

Nonsense. Mak would've known by now if Napier had attempted to circumvent him, cut him out of the plan in favor of some less expensive lackey.

Wouldn't he?

"No special precautions are advised, then?" he inquired. It took a force of sheer will to maintain his casual tone.

"None needed at the present time, sir," his caller replied. "Mr. Napier has asked me to say that he'll be in touch personally within the next twenty-four to forty-eight hours."

"Before any action is required on my part."

"That's affirmative, sir."

Mak glowered at the telephone receiver, wishing the smug young upstart could see his contempt for the double-talk so many Americans affected these days. He wondered sometimes if they were afraid to voice a simple yes or no, as if words of one syllable might somehow bind them to a course of action they would rather not pursue.

"Forty-eight hours," Mak repeated. "Not a moment longer."

"That's a promise," Wagner said.

I'll hold you to it, Mak thought, settling for a curt "Goodbye" as he returned the handset to its cradle.

He hadn't asked about Ammar Samman, since the Arab's fate held no meaning for him, one way or the other. Revolutionaries were a yen a dozen in the Middle East, lining up to sacrifice themselves for Allah in true fanatic's style. In Mak's view, they were living proof that Marx was right about religion: it not only lulled the captive masses into willing servitude, but also sent young warriors to their futile deaths, propelled by superstition to expect a glorious reward in the afterlife.

What sort of fool believed that strapping C-4 to his body and blowing himself to bits in a crowded marketplace would guarantee passage to Paradise and eternity in the arms of willing, nubile virgins? The very notion reeked of insanity, a product of peasant brainwashing from cradle to premature grave.

He didn't worry, then, about Samman or the young men who served him. There would always be more, ready to squander their lives for a chance to uproot the Israeli state and recapture their ancestral homeland. The fact that they and their predecessors had failed to achieve the common goal, after fifty-odd years of ceaseless effort, spoke more to their resources and their innate ability than to the mission itself.

There was still hope, Mak believed.

If not, then *his* time had been wasted, too, and that was unacceptable. It made him vulnerable, placed his very life at risk.

It made Lin Mak a fool.

Scowling, he reached out for the telephone once more. Napier and his lackey might not believe increased security precautions were necessary, but Mak trusted his own judgment in such matters. What good was it being an official of the People's Republic, if he couldn't flex his political muscles from time to time?

Lin Mak would mount a defense.

And if he found that Arnold Napier or Christos Andrastus were scheming against him, he could mount an offensive, as well.

In fact, it would be his pleasure.

CHAPTER FOUR

The Bekaa Valley

Bolan was a hundred yards from the drop zone when Grimaldi lifted off and took the chopper back toward Israel, running low and dark. He waited in the darkness, hidden by a stand of trees, and watched the chopper go. He hoped Grimaldi made it back, as much for friendship's sake as for his own.

One friend was more than Bolan cared to lose this time around.

He saw Rebecca Mindel coming through the moonlight, whistled softly in the night to redirect her. After the Sikorsky's racket, Bolan guessed he could've called her name out through a megaphone without attracting any more attention, but there was no point in taking chances.

Close behind her, bringing up the rear, McCarter saw Mindel adjust her course and followed, sliding into cover with a rustle of shrubbery. They waited for the helicopter's echo to recede and normal night sounds to return, Bolan alert to any clink or whisper that would target hunters closing in.

Nothing.

When Bolan judged that they had waited long enough, he whispered to the pair of them, "Let's go," and started moving north. Mindel gave him a twenty-yard lead before following, McCarter leaving the same space between himself and the woman, still taking rear guard.

The drop was roughly two miles due south of their intended target, a patch of undeveloped scrub and woodland where no one had yet planted opium poppies or laid out a guerrilla training camp. They'd been lucky to find an LZ that close to their quarry, Bolan knew, since a longer walk through the Bekaa would've increased their peril and might've put them at the target after daybreak.

This way, at least, they had the night to cover them.

They were armed as before, with Kalashnikov rifles, untraceable side arms and Russian frag grenades, the RGD-5 antipersonnel model. They wore generic fatigues in desert-camouflage patterns, with labels removed. Their combat boots were Army-surplus, broken in by prior owners they would never meet. Combat cosmetics darkened their faces and their fingers protruded from their cut-down shooter's gloves.

It was an hour past midnight. A waning moon provided all the light Bolan required to hold his course. There was a road off to his right, but he kept his distance from the broken pavement, ready to go belly down and take the others with him at the first sound of approaching vehicles. They had no friends within the Bekaa Valley, and if they met anyone along the way tonight, they could assume the chance encounter was with an enemy.

Bolan focused on the ground ahead of him, ever watchful. Halfway to the target, he began to slow his pace, watching and listening for sentries. His first choice was a quiet probe, but that could go to hell in seconds flat if they ran into pickets on the outskirts of the camp. He didn't know how skittish Ammar Samman might be, but with the recent losses Allah's Lance had suffered in Israel and Syria, smart money said his nerves would be stretched tighter than piano wire.

Assuming he was even there at all.

Bolan dismissed the thought of missing his quarry a second time in as many days. He still didn't think their terrified informant had been lying, though the information might be out of date or simply incorrect.

The soldier smelled the camp before he saw it, a lingering odor of fried meat competing with the smell of untended latrines. The combination would've made an effective appetite suppressant had Bolan been thinking of food. As it was, his mind had zeroed in on another odor, sharper and closer at hand.

Tobacco smoke.

Bolan signaled the others to wait, drawing his knife before he followed the aroma to its source. He found the sentry idly smoking, staring back toward camp when he should've known the danger lay without.

It was the young man's last mistake.

Bolan came up behind him in a rush, silenced the sentry's outcry with an arm across his throat and drove the knife between his ribs, twisting hard and deep to make it count. The sentry shivered, then went slack in his grip. Gravity helped him set the young man down. He wiped the knife and sheathed it, motioning for Mindel and McCarter to close up.

"There may be more," he said. "You'll have to watch it, going in."

"No sweat," McCarter said. Mindel frowned at the body and said nothing.

"Ready, then?" Bolan asked.

"Ready," Mindel said this time.

"As ready as I'll ever be." McCarter smiled.

Bolan eased his rifle off its shoulder sling.

"Let's do it," he said.

AERIAL PHOTOS HAD GIVEN them a clear view of the camp's layout and allowed them to estimate its population. Based on the number of tents and latrines, McCarter knew roughly a hundred fighting men of Allah's Lance were currently in residence. Call it thirty-to-one, then, and there was only so much that surprise could do to trim those odds.

A man worried about his future would've likely let it pass, but McCarter still owed something to Yakov Katzenelenbogen and to the men who'd killed him. This night, perhaps, another overdue installment on that debt would be paid, and he would be that much closer to settling the full account.

The Briton entered the camp from the west, slightly closer to the apparent command post than either Bolan—east—or Mindel—south. It was pure luck of the draw, maybe a break and maybe not. Fortune was with him so far, no more sentries on his part of the perimeter, but the plan didn't rely wholly on stealth.

They could search the camp all night, one darkened tent at a time, without finding Ammar Samman. This time, to improve the odds, they had agreed to let chaos assist them for a change.

Beginning now.

McCarter's first stop was the motor pool, midway between his point of entry to the camp and the CP that was his final destination. The camp's rolling stock included two covered trucks, three old-model military jeeps and a half-dozen mismatched civilian vehicles ranging in size from a two-door subcompact model to an old station wagon with dramatic, rust-flecked fins in back. Three dirt bikes at the far end of the line completed the collection.

McCarter passed along the line of dusty vehicles, stopping at the first, the fourth and so on down the row. Each time he paused, a gas cap was removed and twisted cloth inserted in its place. When one end of the cloth was soaked with gasoline, McCarter pulled out the wick and reversed it, feeling the brief chill of gas on his fingertips, breathing its fumes. He finished rigging all the chosen vehicles—including one of the trucks, one jeep, two cars and one of the dirt bikes— before he started back along the line, lighting the fuel-soaked wicks in reverse order.

No dawdling now. Time to move.

He broke cover and started for the CP, not running, rather "walking with a purpose" as his SAS instructors used to say. Most of the compound lay in darkness. He couldn't escape a challenge if he met one of its tenants face-to-face, but from a distance there was still a chance that he could pass, at least until—

The dirt bike went up like a rocket on Guy Fawkes day, bouncing on its shock absorbers as the fuel tank blew, then flipping over on its back with the concussive force of the explosion. McCarter was prepared for it, and still he winced, ears battered by the blast.

The station wagon, next in line to blow, was twice as loud, its booming echo rousing anyone in camp who wasn't on his feet already, scrambling for a weapon or a pair of pants. Bright arcs of flaming gasoline were sprayed in all directions, setting fire to vehicles on either side of ground zero. They were burning fiercely by the time a second car detonated, shattering the windows of its neighbors, settling on melted tires in a lake of flame.

Bedlam. The saving grace.

McCarter's luck went sour when he was still twenty yards or so from the camp command post. The CP's door flew open and disgorged a slender rifleman. He wore a khaki cap and rumpled pants to match, but he was barefoot and bare-chested, clutching an AK-47. McCarter stood between him and the motor pool, backlit by fire, his face invisible, but something in his look or attitude alarmed the enemy.

The gunman wasn't Ammar Samman; that much was obvious. He shouted something in Arabic, lips twisting in a snarl, and began to raise his weapon.

Sod it, McCarter thought. This one was expendable. He fired from the waist, near enough to his target that aiming was superfluous. A short burst of 5.45 mm rounds tore through the Arab's bony chest and pitched him backward, bare arms flailing as he fell.

McCarter glanced around, keeping the CP covered, still advancing, but the final detonation from the motor pool appeared to mask his gunfire. Nearly all the vehicles were burning now, only a matter of time before their gas tanks added secondary blasts to the confusion. One thing at least was obvious: whoever fled the camp this night—McCarter and his friends included—would be traveling on foot.

McCarter reached the CP, spared the young man he had killed a passing glance and stood before the open doorway, ready for whatever lay within.

"Sod all you bastards, then," he said, and stepped inside.

AMMAR SAMMAN SWALLOWED panic, nearly retching from its bitter taste. His hands trembled, defeated by the simple task of buttoning his shirt. He gave it up and left the garment hanging open. More than anything, he craved the pistol belt around his waist, buckling it snugly on the second try.

A Kalashnikov assault rifle stood in the corner, near his bunk. Samman picked it up, feeling better already with the gun's solid weight in his hands. He crossed to the door of his quarters, where Moukib had knocked and shouted for him moments earlier, wailing as if he thought Samman could sleep through the explosions shattering the night.

Young fool. But he was loyal and brave. It wouldn't

do for him to know Samman was terrified, about to
lose his grip.

The enemy had found him, somehow. After all the
killing of the past few days in Syria and Israel, after
he had fled to what he thought were safer quarters in
the Bekaa, still he couldn't shake them.

And he still didn't know who they were.

Samman opened the door and saw Moukib standing
just outside, his weapon leveled toward some target
out of sight, away to the west. Samman opened his
mouth to speak, demand an explanation, but before the
words could clear his throat Moukib was driven backward, going limp as bullets tore his chest apart.

There was no swallowing the panic, then. Samman
saw death before him, knew that in another moment
it would peer around the doorjamb, whispering his
name.

Samman closed his door, locked it and moved toward the window, mouthing a silent prayer. Let it be
large enough.

It seemed to be, if only just. He slid the window
open, fumbling in an ecstasy of fear, and used the butt
of his Kalashnikov to batter out the flimsy screen. Outside, another thunderous explosion rocked the compound, rattling the command post walls.

He couldn't place the source of the explosions.
Somewhere from the west side of the compound,
surely, but he heard no aircraft overhead, no whistle
of incoming artillery shells. In his panic, Samman dismissed the question, concentrating on escape.

His first attempt, with rifle slung across his shoulder, sent Samman tumbling back into the room, head over heels. He came up cursing, jerked the rifle off its sling and worked his aching shoulder as he strode back to the window. This time, he leaned out and let the rifle drop, first making sure its safety was engaged. That done, Samman edged head-first through the window, gasping as the sill ground painfully against his ribs, his stomach, then snagged on his belt buckle.

Half in, half out, he suddenly imagined being stuck there, trapped as enemies surrounded him and opened fire from point-blank range. He rocked his hips with desperate urgency, sweat beading on his face despite the chill night breeze.

Why had he even put the pistol on? It was about to get him killed, unless he could—

The sudden drop took Samman by surprise. His heels banged hard against the upper window frame, pain lancing through his feet and shins, while Samman raised both arms to protect his face from the uprushing earth. The drop was no more than five feet, but he still skinned his palms, bruising his cheek on the Kalashnikov when his arms wouldn't hold him.

Rolling away, Samman ate dust and spit it out again, cursing. He scrabbled for the weapon that had wounded him, knowing that it could mean the difference between life and death.

Struggling to his feet, he used the rifle as a crutch to push himself upright. A burst of gunfire sounded from within the CP hut itself, shocking him out of immobility. Samman imagined grim Israelis with their blacked-out faces, pouring through the rooms in search

of him and lighting up the shadows with their muzzle-
blasts.

He turned and ran.

Safety lay elsewhere, in the desert's outer darkness.
He could reach it yet, if he was resolute and didn't
falter. Those he left behind could do without him.
They need never know his courage had deserted him.

Samman cleared the first row of tents beside his
quarters, then glanced back to see if anyone was following. A dark shape backed by firelight stood in front
of the command post. Was it staring after him, or
turned away? He couldn't tell and was afraid to wait.

Samman faced forward, lurching in the split second
before collision with another form that barred his path.
This one was smaller, verging on petite, but there was
nothing small about the AKS rifle it held.

"Bastard!" a woman's voice spit at him.

He had time to register that she was speaking Arabic, before the rifle swung and clubbed him down.

REBECCA MINDEL TOOK a pair of handcuffs from her
pocket, snapped one of the bracelets on Samman's left
wrist, then pulled the arm behind his back and cuffed
it to his right. She had already checked to make sure
he was breathing, that she hadn't killed him with the
blow that put him down.

It would've been so easy to finish him, but he was
needed breathing. For the moment, anyhow. Perhaps
later, when he had spilled his guts, Mindel could put
a word in someone's ear to see that he was shot while
trying to escape. Or maybe Samman would simply dis-

appear into a prison cell and be forgotten there until he died, one of the worst fates any ardent revolutionary could endure.

But first, she had to get him out of there alive and back to Israel, where he could be questioned on the whereabouts of his associates, the men who paid the bills and kept their distance while the bloody war dragged on.

Mindel was trying to revive Samman and get him on his feet, slapping his face and none too gently, when she heard footsteps approaching through the darkness. In a heartbeat she was ready with her AKS, tracking a form that filled her sights, before she recognized McCarter.

"I'd prefer you didn't shoot me, if it's all the same," he said.

"All right."

"You bagged him, then."

"I did."

"Good job. I got some of his papers from the CP, but I was afraid he'd given us the slip."

"Not this time. Help me get him up, will you?"

Around them, automatic weapons spewed tracers into the darkness. As before, most of the guns were turned outward, laying down fire on the perimeter, searching for enemies the shooters couldn't see. They'd have to clear that ring of fire to get out with their captive, but they hadn't reached it yet.

Samman came grudgingly around after McCarter grabbed one of his ears and twisted it. The Arab sputtered, tried to struggle free, then gave it up when Mindel pressed the muzzle of her AKS into his groin.

"We're leaving now," she said in Arabic. "Your life depends on making sure nobody tries to stop us. Understand me?"

He defied her for a moment, felt the rifle gouge deeper and nodded. "I understand."

McCarter was half-turned away from her, speaking into his microphone. He barely whispered, but the words were loud and clear in Mindel's earpiece. "Striker, we've retrieved the package. Do you read me?"

Bolan's voice came back a heartbeat later, gunfire in the background, making for a chilling stereo effect. "I read. Where are you?"

"Thirty meters out from the CP, southeast."

"I'm halfway there. Make for the south perimeter. We'll regroup there."

"We're moving," said McCarter. "Out."

"Get moving," Mindel told Samman, prodding him. "That way."

McCarter joined them, flanking the prisoner, ending any feeble hope Samman may have cherished that he could escape. He was theirs now, and the only way Mindel would release him, short of delivery to Mossad handlers, was if Samman forced her to kill him.

That could still happen, she knew, but it wasn't her first choice. Not while he could direct her to the men behind her uncle Yakov's death. She hated Ammar Samman and all he stood for, but Mindel was ready to defend his worthless life against all comers if it would advance her quest.

She pegged the distance they had to travel at 150 meters, more or less. The good news was that most of the guerrillas in the camp had gravitated toward the motor pool, either believing they would find live targets there or simply hoping to find out what produced the string of fiery blasts. Around them, aimless gunfire had begun to sputter out on the perimeter, as nervous sentries or their officers regained a measure of control.

That could be good or bad, depending on how many shooters lay between the three of them and their escape route. She experienced a moment's worry for Mike Blanski, then focused with deadly clarity on covering the ground in front of her and getting to the other side of the perimeter alive.

Call it two hundred paces. On a city street or in a quiet park, it would be nothing. Here, surrounded by the enemy, each step could be her last. The split second she used to take that step could be a lifetime.

Samman broke stride and she reached out to shove him forward, keep him going. "Move," she snapped, "unless you want to die!"

No sooner had she spoken than she heard the voice behind them, raised above the echo of gunfire.

"Captain Samman?" it called in Arabic. And when no answer was received, as if to echo Mindel's order, it said, "Stop or die!"

BOLAN MOVED through the semidarkness like a wraith. In the confusion, firelight did as much to hide his fea-

tures from the enemy as to reveal him. Those who
recognized him as an interloper and attempted to de-
tain him died before they recognized their critical mistake.

Until the last three, anyway.

They had to have seen him coming, maybe watched
him drop one of their comrades moments earlier, outside the mess tent, where a young guerrilla with more
guts than brains had tried to take him down. It wasn't
even close, the Arab dead before he fell into the ash-
strewn pit they used for roasting meat and vegetables.
Bolan was past it, moving on, when his two shadows
came from nowhere, flanking him, and tried to close
the trap.

They almost pulled it off; he gave them that. The
set was adequate, their timing likewise, but he caught
a break when one of them surrendered to a case of
nerves and jerked the trigger of his AK-47, not remembering the slow and steady squeeze required to
do it right.

Bolan had seen the muzzle-flash and gone to ground
as hasty bullets fanned the air above his head. Between
the AK's tendency to climb when firing on full-
automatic and the shooter's poor technique, Bolan had
room to spare between himself and first rounds that
rippled past. The other shooter tried to compensate,
but by the time he started firing, Bolan had rolled out
of view behind a two-man tent.

He found no safety there—canvas no match for military rounds—but his assailants hesitated in the moment they lost sight of him. Instead of pouring fire

into the tent and through it, as they should've done, they waited for a moment to find out if he would re-emerge.

And when he did, their fate was sealed.

Bolan went left, rolling across the sand, and came up with a frag grenade already primed. He pitched it toward the gunner who had missed him first, crouching between two tents but making no real effort to conceal himself. The Arab either didn't see it coming or he didn't know quite what to make of it. In either case, he stood his ground and let the green egg drop a yard in front of him, rolling almost between his feet before it blew.

The blast tore him apart and left his partner suddenly alone. He was recovering after a fashion, trying to lay down a screen of fire and save himself, when Bolan framed the young man in his sights and cut him dead with half a dozen armor-piercing rounds.

He moved on, making tracks before any of their comrades could respond to the grenade blast and encircle him. Mindel and McCarter were already moving, counting on Bolan to join them and help move their hostage safely out of camp. He planned to be there when they needed him, even if it meant wading knee-deep through the blood of enemies to get there.

Another shape reared up in front of him, and Bolan chopped it down with automatic fire. He didn't have to see a face or uniform to know his only friends in camp were well ahead of him, embroiled in trouble of their own. Whatever moved between him and the compound's south perimeter was fair game for the kill.

The soldier picked up his pace, pushing it. If he was late and missed the others, it would be McCarter's job to leave without him, and he counted on the rugged Brit to do exactly that. The signal should've already gone out for Jack Grimaldi to meet them at the pickup point, but Bolan reached down to his belt and keyed his own transmitter, just in case.

He didn't think about the odds against them, or the risk Grimaldi faced in coming back across those darkened miles of hostile territory. So much could go wrong before the rendezvous, that even thinking of it seemed to amplify the risk, as if he'd thumbed his nose at Fate.

Be there, he willed Grimaldi, from across the miles of midnight desert. Be alive.

Pressing forward, Bolan concentrated on his progress, taking one step at a time.

THE ARAB STUMBLED, nearly falling in midstride, cursing when he couldn't use his handcuffed arms to catch himself. Rebecca Mindel caught him instead, hauling him upright by sheer will alone, lashing out at him in Arabic to watch his step.

McCarter covered them, spinning like a dancer and firing from the hip with his AKS and toppling two guerrillas who were close enough to be a threat. Others were following, but they peeled off to either side and looked for cover as a second short burst from McCarter's Kalashnikov fanned the air close to their faces.

"Faster!" he snapped at the others, catching Mindel's baleful glare in return.

"Tell this one!" she answered.

"You tell him," McCarter said, striking Samman across one shoulder with the barrel of his AKS for emphasis. "Whatever happens, win or lose, he isn't staying here alive."

Mindel translated on the run, shoving Samman in front of her. The ranking officer of Allah's Lance made no reply, but he picked up his pace a fraction, laboring to stay a length or two ahead of them. His breathing came in ragged gasps, as if his lungs were on the verge of bursting.

Some commando, McCarter thought. This one couldn't run a half mile without laboring. He'd lose his dinner at a mile and probably collapse soon after. The Briton hoped he wouldn't have to haul Samman's deadweight across the desert to the rendezvous.

A shadow moved to intercept them in the darkness, both assault rifles swinging around to meet the challenge before McCarter recognized Bolan. "You made it, then," he said.

"Looks like," Bolan replied, and fired a burst along their back trail, scattering pursuers.

McCarter triggered a burst of his own but the human targets eluded him, ducking and weaving like reeds in a windstorm. They were good at that part of it, anyway. He only hoped their marksmanship wouldn't improve dramatically within the next few minutes.

"How much farther?" Mindel asked.

"Another klick," Bolan stated, "give or take."

Three-quarters of a mile, approximately. With sporadic gunfire snapping at his heels, McCarter knew he wouldn't hear the helicopter until it was right on top of them, assuming that Grimaldi could get through this time. If he'd been shot out of the sky somewhere along the way, they were as good as dead.

A bullet whistled past McCarter's head. He ducked reflexively and palmed a Russian frag grenade from its loop on his combat harness, tearing the pin free as he turned and cocked his arm for the pitch.

Their pursuers had closed the gap, some firing on the run without success, others dropping to one knee and trying for a clear shot at their zigzagging targets. Darkness and movement had foiled them so far, but McCarter knew it was only a matter of time before one of the Arabs got lucky.

He pitched the grenade, losing sight of it immediately as he raked the desert with another burst of autofire. Most of his adversaries went to ground, but two or three were on their feet when the grenade fell among them, detonating in a smoky thunderclap. A storm of shrapnel turned them into screaming pincushions, their comrades scrambling for better concealment in case a second blast followed the first.

It didn't.

McCarter was too busy running for his life, catching up with the others—and in the lull that followed the explosion, he could hear another sound approaching from the front.

The Sikorsky!

McCarter couldn't see the chopper yet, but from the

sound of it they were on a direct interception course. Grimaldi would be running dark for safety's sake. He could be right on top of them before—

A floodlight blazed in front of them, searing the desert sand a hundred yards away before it was extinguished, just as suddenly. Beside McCarter, Ammar Samman stumbled again, grunting. The Briton grabbed the prisoner's right arm and tried to hold him upright, but deadweight defeated him.

Deadweight.

He crouched beside Samman and found the wound between their captive's shoulder blades. His life was shuddering away before McCarter's eyes, and there was nothing to be done. From the position of the wound, McCarter knew the spine was clipped, the heart and left lung almost certainly mangled by the projectile or bone fragments.

"Dammit!"

Mindel dropped to her knees beside Samman, in time to watch him die. Enraged, she turned back toward the trailing gunmen, emptying her AKS in one ferocious burst.

"Leave it!" Bolan snapped, dragging Mindel to her feet and toward the helicopter where it hovered, thirty yards in front of them. "It's too late now."

Too late.

McCarter cursed again and left Samman slumped in the dirt, pushing off toward the waiting Sikorsky.

Inside the cockpit, Jack Grimaldi saw them coming and unleashed hellfire upon the enemy, a rippling wave of rockets springing from the chopper's undercarriage, riding brilliant tails of flame to meet the enemy.

McCarter felt the sheaf of papers slapping at his thigh, inside the cargo pocket of his pants, as he ran toward the helicopter. They had been a kind of consolation prize, before Mindel had snagged Samman, and now they would be all he had to show for this excursion into hell.

Too late, his mind repeated numbingly. Too bloody late.

He leaped aboard the helicopter as Grimaldi fired another wave of rockets toward the camp and their pursuers, raising hell with those who weren't already dead or dying.

A bloody waste, McCarter thought, before the thunder ended and the helicopter swung back toward the south, racing across the pitch-black killing ground toward friendly lines.

CHAPTER FIVE

Tel Aviv, Israel

There'd been a brief dispute with Mossad over the disposition of Ammar Samman's private papers, retrieved by McCarter from the Bekaa encampment, but Bolan had settled the matter by offering to give them up if the Israelis would pursue all principal conspirators regardless of their influence, wherever they were found. The agents he'd faced off against would probably have liked nothing better, but they understood political reality and knew they'd never be unleashed against high-profile residents of China, Greece or the United States.

Mindel had made her stand with Bolan and McCarter at the airstrip, moments after they'd returned from Lebanon. Her handlers had been waiting to receive Samman, and failing that, they'd wanted to review his notes for anything of value for their long war against Allah's Lance. Bolan had balked at handing off the papers without getting a translation for himself, first thing, and when push came to shove the Israelis had stopped short of forcing a violent confrontation on the helipad. It was agreed that Mindel would retrieve the documents and file them after Bolan's team had extracted the pertinent data.

It was a leap of faith for Mossad, not known for trust at the best of times, but they had nothing to lose in the long run. The documents might provide no information of value—and if they paid off, Bolan's squad would be taking the risks, diverting attention and potential scandal from the Israeli regime. The most they stood to lose so far was one agent, covered with enough layers of deniability to satisfy headquarters on that score. If Bolan's people blew it, Tel Aviv could always find another way around the problem, using stealth in lieu of a frontal assault.

But first, it had to be determined if the papers lifted by McCarter offered any hope at all.

They drove from the air base to Mindel's apartment, the first time Bolan had seen where she lived. It was a small place, but homey—the female equivalent of a bachelor pad, he supposed. Mindel had decorated it with photographs of family and friends, including several shots of Yakov Katzenelenbogen taken during rare family reunions. From his hair and the lines in his face, Bolan guessed the photos spanned two decades, charting way stations in a transient life.

At least he left something, Bolan reflected. His own photo album, had it existed, would've been blank since the day he'd supposedly died in New York. His new face, his new life, had left no more permanent trace than a handful of ashes tossed into the wind.

Unless he counted graves.

They sat around a table barely big enough for four, with coffee mugs in front of them, watching Mindel page through the sheaf of documents. Some of the items concerned camp logistics, she explained, an accounting of movements and material received. There was a record of guerrilla actions dating back some eighteen months that held Mindel's attention for a while, confirming official suspicion in several unsolved cases, surprising her in one instance—a school bombing that her superiors had blamed on Hezbollah.

"Eight children murdered," she said, with a break in her voice.

"You paid them back with interest tonight," McCarter said. "Stay focused."

"I'm looking."

And five minutes later she found it, skimming through the entries of a combination diary and appointment ledger, written out by Samman in a spiral notebook similar to those Bolan had carried to his classes in high school. It seemed out of place on the table, surrounded by loose foolscap pages and flimsy invoices. Mindel was riffling through its pages, pausing here and there to comment on some entry, noting Samman's movements and meetings with the late Wasim Jabbar, when she stopped, finger pinning a short entry written in blue ink.

"'Received message from Lin Mak in Macao,'" she read aloud. "'Delivery accomplished on schedule. Payment forthcoming.'"

"Delivery of what?" McCarter asked.

"It doesn't say. There's nothing in the notes beforehand to explain it. I suppose he didn't feel the need to note details that he already knew.''

"Or details that could make things hot for him," Grimaldi said, "if they fell into the wrong hands.''

"In that case," McCarter added, "why make notes at all?''

"Payment forthcoming," Bolan said. "My guess would be that he wanted a record of the date, in case the money was delayed.''

"Macao. That doesn't tell us much," McCarter said. "It still leaves, what, six hundred thousand targets, give or take?''

"It's more than we had two minutes ago," Bolan reminded him. "Maybe something else in the notes pins it down.''

But it didn't. Mindel went through the rest of the diary without discovering an address for Lin Mak. She found no mention at all of the other targets, Arnold Napier or Christos Andrastus.

"He's some kind of government official, right?" Grimaldi asked.

"Something to do with trade," Bolan replied. "Not ministerial, from what I gather, but he's got the pull.''

"So the chances are," Grimaldi continued, "that he'll have some kind of an official residence, maybe some primo office space. That has to narrow down the possibilities.''

"It couldn't hurt," Bolan replied.

"I find it strange that there's no mention of the others," Mindel said.

"That would depend on the transaction," Bolan

said. "It could've been something specific to China, or even a personal contract. Either way, it's someplace to start."

"Bloody China," McCarter groused. "We'll fit right in there."

"At least it's Macao," Bolan said, "not Beijing."

"Hal may have a connection we can use," Grimaldi said.

"There's no time like the present to find out," Bolan replied.

REBECCA MINDEL DIDN'T trust her cell phone for the call to Mossad headquarters. Blanski had balked at using the landline from her apartment, making some excuse about his scrambler unit, when they both knew he was more concerned about the possibility of built-in traps that would allow Mossad to trace and monitor his call to the United States. Mindel had reason to believe her people knew Blanski's superior by name— or title, at the very least—but she couldn't fault him for being cautious in a foreign land where even so-called friends seemed hostile.

After Blanski left to find another telephone, Mindel retreated to her bedroom and called headquarters, waiting for the operator in her section to raise Gideon Herzhaft.

"Rebecca," her controller said when he came on the line. "How goes it?"

"It goes east," she said. "We have a lead on Lin Yuan Mak."

"Ah, yes?"

"He's in Macao," she said. "Or was, three weeks ago."

"Macao," Herzhaft repeated. "That's outside our normal sphere of operation, as you're well aware."

"Yes, sir."

"You don't exactly fit the standard profile over there."

"Nor do the others, sir."

"That's not our problem, is it, Mindel? I suspect the wisest course of action now would be for us to watch and wait. If they proceed and are successful, then the issue should resolve itself. And it they fail…"

She knew the rest, although he didn't finish it. If Blanski and McCarter failed, Mossad could reconsider its options, decide whether a covert operation with Israeli personnel was wise or even possible.

Mindel knew that she couldn't let it go at that.

"Sir," she replied, "I have a special interest in this mission, as you know."

"A personal involvement, I believe you meant to say." Herzhaft made no attempt to mask his disapproval. "The loyalty to your uncle does you credit, Mindel, but we still have rules. I've risked a reprimand or worse by letting you proceed this far. As for Macao—"

She interrupted him, saying, "You know me well enough to realize I'd never compromise the service, sir. I won't embarrass Israel or Mossad."

"You won't intentionally compromise the service or your country, Mindel. That I take for granted. What you fail to grasp, in your excitement, is that simply being found in China, on whatever errand, could be compromise enough. Don't mind that blather out of Washington about the axis of evil. They're as keen for trade with China as the Chinese are to gain commercial footholds in the West. They won't look kindly on us muddying the waters, I can promise you.''

She understood then that the choice had already been made. The men responsible for her uncle's death weren't to be pursued outside the Middle East, if there was any chance at all of Israel being linked to the campaign.

''In that case, sir, I think it only fitting for the service that I should resign immediately and continue as a private citizen.''

''Mindel—''

''Of course, I understand deniability must be preserved. I have replacement travel documents, Canadian and Swiss. There should be ample time to purge the necessary files and—''

''Mindel, please! You must understand—''

''I understand perfectly, as I've explained. You'll have my resignation via fax within the hour.''

''I'm afraid that's unacceptable.''

''And how do you propose to stop me, sir?''

''It's well within my power, as you know.''

''Best make it permanent,'' she said. ''I won't forgive the interference, if you understand me, sir.''

''I think we understand each other, Mindel. Now, are you prepared to listen and be reasonable?''

"I'm prepared to listen, sir," she answered. "As for being reasonable, I suspect our definitions of the term may be at odds."

Herzhaft surprised her with an honest laugh. "You make me proud, Mindel," he said. "Such fire, such dedication. If you weren't completely insubordinate, we'd get along much better, though."

"Sir, I don't mean to be—"

"Spare me, for heaven's sake! I'm about to grant your wish, unless you muck about and make me change my mind."

"That isn't my intention, sir."

"I shouldn't think so. Now, the compromise I'm going to suggest is this," Herzhaft went on. "Fax in the resignation you've described, backdated before this business started. I'll keep it on file until you're finished in Macao or wherever this business takes you in the end. If any mischief should befall you, God forbid, deniability will be preserved. Of course, I can't assist you, once you've left our local sphere of influence. If you have certain contacts in the field who might be helpful, use them sparingly and leave no tracks."

"Yes, sir. I mean, no, sir."

"We have an understanding, then," Herzhaft said. "When we speak again, if everything's all right, the resignation will be lost, shredded. If by some chance we never speak again..."

"Yes, sir. Goodbye, sir."

"Make it 'farewell,' Mindel," he corrected her. "Farewell."

Washington, D.C.

HAL BROGNOLA TOOK the call an hour past quitting time. His secretary had left for the day, but since the call was on his private outside line, he didn't need her help to patch it through.

"Brognola."

"Working late?" There was a faint trace of amusement in the deep, familiar voice.

"The usual," Brognola said. "I guess I never shook J. Edgar's so-called voluntary overtime routine."

"That's why you get the big bucks," Bolan quipped.

"Don't tell the IRS, all right? They don't know anything about my oil wells or the diamond mine."

"Your secret's safe with me."

"Speaking of secrets…"

"Right. We lost the package," Bolan told him. The big Fed could almost hear the big guy frowning. Then he added, "But we caught a lucky break."

"How's that?" Without Samman, Brognola couldn't think of any other way to nail down the top-rank plotters. He kept his fingers crossed.

"Our boy kept notes," Bolan replied. "They're not complete, but we have a lead on one of the players."

"Which one?" Brognola asked.

"Lin Mak. If our source got it right, we should find him somewhere in Macao."

"Somewhere," Brognola repeated. "That's not exactly GPS precision."

"It's a start," Bolan reminded him.

"Okay. It makes me nervous, though."

"I know the feeling."

China was a bitch to infiltrate. Forget about the vast interior, where any Western face stood out like the proverbial sore thumb. Macao, Hong Kong and Guangzhou—formerly Canton—were cosmopolitan enough for foreigners to pass without creating a commotion on the street, but "round-eyed" visitors were still monitored by local authorities, any unorthodox behavior reported to Beijing with all dispatch.

Unless local authorities screwed up, that was. Unless they could be bought.

"I may know someone in Macao," Brognola told his friend. It was a stretch, but he knew people who knew people on the Chinese mainland. "I'll put out some feelers. What kind of deadline are we looking at?"

"ASAP," Bolan replied. "Mak may be in the wind already. I don't want to give him any more time than we have to."

"Right. I'm on it. You'll need visas, something on those lines?"

"I was about to ask you," Bolan answered. "Right now, all we have is passports."

"That's the easy part. Give me a couple hours, then swing by the embassy in Tel Aviv. You'll find them holding paperwork for three."

"We'll need a fourth," Bolan said.

That was a surprise to Hal. "I thought Mossad would drop you flat," he said.

"They did the next-best thing," Bolan explained. "The niece gets a green light but no field support. If the Chinese ask questions, she doesn't exist."

"We've got some nervous Nellies here in D.C., too. I'm not sure how much I can do for you, beyond arrangements for a local contact."

"If the contact knows Macao, that should be plenty," Bolan said.

Brognola hoped so, but he wasn't long on confidence where mainland China was concerned. Whole armies could be swallowed up there, much less four field agents operating on a shoestring, bucking killer odds. If Bolan or his people dropped the ball in China, it would take a miracle to get them back for burial, much less alive.

The big Fed checked his watch and wondered if he'd have to call his CIA contact at home. If so, too bad. A lifer in the cloak-and-dagger trade should know that there was no such thing as being off the clock.

"I don't suppose you have a contact number there?" he asked.

"I'll have to call you back," Bolan replied.

"Okay. I'll get the wheels in motion for your travel documents, first thing. The contact in Macao may take a little time. Say ninety minutes, for the sake of argument. If I don't have an answer for you then, I'll light a fire under some lazy asses, PDQ."

"Appreciate it," Bolan said. "If you come up with someone, great, but we can't pass on Mak, regardless."

No, Brognola thought, you couldn't do that, just this once.

"I'm working on the others," he assured Bolan. "Andrastus took one of his yachts out for a spin around the Med, but so far we can't pin him down. Nothing on Napier, anywhere we look.''

"Which only makes Macao more critical," Bolan replied.

"You'll have support," Brognola promised, "even if I have to learn Chinese and do the job myself."

"We need to get it done this year," Bolan reminded him.

"Nobody likes a wiseacre."

"Sorry."

"That's ninety minutes," Brognola repeated. "I'll have something, one way or another."

"Home or office?" Bolan asked.

"Office," Brognola said. "If anybody tries to slow me down, I've got a nice fat stash of midnight oil. Nobody sleeps until they come around."

"Okay. I'll be in touch."

Brognola cradled the receiver, conscious of a sudden hollow feeling underneath his ribs. He had the Langley number memorized, tapping the digits out before he had a chance to think of what he'd say, how he'd approach the matter of procuring assistance from a contract agent in Macao.

He only knew he had to get it done, and soon.

GRIMALDI WAITED until Bolan, fresh back from his call to Washington, had finished speaking. While he listened, the pilot had eyed the map spread out before him. It portrayed Macao in fair detail, enough to make him feel like a fifth wheel with a flat tire, destined to make the team more vulnerable than it had to be.

"Questions?" Bolan asked.

"Call it a comment," Grimaldi replied. "I'm with you one hundred percent if you want me, but looking at this—" he fanned a palm over the map, "—and knowing what little I know about China, something tells me I won't be much good on this run."

McCarter flashed a crooked smile at him. "Don't say you're tired of us already."

"I'm thinking I might be a liability," Grimaldi said. "It's not an airborne mission, and unless you've got a carrier floating around somewhere in the South China Sea, the nearest friendly air base will be on Taiwan, five hundred miles away. That's damn near useless for a hurry call, assuming I could sneak in past the Chinese air force in the first place."

"I was hoping for a bit more subtlety," Bolan replied. "To get us started, anyway."

"Okay," Grimaldi told him. "Break it down."

"Macao comes close to rivaling Hong Kong, in terms of international finance," Bolan said. "They've got round-eyes in and out of there like a revolving door. Four more won't make a ripple, if we have the paperwork in order."

"Would the four have wings, by any chance?" Grimaldi asked.

"I'm working on it. Something in a nice Learjet to get us started, maybe with a chopper if we need to make side trips."

"High-ticket items," McCarter pointed out. "Can we swing it?"

"Washington still wants results," Bolan replied.

"As long as there's no paper trail, I think we've got a decent shot."

"There's still the matter of a contact on the ground," Jack reminded them. "I know English is like the second language where we're headed, but I never feel quite right if I can't eavesdrop on the locals."

"You afraid they'll talk behind your back?" McCarter asked.

"I don't mind talk," Grimaldi answered. "It's the sticks and stones that worry me."

"And bullets," Rebecca Mindel added.

"Bullets are a problem, too," the pilot readily agreed. "I make an effort to avoid them when I can."

"We have a contact in the works," Bolan confirmed. "I'll know more details when I check back in an hour."

Trusting anyone in China would be problematic, Grimaldi thought. The Communist regime had deviated so much from its former hard-line stance in recent years that it was sometimes difficult to separate the party spokesmen from dedicated capitalists, but any one of them could spring a trap if he—or she—was so inclined. The vast nation still nurtured a thriving network of spies at all levels, from high-rise office suites to steaming rice paddies. Reds aside, there were also right-wing Chinese nationalists with their own ax to grind, triad gangsters, party loyalists or straight-up businessmen and enough outsiders to maximize confusion at the best of times. The old rules had been cautiously relaxed, but China still reminded him of a bear trap, cocked and ready to snap shut on the first unwary soul who brushed unwittingly against its trigger.

And once the trap closed, getting out alive would be next to impossible.

Grimaldi kept those worries to himself and gave the map another look. "Okay," he said. "Learjet or chopper, take your pick. Unless they've got MiGs waiting for us on arrival, I can get us in. As far as getting out, it may be touch-and-go."

"One step at a time," Bolan answered. "Unless we have a clear fix on Lin Mak, it's all for nothing anyway."

"And how's that coming?" McCarter asked.

"It's confirmed he has an office in Macao," Bolan replied, "as well as Hong Kong and Beijing. He obviously gets around. Hal's working on a confirmation of his present situation, as we speak."

"Sooner the better," Grimaldi said. "If the mark gets wind of what's been happening out here and takes a powder, finding him in China will be damn near impossible."

"I'm counting on a fair amount of arrogance," Bolan replied. "He should feel reasonably safe at home, particularly if he thinks we're busy tearing up the Middle East, looking for Napier."

"Someone ought to be," McCarter said. "No word on that one yet?"

"Nothing," Bolan told him, "but he has to surface sometime. When he does—"

"Let's hope we're there to greet him," Grimaldi quipped.

"Bloody right," McCarter said. "Let's hope we're somewhere, anyhow."

"We made it this far," Bolan told his British comrade.

"True enough." Frowning, McCarter added, "But I'd hate to see the cost go any higher, if you get my drift."

"I hear you," Bolan said. "From now on, we're collecting due, paying them."

WHEN THE MEETING broke up, McCarter retired to the kitchen and helped himself to a soda from Mindel's refrigerator. Unlike most people he knew, the caffeine seemed to help him relax, while sharpening his wits at the same time. Draining a quarter of the can's contents in one long swallow, he leaned against the kitchen counter, tuning out the others in the dining room, thinking about what was supposed to happen next.

They would be leaving Israel, which was good news any way McCarter looked at it. The team had worn out its welcome, with allies and adversaries alike. Mossad had suffered their presence out of respect for Yakov Katzenelenbogen—and a desire to have someone else do the dirty work for a change—but there'd been so much killing now, without concrete results, that official patience was nearly exhausted.

China would be another kind of war zone altogether. Instead of hunting terrorists with the covert collaboration of the government in power, McCarter and his colleagues would be operating as "illegals," covert agents with no official allies to help them if the mission began to unravel, stalking a member of the Chinese communist establishment. It was a rough way to go, exacerbated by the drawbacks of ethnicity and language.

Bottom line: there was a solid chance that none of them would ever leave Macao alive.

McCarter didn't take such things to heart in normal circumstances, but the present situation wasn't normal. Gruff old Katz had once seemed indestructible, but he was dead. McCarter got the message loud and clear.

None of them were invulnerable.

Anyone could die, at any time.

The choice of action they'd just chosen brought death closer to them, virtually breathing down their necks. McCarter knew the feeling, was experienced enough to cope with it, but nothing in his training said he had to like it.

Going into China meant they'd have to fly unarmed and trust a contact still unknown, a person none of them had ever met, to hook them up with gear and weapons on the other end. If anything went wrong— say their connection proved to be a traitor, for example—they'd not only be on hostile ground, cut off from any kind of help, but they'd also be unable to defend themselves.

Luck of the draw, McCarter thought, knowing he'd go ahead with it regardless of the odds, the risks, the chance of never coming home again. Besides, he wasn't sure where home was, anymore. He was a British citizen who didn't live in England. He was di-

vorced, without children. His closest friends were warriors, constantly at risk, their meager number recently
reduced by one.

McCarter could've counted those who'd mourn his
passing on his fingers, but he also knew how they'd
react in that event.

The same way he was doing now, for Katz.

A soldier's code of honor would permit no less.

He drained the can of soda, crumpled it in one
strong hand and dropped it in the kitchen wastebasket.
When he rejoined the others, they were running down
potential arms sources in the Far East.

It didn't sound encouraging, so far.

"THE PHILIPPINES are easy," Grimaldi said. "They've
been stashing military hardware on the islands there
for fifty years."

"For all the good it does us," Bolan answered. "If
we have to go that far afield, we still have import
problems. And we can't expect to catch a break at
customs while we're at it, either."

"Macao may yet surprise you," Mindel said. "My
people work through contract agents there, from time
to time—also Hong Kong. We take advantage of the
European influence whenever possible. The triads
haven't been suppressed, by any means, and there are
dissidents who trade in contraband to fund their
causes."

"Same thing anywhere you go," Grimaldi said.

"Except in China, if they're caught, it could mean
more than prison time," Mindel replied.

"I heard about their organ-donor program," Grimaldi agreed. "That's pretty cold."

Mindel responded with a shrug. "Some feel a criminal should have no rights."

"I hear you," Grimaldi said, "but I still don't want to wake up on a gurney someday with some murderer's kidney."

"Ah," She smiled. "A man of principle."

"Good taste."

"It's not kidneys we need," McCarter interrupted. "Try Kalashnikovs."

"We're working on it," Bolan answered.

"Wings and weapons," Grimaldi said. "Is that so much to ask?"

"I hope not," Bolan said.

To which McCarter answered, silently, I hope not, too.

BROGNOLA HAD the name waiting for Bolan when he called again at the appointed time. Their guide would be one Ming Cho-Hei, described by the contact at Langley as reliable and trustworthy.

"What's that worth in the real world?" Bolan asked.

"My guess," Brognola said, "it means he hasn't screwed them lately, or they haven't caught him at it."

"I was hoping for a little reassurance here," Bolan replied.

"I'd give it to you if I could. The Company works through him, and he's not officially connected to the other side. Some kind of merchant in Macao, from what I gather.''

"Triad?" Bolan inquired.

"They tell me no," Brognola said. "Of course, that doesn't mean he's strictly on the straight and narrow, either."

Bolan hoped not, for his own sake. A completely honest man wouldn't have the connections he required for weapons and the rest of it.

"I guess I'll take my chances," he allowed. "Where is he meeting us?"

"He'll be there when you land and help you get through customs. What I'm hearing at this end, it's not too rigorous for Western business types, unless you've done something to get your name put on the shit list."

"Speaking of names," Bolan told him, "the passports and visas look fine. You must've turned the heat up pretty good to get them done that quickly."

"Nothing to it," Brognola replied. "A word in the right ear gets the job done."

Bolan knew there was more to it than that, but he didn't challenge Brognola's humility. Instead, he asked, "Will he have what we need?"

"Should have connections to supply you, anyway. I gather that he's not an arms dealer himself, but that he knows someone who knows someone, that kind of thing."

"That kind of thing" was common in the Far East—and around the world, for that matter. Wherever Bolan's war had taken him, there were always people with illicit connections, some of them doing more good in their own way than those who were oath bound to uphold the law.

And some of them would stab a stranger in the back without a second thought.

He didn't know which kind of person Ming Cho-Hei would prove to be, but they were short on options at the moment and would have to play the cards as dealt. If Ming betrayed them, Bolan would exert himself to pay the stranger back, even if it turned out to be his final act on Earth.

"That covers hardware on the ground," Bolan said. "Jack's a little curious about the air."

"He would be. I've lined up a Lockheed Jetstar, coming your way out of Cyprus. Should be landing in an hour or so."

"Cyprus?"

"Don't ask," Brognola said. "The pilot's already been paid. He doesn't need a tip. You've got a long trip still ahead of you, before it hits the fan. You'll have to do this thing in hops."

Bolan guessed they were looking at six thousand miles, one way, from Israel to Macao. He didn't know the Lockheed's range, but left that part of it to Jack. If a machine had wings and engines, odds were excellent that Grimaldi could handle it as if he were born in the cockpit. As far as fuel stops, there were various airports en route from Israel to Macao where money talked and all comers were welcome, as long as they'd filed a flight plan.

No problem, right.

Barring extraordinary, unexpected difficulties with the weather or machinery, their trouble wouldn't start until they touched down at the other end, on Chinese territory.

Bolan had scores to settle with the men responsible for Katz's death, and not entirely for the fact that they had killed one of his friends. Lin Mak and his accomplices had more to answer for than one man's death. With Napier and Andrastus, he'd been playing God, manipulating governments and armies, terrorizing thousands, pushing nations to the brink of all-out war.

It had to stop, and Bolan meant to see that done.

The Executioner was pulling out all stops and shifting into scorched-earth mode.

CHAPTER SIX

Jakarta

Arnold Napier glowered at the screen of his computer monitor, reading through the cryptic e-mail message for the fourth time. The message hadn't changed, of course. It never would, no matter how long he sat there, staring dumbly at the screen.

It wasn't Worthington this time. The action had apparently moved on to Lebanon, and this e-mail had come from Dandridge, in Beirut. His style varied from Worthington's, but like all Napier's spotters, he played his cards close to the vest.

> Reports of contact from the Bekaa AL unit are officially confirmed. No final tally, but I'm told the group has been downsized. Late word has AS among those cut. No leads so far. Advise at your convenience. D.

"AL" was Allah's Lance, and Napier didn't need a Cracker Jack decoder ring to know that "AS" was

Ammar Samman. Make that had been, since he was dead now, just like Wasim Jabbar before him, not to mention several dozen of their best commandos.

Best, my ass, Napier thought, glaring daggers at the flat computer screen. He would've loved to smash it, pick the damn thing up and fling it right across the room, but what would that accomplish?

Nothing.

Instead, he read the message one more time, then tapped out his response on the keyboard: "Maintain contact with locals and advise on any new developments. No further action indicated."

That was starting to feel like his personal mantra. No action. Napier prided himself on his prudence, minimizing risk whenever possible, but he hadn't built a multibillion-dollar empire from scratch by sitting on his hands. The Palestinians were getting their asses kicked right and left, compromising their effectiveness as a strike force—assuming they had any left, by now—and so far his one attempt to help had only made things worse. The ambush he'd planned in Israel had gone bitterly awry, costing him one expendable vice president of Global Petroleum and half a dozen high-priced shooters, in addition to God only knew how many Arab allies.

All to kill an aging, one-armed ex-Mossad agent whose role in the fiasco was still undefined, a mystery that tantalized Napier and enraged him, all at once.

He had the old bastard's name, from a contact inside the Tel Aviv legal establishment, but who in hell was Yakov Katzenelenbogen anyway? The name meant nothing to Napier, and the dead man's files were sealed, classified beyond the ability of his toadies to crack them.

So far.

He'd keep trying, of course, but in the meantime someone else was tearing up the allies he had left in Israel and environs. Try as he would, even after speaking to one of his adversaries on the telephone, Napier still had no idea who the shooters were or who had fielded the team.

He switched off the computer and spun his swivel chair to face Jared Wagner. The new VP was holding up all right so far, but he hadn't come under fire yet. With any luck, Napier thought, that was a test they could avoid. But if it came to that, he was prepared to make another sacrifice.

"Samman?" Wagner asked.

"Dead," Napier replied. "More of his men, as well."

"Jesus!"

"I doubt that He had anything to do with it, Jared."

Wagner was caught somewhere between a smile and an apology. He settled for a grunt and nodded, as if some great insight had been shared between them.

"So, what next?" Wagner asked when the silence had begun to stretch too thin between them.

. "I believe we need to reassess our options," Napier said. "Keep it low-profile, nothing that would draw attention to ourselves. I've still got people working on the Middle Eastern problem, trying to learn more about this Yakov what's-his-name."

"Nothing so far?"

Napier suppressed a sudden urge to laugh out loud. "A one-armed senior citizen, for God's sake. What is this, a remake of *The Fugitive*? I swear, sometimes I feel like giving up and letting someone else handle the dirty work."

"You don't mean that, sir?" There was just the proper lilt in Wagner's voice to make a question of it. Napier smelled the younger man's ambition like a jolt of musk at mating time.

"Of course not," he replied, and watched the spark of hope extinguished in the depths of Wagner's eyes. "You'll have to wait a damn sight longer, son, before you take my place."

"I didn't mean—"

"Please don't embarrass either one of us with an apology, Jared. You wouldn't have come this far without a healthy dose of ambition."

"Well—"

"False modesty has its place, I suppose," Napier said, "but save it for someone who doesn't know your life story, chapter and verse."

Wagner paled a bit at that, or maybe it was only the fluorescent lighting in the office, but he still responded with a crisp "Yes, sir."

"Our Palestinian associates are in a state of total disarray," Napier continued. "If we want to save the operation—and I don't see any choice in that regard, agreed?"

"Yes, sir!"

"Then what we need to do is quietly divorce ourselves from Allah's Lance and find another team that's worthy of support. I take responsibility for any setbacks that we've suffered up to now.''

''It's not your fault, sir.''

''When you steer the ship, Jared, it's *all* your fault. That's lesson number one. Make no mistake on that score.''

''No, sir.''

''But responsibility is only part of it. The more important part, in situations like the present one, is smooth recovery. Unless we want to lose the confidence of our associates in Greece and China, we must turn this thing around without delay and get the operation on a solid footing. Right?''

''Right, sir!''

''Okay, then. We can't change the basic goals, but maybe we can fudge the game plan without taking any more decisive hits. See where I'm going with this, Jared?''

''Well...''

He didn't see a goddamn thing, but that was understandable. The plan had only come to Napier in the past few moments. There'd been no discussion of it, nothing to prepare Wagner for Napier's leap.

''We need new allies,'' he repeated. ''Someone with more staying power than the Lance, maybe an outfit on a par with Black September or Hamas. They all need money and they all hate Israel. How resistant can they be to new investors with a plan for victory?''

''Good thinking, sir.''

''My big mistake, I think, was trusting in the Palestinians to do the job alone. Hell, they've been trying to get rid of the Israelis since 1948. There's obviously something wrong with their approach, agreed?''

"Yes, sir."

"So, here's my thinking on the matter, and correct me if I'm wrong—they fail because they're in a rut, committed to these endless hit-and-run techniques that only make Israelis more determined to stand fast. Deep down, I have a feeling they're afraid of victory.''

"How's that, sir?"

"Look at Arafat," Napier said. "Since he went legitimate, he's nothing but a tired old man—a whipping boy for Tel Aviv whenever militants slip off the reservation. He's about as influential in the Arab world today as T. S. Lawrence.''

"Who, sir?"

"Never mind. Just follow me on this. Whoever we're allied with in the next half of the game, let's take for granted that they need a jump-start and some technical assistance.''

"Sir?"

Napier was smiling as he asked, "You keep in touch with any of the Russians you got acquainted with while you were working on the Eastern European beat?''

"Yes, sir."

"Reach out to them and see if you can find someone with excess hardware on his hands.''

"Hardware?"

"Nothing extravagant," Napier replied. "I'm thinking of a compact unit, portable, simple to operate. A couple megatons should do the trick.''

Tel Aviv

THE AIRCRAFT Brognola had sent from Cyprus was a Lockheed Jetstar C-140, instantly recognizable from its four rear-mounted engines and the massive fuel tanks attached to each wing, resembling Exocet missiles without the tailfins.

The Jetstar was shorter than some jet fighters, at that—a few inches over sixty feet, from nose to tail— but with a fifty-four-foot wingspan that dwarfed any fighter flying today. It cruised at 508 miles per hour, carrying a maximum complement of ten passengers. The C-140 was built for a two-man crew, but Grimaldi had flown larger planes alone and knew he'd have no trouble handling this one. There would be no in-flight service for his comrades, but the team was seeking speed, not luxury.

The jetliner would get them where they had to go, if Grimaldi could hold fatigue at bay for twelve more hours in the air.

No sweat, he told himself. It's just like falling off a log.

Except the fall, in this case, would be thirty thousand feet if anything went wrong.

Grimaldi spent ten minutes with the pilot who'd delivered the jetliner, looking over charts and flight plans, running down the preflight checklist. It was standard for a pressurized highflier with complete airliner appointments, including automatic oxygen mask delivery in case pressure was lost at maximum altitude. After that, he watched an airport ground crew going through its paces, taking care of maintenance, topping off the plane's long-distance tanks. When they were done, Grimaldi spent some time inside the cockpit, looking over the controls.

They could've carried guns aboard the jetliner, since there would be no customs hassle on departure, but arrival in Macao would be another story. Bolan didn't want to risk being caught with hardware on the plane when they touched down. It would mean expulsion, at least, with no chance to reenter China openly and damn poor odds of sneaking past tightened security. At worst, they could wind up in prison, charged with spying for the West, which, even with deniability in place, would mean red faces all around for Israel and America.

Grimaldi dismissed that part of the mission from his mind. He was the pilot, and as such was presently concerned more with mechanics than strategy. They would be covering six thousand miles in the next fourteen hours, give or take, if the refueling stops went smoothly. The Jetstar had a cruising range of 2,200 miles, which meant two stops en route from Israel to Macao. Grimaldi's picks had been Karachi and Bangkok, because the airports were reliable and fairly well maintained. They were less likely to be hijacked, sabotaged or otherwise detained in either place than if they stopped at Kabul or Tashkent. It was a choice of lesser evils on a jaunt like this, and Grimaldi would've felt better if they could have traveled armed, but he would do his best with what they had.

And on arrival he would take a back seat to the infantry.

Bolan was waiting on the tarmac for Grimaldi when the pilot stepped down from the jet. "All ready?" he inquired.

"We're good to go."

"How soon?"

Grimaldi checked his watch. "We're scheduled to lift off in twenty-seven minutes."

"Good," Bolan replied. "We need to do this thing."

"For Katz," Grimaldi said.

"For Katz," the tall man echoed him. "For all of us."

Macao

IT WAS A POINT of pride with Lin Yuan Mak that he never lost his temper. He was subject to anger, of course, but the trick lay in rigid self-control. The moment any man revealed his secret feelings to another, Mak believed, that man was lost.

He didn't curse or shout, therefore, when Jared Wagner telephoned from Jakarta to report the latest in a growing series of disasters. Instead of flying off the handle, demanding empty assurances or threatening to withdraw from the project, he listened carefully and questioned Wagner briefly in a civil tone. He made a point of cradling the receiver gently, even though he longed to smash it down with crushing force.

Bad news again, from the pathetic Palestinians. Sometimes it seemed to Mak as if no other kind of news ever emerged from the benighted Middle East. Turmoil was constant in the region, and despite his recognition of the fact that violence was essential to their plans, Mak wondered why his allies—or their stooges—always seemed to be on the receiving end.

There was a flaw in Napier's plan somewhere. If only Mak could put his finger on it, he might be the hero of the hour.

He might even save himself before it was too late.

He wasn't pulling out, of course. The plan had progressed too far for that, and Mak still hoped the plan could work—if not exactly as conceived, at least to the extent that none of the conspirators was damaged by it. Truth be told, he only cared about himself, but if the others toppled, Mak knew he would be less likely to survive.

Beijing appeared to favor dealings with the West—for now, at any rate, but there was zero tolerance for private operators who sought profits solely for themselves. Mak had pursued the risky avenue because he knew his government wouldn't approve, and the amount he stood to earn was too seductive to refuse.

Billions.

The very word itself was succulent. It had a texture and a flavor all its own. Beside it, tawdry millions paled to insignificance. Mak thought of all that he could do with such a fortune—all the places he could visit, all the women he could have—and nowhere in his thinking did the sacred People's Revolution play a part.

The money and the power would he *his*.

Assuming that his partners didn't get him killed.

That image drew his thoughts back to the blighted Middle East, where all their fortunes lay beneath the soil, waiting to be extracted, processed, sold to greedy nations that could never get enough black gold. China itself would be a vast new market, and his hand would be the one that turned the tap.

If they succeeded.

If they managed to survive.

Mak wasn't clear on every detail of the problem, but he knew their plans had hit a major snag in Israel and environs. First, it seemed, some meddling Israeli had stumbled on the scheme and Napier's efforts to eliminate the threat had been spectacularly unsuccessful. Now, instead of killing one man, they had a small war on their hands—and from the periodic bulletins Mak had received, it seemed that they were losing. Adding insult to the injury, Napier and his associates had thus far been unable to identify their enemies, much less destroy them.

They could write off Allah's Lance. That much was clear. Within a week, two leaders of the Palestinian guerrilla army had been killed, along with dozens of their soldiers, and they had nothing to show for it. Their allies were disrupted and demoralized, unable even to describe their enemies coherently.

And Napier had decided that enough was enough.

He was initiating the contingency he liked to call Plan B.

So be it.

It was dangerous, no doubt. Thousands would die, and some form of retaliation was inevitable, but it wouldn't touch Lin Mak. His hands, if not precisely clean, at least had left no fingerprints behind to link them with the plot.

Or had they?

That, above all else, troubled his mind. If Napier left a trail—and it was true, one of his aides had already been killed near Tel Aviv—and if the nameless enemy tracked down Napier, what might the oilman do or say to save himself? Or if he kept his faith and silence to the point of death, what evidence might be uncovered in his files, extracted from subordinates, to jeopardize the other principals?

Lin Mak had been invited into the cartel because he had influence with the Chinese government and held a post that let him carry out certain maneuvers without being caught. He had already paved the way for trade agreements with the new state that would rise from Israel's ashes. After public lamentation and condolences, self-interest would assert itself once more, as it had always done. Money would talk, and men would fall in line with its demands.

Mak had accepted Napier's invitation to the game because he wanted to be rich beyond his wildest dreams, beyond the dreams of any proper socialist raised on Marxist doctrines from the cradle onward.

But the money would be useless to a corpse.

Plan B was set to roll, and there was nothing Mak could do about it now. He could, however, take pre-emptive steps to save himself if this—like Napier's other "foolproof" plan—should go disastrously, irreparably wrong.

Plan B would set the Middle East ablaze.

Lin Mak decided it was time to take out fire insurance, just in case an unexpected wind should blow the flames his way.

Aboard the Aristotle, *Tyrrhenian Sea*

"YOU'RE CERTAIN it's the thing to do?" Christos Andrastus asked.

"We're confident of ultimate success," the young American replied. His disembodied voice seemed cheery, almost flippant, in a manner unbefitting such grim topics.

Andrastus didn't know this Jared Wagner, had spoken to him only once previously, and was disinclined to trust him. If he hadn't given Napier's password to authenticate himself, Andrastus would have switched off the cell phone and ordered Nikos to block all incoming calls.

"Plan B," Andrastus said.

"Yes, sir."

A shadow seemed to slide across the sun, although no clouds were visible for miles around. Andrastus felt a sudden chill, entirely unrelated to the brilliant day.

"Is there a schedule, then?" he asked.

"Not yet, sir. You will be apprised, of course."

"Of course."

"There's no reason to be concerned."

"I see. Thank you."

"Good day, sir."

"Yes. Good day to you."

There'd be no reason for concern if he was sitting in Sri Lanka or wherever Napier had gone to ground after the bloody mess in Tel Aviv. Andrastus wasn't halfway around the world, however. He was twelve miles out from Naples, homeward bound at a lethargic pace, and when his yacht reached the Aegean he would be within five hundred miles of ground zero.

Too damn close for comfort.

Even if Napier was right, and the payload was clean—a fact Andrastus couldn't take for granted, in the circumstances—it still made him nervous. The Israelis might be taken by surprise, their government decapitated, but they were tenacious fighters and a strike on Tel Aviv wouldn't prevent them from retaliating. As to where and whom they struck, that would be anybody's guess.

It made no difference to Andrastus. He imagined the destruction, chaos, loss of life—and cared for no one but himself. Returning home placed him at risk, and he wasn't prepared to take that chance.

Not now, with so much still at stake.

Andrastus set the cell phone beside his sweating glass of ouzo and retrieved the compact two-way radio he used to speak with members of the crew. His thumb depressed a button labeled 3 before he spoke into the mouthpiece.

"Kolya!"

Static whispered back at him before a gruff voice answered from the *Aristotle*'s bridge. "Yes, sir?"

"I've changed my mind," Andrastus said. "I feel like visiting Tangier, perhaps Lisbon. Adjust our course accordingly."

"Yes, sir." The captain didn't sound surprised. He'd learned that working for Christos Andrastus meant all plans were fluid; anything could change at the last moment. It played hell with private lives, but the rewards were such that few complained and fewer still saw fit to throw their jobs away.

Andrastus felt the yacht start its long, slow turn westward, leaving Naples and the boot of Italy behind. The Med lay glistening before them, with Sardinia to starboard, Sicily to port, North Africa barely a shadow on the far horizon, still three hundred miles ahead.

Andrastus would feel safer in Tangier than at his home in Greece, and safer yet in Lisbon, if he chose to sail that far. He didn't know when Napier meant to activate Plan B, but he could wait it out. And in the meantime, he would issue orders to recall his cargo fleet from any point within three hundred miles of the selected target zone. That meant the eastern quarter of the Med, along with the Red Sea and Persian Gulf.

How many ships, in all? No less than half a dozen, he supposed, at any given time. Andrastus thought of sacrificing one, to divert any vestige of attention from himself, but just as rapidly dismissed it as a foolish notion.

Why should he lose anything, when he had joined the game to make huge profits for himself?

When histories were written of this moment—as they would be, after he was dead and gone—Andrastus knew his critics would attempt to make the worst of it. They would "discover" that his father had collaborated with the Germans during World War II, to make a profit, and had suffered for it afterward—which was to say, he lost respect and certain friends, but kept the cash. They might suppose that he'd inherited some strain of anti-Semitism from his parents, predisposing him to use his wealth and power against Israel all these decades later. When the presses rolled, it would become a grand conspiracy, something he'd dreamed up to avenge his father's honor.

As it happened, nothing could be farther from the truth.

Thanos Andrastus *had* collaborated with the Nazis; it was true. He'd seen a chance to make a fortune from the war and seized the opportunity without a second thought. That didn't mean he hated Jews, of course. In fact, he cared no more or less for them than for the members of his own devoted family, which was to say, not very much at all. Christos would have been very much surprised to learn his father thought about the Jews at all.

His mind was always on the money, and in that one aspect he had schooled his only son to emulate the old man he despised.

Christos Andrastus hadn't missed his father once in twenty-seven years since the old man collapsed and died atop a whore one-third his age. He had ascended to his father's seat of power in the shipping trade and then expanded to a point the old man never thought attainable.

He wouldn't willingly surrender any of it now.

Andrastus felt a stirring, palmed the walkie-talkie once again and thumbed another button. "Irina?"

She responded without hesitation. "Yes, Christos?"

"Meet me in the sauna. Ten minutes."

"Of course."

Andrastus sipped his ouzo, smiling. Life was good.

Macao

MING CHO-HEI LIT a fresh cigarette from the butt of his last one, chain-smoking in a vain attempt to soothe his nerves. It wasn't working, but he had no other antidote for the uneasiness that plagued him. Drinking would be foolish in the circumstances, since he needed all his wits about him when he met the foreigners and put himself at their disposal.

Ming didn't know exactly what the foreigners required of him, but it would almost certainly be dangerous. His contact at the U.S. embassy only reached out for Ming when he—that was, the CIA—had need of special services beyond the scope of normal burglars, pickpockets and thugs. He had contacts the Agency couldn't maintain without endangering its people in Macao, risking exposure of their function and a deportation order from Beijing.

Instead, Ming Cho-Hei was retained to risk *his* life

for strangers, facing life in prison or a firing squad if he was caught. It pleased him to subvert the masters in Beijing, who had labeled his parents "politically unreliable" in the late 1970s, packing them off to a reeducation camp in Mongolia. There, his father had been shot while trying to escape—or so the bastards said, at any rate. Ming's mother had returned a broken woman, mind and spirit shattered, which was doubtless what her persecutors had in mind. It was a secret blessing when she took her own life six months later. Ming Cho-Hei had wept with shame, because he felt relief.

And he had turned his full attention to revenge.

Ming was a translator for China's tourist bureau, which explained his work with sundry foreigners. Part of his job was watching, eavesdropping and then reporting back what he had seen or heard. Sometimes Ming told the truth to his superiors; more often—and particularly if he learned of some activity inimical to the Beijing establishment—he lied to help the outsiders maintain their secrets.

And for six years now, he'd been a contract agent of the CIA. It paid more than his day job, but Ming told himself the cash was secondary. He was fighting for his parents, and for friends who had fallen before the Communist guns at Tiananmen Square. Ming didn't delude himself into thinking that anything he did would topple the Communist government, but he did what he could, one man working alone.

Until now.

If he understood the latest mission, it might involve

more than simply translating or giving directions. He'd
been warned that there would be hazards above and
beyond the usual, and that his compensation would be
increased accordingly. He'd even been given the opportunity to decline, with an understanding that no one
would hold it against him.

And he had accepted the mission, regardless.

Ming felt a sense of having crossed a line, working
without a net, as the Americans might say. He didn't
know exactly what the mission would entail yet, but
Ming knew what he'd be risking.

The same thing as always.

His life.

Ming had a flight schedule for the incoming strangers and the number of their party: three men and a
woman, all round-eyes. His contact had given him
names, which Ming assumed to be false. Never mind.
He would address the newcomers however they preferred. Such things were standard in the world he occupied, a precaution against betrayal.

Ming checked his watch: nine hours before he had
to meet the Westerners whose lives were in his hands.
Meanwhile, he took the lockbox from its place beneath
the flooring of his tiny bedroom closet, placed it on
the narrow bed where he habitually slept alone and
used a small brass key to open it.

Inside, the Type 59 semiautomatic pistol lay
wrapped in an oiled chamois cloth with six spare magazines. Two pasteboard boxes of 9 mm cartridges
filled the rest of the box, but Ming left them alone as

he took out the weapon, unwrapped it and prepared to wipe it with a paper towel.

The Type 59, like all state-produced Chinese weapons, was a copy of a Russian gun—in this case the venerable Makarov PM, itself patterned on the German Walther PP. Each magazine held eight rounds, the loaded weapon weighing a solid two pounds in Ming's hand.

When he was satisfied in terms of cleanliness, no risk of gun oil staining his clothes, Ming jacked the pistol's slide to put a live round in the chamber. It was double-action, safe to carry with the safety off and hammer down. Ming didn't have a holster, but the pistol fit nicely inside his waistband, at the back, or he could hide it in the pocket of an overcoat, depending on the weather. Usually he left the gun at home, but this wasn't a usual situation.

If he had to fight, at least he'd be prepared.

And if he had to die, perhaps he wouldn't go alone.

Ming Cho-Hei had never shot another human being, or attempted to, but in his mind he had rehearsed the moves a thousand times. When he put faces on the targets in his mind, he visualized the judge and prosecutor who had sent his father off to die, the captain of police who'd smiled and made suggestive comments to his mother afterward. There was no shortage of potential targets in the Workers' Paradise.

The strangers who were coming would need weapons, he'd been told, and that spelled trouble. There were weapons to be had, of course, for those with ready cash, and Ming knew where they could be found. He'd purchased his own pistol from one such black-market dealer, though not in Macao. There were others, much closer to home.

Ming was surprised to find himself smiling. He crossed the room, confirmed it in a mirror. Yes, that was a smile. It felt suspicious on his face, an alien expression that belonged to someone else, stolen for him to use as a disguise.

And in that moment, Ming knew he wasn't afraid to die.

CHAPTER SEVEN

Karachi, Pakistan

Their first stop for refueling was a choice of lesser evils, as far as Bolan was concerned. Pakistan had been a tinderbox of violence for more than half a century, created as a refuge for India's Muslim minority, battling through long generations along the ragged border with its mother country. Military coups and a flood of Afghan refugees in the 1970s had done nothing to insure national stability, while a nuclear arms race with India in the late 1990s brought down U.S. sanctions on both sides. The border wars continued into a new century, with ambiguous reactions to the U.S. war on terrorism in neighboring Afghanistan and reports that die-hard al-Qaeda fighters were sheltered by elements of the Pakistani power structure.

So, why were they here? Bolan asked himself as he stood in shadow, watching technicians refuel the Lockheed Jetstar under Jack Grimaldi's watchful eye.

And he already knew the answer: because it was the best of their several poor choices. Iran and Afghanistan posed even greater risks to Westerners in transit, while "friendly" India's nearest major airport was beyond their reach, at Bombay. They needed fuel for the next leg of the journey, and Karachi had been chosen as the least likely scene of a major snafu.

In fact, Bolan knew, Hal Brognola had been pulling strings from Washington to help them on their way. Uniformed Pakistani police had been waiting for them on touchdown, to secure the plane and parking area while a ground crew did its job. There'd been no questions or hassles, but Bolan was cautious by nature, a trait that had helped him survive up to now. Unarmed though he was, he'd elected to stand guard himself, outside the Jetstar, while Grimaldi supervised the refueling and maintenance, McCarter and Mindel lying in wait to surprise any saboteurs who might slip past them.

The police left him alone, pretending not to notice Bolan as they stalked the perimeter, holding their Swiss SG540 assault rifles at the ready. Commanded by a stern-faced officer who held himself apart from the others, they'd clearly been ordered to keep their distance from the Jetstar and ignore its occupants, if they were seen.

So far, so good.

Grimaldi had told him to expect an hour on the ground, give or take, and they were coming up on the halfway mark without incident. Refueling was nearly completed, and aircraft mechanics were giving the Jetstar a checkup, inspecting the landing gear, rudders, whatever. Grimaldi crouched beneath the starboard wing with one of the ground crew, reaching up to rap his knuckles on the metal there. As Bolan watched, the Pakistani frowned, nodded and bobbed his head in something like a jerky little bow.

Their conference concluded, Grimaldi duck-walked from under the wing and rose to full height, stretching to relieve muscle cramps in his legs. He crossed the tarmac to stand beside Bolan, flicking glances between their perimeter guards and the busy mechanics.

"About half an hour," he said.

"What was that, with the wing?" Bolan asked.

"The starboard ailerons are just a trifle sluggish. No biggee. He'll take care of it."

"It's not a problem?"

"Shouldn't be," Grimaldi said.

Bolan did everything within his power to blot out an image of the Jetstar plummeting to the ground, dense jungle rushing up to meet them at the speed of fright.

It almost worked.

Another time and place, he might have argued, but Grimaldi was among the warrior's oldest and most trusted friends. He had been there for Bolan when the chips were down on countless battlefields, and Bolan knew the pilot well enough to realize he'd never risk his own life—much less someone else's—for the sake of haste in checking or repairing some mechanical device.

Grimaldi was a gambler, but he'd never be a fool.

Bolan dismissed the matter from his mind, casting forward to their next stop and the touchdown after that. They were still some four thousand miles from

Macao, and Lin Mak's power would increase the closer they came. An ambush was more likely in Bangkok than in Karachi, and more likely still at their final destination. Mak shouldn't know they were coming, but that was expectation, fueled in equal parts by strategy and wishful thinking.

They could still be wrong.

Dead wrong.

There were still too many ways they could die for Bolan to linger on any single hazard. Simple accident. Equipment failure in midair. Stormy weather. Sabotage by the ground crew. Surface-to-air missiles. Interceptor aircraft.

It was a veritable smorgasbord of death, but Bolan wasn't buying. Not just yet.

Not if he had a choice.

It was a challenge not to check his watch or mentally urge the mechanics to hurry. He watched a pair of techs working in the starboard ailerons, testing them by hand, one of them signaling Grimaldi to give it a try from the cockpit. Jack disappeared inside the Jetstar and the wing flaps waved at Bolan, whirring smoothly up and down.

Emerging from the aircraft once again, Grimaldi signed a sheaf of papers offered to him on a clipboard, flashed a thumbs-up sign at Bolan and ducked back inside the plane. Crossing the pavement to rejoin his comrades, Bolan didn't ask himself whether the techs had done their job correctly. That part was out of his hands now.

He was already beyond Karachi, winging his way

toward Bangkok and the next threat assessment, wondering if their luck would hold.

A few more hours, Bolan thought. That's all we need.

That, and a world of luck.

Macao International Airport

THE AIRPORT LAYOUT was unique in Bolan's personal experience. He's never seen a runway flanked by water on all sides, linked to a terminal by taxiways that were, in essence, bridges spanning a thousand yards or more of open sea. He didn't want to think about the beatings aircraft and their passengers had to take when tropical storms came roaring out of the South China Sea to flog Macao and its adjacent islands with the wrath of God.

They had clear skies, at least, for their approach. As far as what lay waiting for them on the ground below, Bolan could only guess—and that had never been his style.

His last check-in with Hal Brognola, during a refueling stop in Bangkok, had added no new information to the warrior's mental file. Their contact in Macao would have a line on Lin Yuan Mak or someone who could find him, the big Fed reiterated. Otherwise, the team would have to forge ahead without a detailed plan, making up strategy as they went along.

Been there, done that, Bolan thought. Living on the edge was nothing new for him, but he still balked at giving up control to total strangers when he had a mission cooking and the odds were stacked against him.

Touchdown was the usual Grimaldi special, smooth and gentle. Never mind the cross-wind whipping east to west across the runway, or the flight of seagulls wheeling up in front of them. Jack made each landing feel as if there was nothing to it, a routine and simple exercise. It was part of his magic, taken for granted by those who'd flown with him repeatedly.

As if on cue, Grimaldi's voice addressed them from the Jetstar's intercom. "We've been directed to the northern taxiway," he said. "Call it another three klicks before we reach the terminal. Grimaldi Airways recommends that everyone stay seated till we've parked and shut the engines off. Keep us in mind for your next jaunt to the inscrutable Far East."

Bolan watched through his window as the Jetstar taxied north, then eastward, never more than thirty yards from water at the farthest. He imagined some fatigued or nervous pilot freezing up at the controls, dumping a 747 in the drink with several hundred passengers on board.

Twenty minutes put them at the terminal, the Lockheed parked outside a hangar at the south end of the sprawling property. Bolan picked out the black sedan with driver standing by before he left his seat, trailing McCarter to the exit with Rebecca Mindel on his heels.

"Our welcoming committee's here," he told them as Grimaldi joined them from the cockpit, opening the door and lowering the Jetstar's folding steps. The ace pilot took the lead, and the sedan's driver was waiting by the time he reached the tarmac.

"Ming Cho-Hei," he introduced himself, smiling mechanically and shaking hands with each of them in turn. In line with their new passports and assorted other documents, Bolan was Mike Belasko; McCarter introduced himself as Daniel Masters; Mindel became Renée Zelig, a British subject; while Grimaldi morphed into James Grafton, his ID including an international pilot's license in that name.

Their contact didn't question any of it. He stood waiting while their luggage was unloaded and Grimaldi made arrangements with the ground crew for the Jetstar to be fueled, serviced and stored. Two customs men in uniform emerged from the hangar to inspect and stamp their passports, but declined to check their bags. That hurdle cleared, Ming showed them to his car and helped them stow their luggage, got them seated, Mindel in the shotgun seat, her three companions wedged in back.

"Now I know how sardines feel," McCarter commented.

"More room at your apartment in Macao," Ming said, putting the car in motion. "You have a one-month lease, the shortest term available. I was instructed to avoid hotels."

"That's fine," Bolan assured him, "but we need to do some shopping first."

"For weapons, yes?" Ming asked.

"That's right."

"No problem in Macao. Sales and possession are

illegal, as you know, but many things are still available."

"And money makes the world go 'round," McCarter said.

"Of course," Ming agreed, his frown reflected in the rearview mirror.

"Aside from weapons," Bolan told their guide, "we need to know what you've uncovered on Lin Mak."

"He's definitely in Macao," Ming answered. "His location is a closely guarded secret—but as Mr. Masters says, money can open doors and loosen tongues."

"You've found him, then?"

"I know where he was staying yesterday," Ming said. "As for today, we'll have to go and see."

CHAPTER EIGHT

Their target was a mansion on a hill. In former times, it would have housed a wealthy merchant or a Western diplomat. This day, it was the home-away-from-home of Lin Yuan Mak, a first assistant to the minister of foreign trade for the People's Republic of China.

Their target.

It had required some persuasion to obtain the address, but Ming Cho-Hei was a man with connections. He'd impressed Bolan favorably so far, with both his network of informers in Macao and his access to dealers in black-market military hardware.

They were armed at last, and none too soon, as they prepared to penetrate mansion on the stroke of 2:00 a.m. They'd chosen Type 56-1 assault rifles, the folding-stock models with 20.5-inch barrels and 30-round box magazines, capable of spewing 7.62 mm Soviet slugs at a cyclic rate of some 600 rounds per minute. Bolan's crew had lucked out on their side arms, bypassing the standard Chinese Type 59s in favor of a newly arrived shipment from Czechoslovakia, the CZ-100s chambered in 9 mm Parabellum with 13-round mags. For real punch, they'd purchased a case of Chinese Type 73 frag grenades, resembling the old Russian RGD-5s with a stubby throwing stick attached in the venerable "potato masher" style. Low-powered but still lethal at close range, the Type 73s were a bargain, selling for mere two dollars each, American.

"You know how it is," McCarter quipped as they were loading up the weapons, making ready for their raid. "An hour later, you're ready to blow up some bastard again."

Ming found the target without difficulty, once they had the address. He had a taxi driver's knowledge of the winding streets and narrow alleyways, choosing shortcuts that actually saved them time instead of making matters worse. By 1:35 a.m. they were parked at the foot of the hill where their target resided, watching the last few lights wink out in the palace.

"Count on guards," Bolan reminded his companions, "and expect them to be armed. You know the drill. Mak holds the key to Napier and Andrastus. If we miss him..."

"Let's not miss him," McCarter said.

"Right. Let's not."

He turned to Ming Cho-Hei and said, "You should be fine, parked here, but if you see it going bad, take off. We'll meet you in the parking lot behind that restaurant, agreed?"

"Of course," Ming said.

The restaurant was just under three-quarters of a mile due east of their target and already closed for the night. Their escape route consisted of narrow back streets, alleyways and a large construction site that could hide a brigade from casual search. Retreating on foot was the worst-case scenario, granted, but Bolan liked to cover all his options and have backup plans for all contingencies.

"All right," he said at last, "let's move."

They climbed the hill together, flitting shadows, Bolan in the lead, with Mindel second and McCarter bringing up the rear. Mak's property was walled but he kept no attack dogs on the premises, according to Ming's informants. Ditto on the high-tech security devices, they were told, but Bolan paused beneath the wall to scan for cameras, wires and sensors, all the same.

It was better to be safe than sorry, right, when "sorry" in the killing fields meant "dead."

When he was satisfied, he faced the others with a curt thumbs-up, received the same in return and scaled the eight-foot wall. It was a measure of the crime rate in Macao that Mak had strung no razor wire along the top, planted no nails or broken glass in concrete to surprise trespassers. Bolan was pleased to think their target felt secure.

It made him easier to kill.

But not before they had a little chat.

Bolan dropped in a crouch onto grass and moved swiftly to the shadow of a tree that grew beside the wall. He heard Mindel land and move off in the other direction, followed seconds later by McCarter. They had planned their movements with a rough plan of the property before them, in the small apartment Ming had rented for them, and so far the layout seemed to match the hand-drawn map.

So far.

They'd come expecting armed guards on the grounds, and Bolan met the first one seconds later, as he closed in toward the house. The sentry had his back turned toward the wall, holding a submachine gun carelessly in the crook of one arm as he bent to light a cigarette. Bolan let him finish and pocket his lighter, then stepped in close and slammed the butt of his rifle against the lookout's skull with crushing force. A second hard chop, this one to the larynx, made sure that he wouldn't rise again in this lifetime.

There was no time to bother with concealment of the corpse, but Bolan pulled the SMG's magazine and tossed it into some nearby shrubbery before moving on. At least he knew another sentry wouldn't come along and use the dead man's gun to shoot him in the back.

The trees ran out some thirty paces from the house, revealing open lawn. Floodlights were mounted at each corner of the mansion, but they weren't turned on, apparently reserved for outdoor parties or perceived emergencies. Someone inside would doubtless throw the switch as soon as any shooting started, but by then it wouldn't matter anyway.

Bolan stepped out of cover, headed for the house. There was supposed to be a door beyond the nearest corner that would grant him entry to the kitchen if it wasn't locked—or even if it was. He didn't know if there were burglar alarms inside the house, but once

they got that far, there would be noise enough to rouse
Mak's distant neighbors from their sleep, in any case.

The Executioner was halfway to the house when
someone challenged him in shrill Chinese, the outcry
coming from his left. He turned in that direction, saw
a shooter sprinting toward him through the dark and
met his adversary with a rising burst of automatic fire.

McCARTER WAS about to spring from ambush on a
passing sentry, when a rattle of gunfire ripped through
the night. Sod it, he thought, and fired a single round
between the target's shoulder blades, watching him
drop as if he were a puppet and some giant blade had
slashed his strings.

"Bad luck," he told the corpse and turned to join
the action on the broad south lawn.

Another sentry tried to intercept the Briton as he
cleared Mak's garden, overgrown with shrubs and
flowers flown in from around the world. The second
shooter had only a pistol, but the gun was aimed directly at McCarter's nose, no time to try negotiating
with the guard who gave no sign of speaking English
anyway.

McCarter gave himself to gravity, legs folding as he
dropped below the shooter's line of fire. He took the
jarring impact on his knees and grimaced at the pistol's muzzle flash, the first round snapping overhead.
Before the sentry could correct his aim and try again,
McCarter shot him in the chest, a 3-round burst that
punched his target over backward, firing once more at
the stars as he went down.

McCarter vaulted to his feet and moved around the corpse, closing the distance to Mak's lawn and the palatial house beyond. Not bad for socialism, he decided as he cleared the garden and advanced into the open.

Bolan had already dropped one sentry on the lawn and he was vanishing around the southeast corner of the mansion as McCarter set foot on the grass. Veering away to the southwest, the Briton raced to reach the front door and the curving asphalt drive that looped in front of it. There would be more guards stationed there, he thought, unless—

Two of them came around the corner, as if summoned by his thoughts. Both carried submachine guns, and they wasted no time cutting loose at their first glimpse of an intruder on the property, one of their own sprawled still and silent on the grass.

McCarter threw himself facedown, firing before he hit the turf. His first short burst was nearly wasted, but it spoiled the gunners' aim and sent them dodging off to either side. The good news was, it saved McCarter's life. The bad news—now his targets were divided and positioned to lay down a deadly cross fire.

The shooter breaking to his left was slightly nearer, so McCarter took him first, tracking with his ersatz Kalashnikov and leading just enough that his next burst would meet the runner in midstride and drop him sprawling to the grass. It worked like magic, and his human target went down in a spray of crimson, dead before he fell.

Mindful of danger on his right, McCarter wasted no

time relishing the shot. Instead, he rolled away and just in time, as a burst of SMG rounds plowed the turf he'd occupied a heartbeat earlier.

The Briton fired at movement and a dancing muzzle-flash, rather than any clear-cut target. The sentry was off balance, firing wildly as he ran, but from a range of less than thirty yards it didn't take much skill to hose a target with an SMG. More spurts of mangled turf were racing toward McCarter when his own fire found its mark and spun the shooter off his feet.

McCarter pushed off from the lawn and sprinted for the house while his last target still lay thrashing on the grass. The shooter might survive his wounds, but he wouldn't rejoin the fight, and that was all that mattered at the moment.

Twenty yards. Fifteen. A dozen.

A shooter dressed in shirtsleeves, with his tie undone and hanging limp around his neck, was opening the front door as McCarter stormed the porch. Squawking, the houseman tried to close it, but he was too late. The Phoenix Force leader chopped him down with automatic fire, slugs gouging divots in the ornate door and thrusting it aside.

Without a pause to think or catch his breath, McCarter barged across the threshold, firing as he went.

LEONG CHUN-SENG had been delighted when he was promoted to command the household guards, but now the honor left a taste of ashes in his mouth. Gunfire from the surrounding grounds had reached the house, and when he tried the telephone to summon help, the line was dead. He tried a cell phone next, frustrated when the warning light told him the battery was low. Enraged, he hurled the device against the nearest wall and watched it shatter.

Instantly, a tremor rocked the house and staggered him. He blinked at the wall where he'd thrown the cell phone, looking for a hole, dazzled momentarily by his own display of strength, until he recognized the smell of smoke and cringed at his mistake.

Explosives.

Whoever the raiders were, they seemed intent on bringing down the house. Leong ran to a nearby standing cabinet and threw it open, reaching in to pluck a Type 79 submachine gun from the rack of weapons hidden there. He rummaged in a drawer, retrieved a magazine containing twenty 7.62 mm Soviet rounds and snapped it into the weapon's receiver. Scooping out three more, he jammed them into his pockets, fumbling awkwardly and hearing fabric rip.

Leong didn't know who his enemies were, but he was ready to face them now, and lay down his life if necessary for the honor of his master's house. Lin Mak would have been proud, if he were present to observe his new chief of security in action.

No, on second thought, Leong was grateful for his master's providential absence. This way, he could try to dream up a convincing lie explaining why his men were taken by surprise.

Another blast rattled the house. Leong suspected they were using hand grenades, since plastic charges would've had more impact, buckling walls and dropping portions of the roof. A burst of gunfire from the parlor told him that the enemy was now inside the house, embarrassing Leong as he repressed an urge to turn and run.

He left the study, barking orders at the men who milled around him. There were seven of them, roughly half the force that he'd been left to guard the house in Lin Mak's absence. Where the others were, he couldn't say, but it wouldn't surprise him to find out that some were dead or wounded on the outer grounds. He hoped they were, in fact, because it would be shameful for the enemy to slip past his first line of guards without a fight.

"The front door!" he commanded as more gunfire echoed through the house. "Go on!"

His men were slow to move, until Leong grabbed one of them and shoved him toward the sounds of battle, followed swiftly by a second. Finally, they moved as one to join the fray, with Leong behind them, blocking their retreat. His choice of battle stations also placed the seven men between himself and any hostile fire they might encounter on the way, which boosted Leong's courage as he moved along the smoky corridor.

Passing the library, he suddenly remembered that his master kept another cell phone there. Watching his soldiers rush along the hall to meet their enemies, Leong hung back, then slipped into the library before one of them had a chance to turn and watch him go.

Alone once more, he spied the cell phone resting

on an antique end table and went to fetch it. Just as Leong's hand closed on the instrument, he heard an outcry from the parlor, followed by another blast of gunfire—and the lights went out.

Cursing, he flipped open the folded cell phone, then realized he couldn't see the numbered buttons. Twice he tried to dial the police emergency number by touch, each time advised by a chirpy recorded voice that his call could not be completed as dialed. The second time, Leong was on the verge of pitching this phone, too, to its destruction, but he stopped himself in time and fumbled back toward the library door.

There was a flashlight in the kitchen, he remembered. Slipping the cell phone into a pocket with one of the SMG's spare magazines, Leong groped his way along a wall of bookcases until he found the door, then slid his fingertips along its frame to grasp the knob. More darkness waited for him in the hallway, lit erratically by muzzle-flashes when he glanced down toward the parlor.

Not that way.

Leong turned toward the kitchen, telling himself that it was his duty to summon police, that he wasn't abandoning his men. They were all trained with weapons. What more could he do than to call reinforcements before they were all overrun? How long before police could reach the scene?

Leong was nearly running when he tripped on something, lurched against the wall, then lost his balance altogether and collapsed. Groping across the floor, he felt fabric with something thick and warm inside it, then a wetness—violently recoiling as he realized he'd stumbled on a dead or wounded man.

One of his own? An enemy?

Leong couldn't tell, and he was in no mood to linger, trying to find out. Panting, he fumbled to retrieve his submachine gun and began to crawl along the hallway toward the kitchen and salvation.

REBECCA MINDEL ENTERED Lin Mak's mansion through a window, just before the lights went out. She didn't know who'd blown the fuse box, and she didn't care. The darkness was a blessing, even when she banged her shins against a bed frame and was limping slightly by the time she found the bedroom door.

She hadn't fired a shot so far this night, but from the racket in the house Mindel surmised that was about to change. She cracked the door an inch or two and listened, since she couldn't see beyond her nose. Someone was speaking in Cantonese, not far away, but distance would be difficult to judge in darkness, moving over unfamiliar ground. Another moment's listening convinced her that the voices emanated from her left, but since she didn't speak the language that was all she knew. It could've been Lin Mak outside the door, scolding one of his flunkies, and Mindel wouldn't be able to distinguish him from any common soldier on the grounds.

The blackout had its uses, but it also tied her hands as far as tracking down their prey. She couldn't hope to recognize Mak's voice or pick him out from conversations overheard in passing. If she didn't find a source of light, and soon—

Jehovah answered prayers, she thought, as someone in the outer hallway switched on a penlight. It wasn't much, but in the utter darkness of the blacked-out house, it shone like a beacon. Mindel watched it pass her door, then leaned out as the light moved farther down the corridor, tracking its progress. For an instant, two grim faces were illuminated by the beam, scowling against the sudden light. One of the gunmen barked a challenge and the light swung upward to reveal its owner's face.

Even in profile, Mindel knew he wasn't Lin Mak.

Three targets, then.

Holding her breath, she stepped into the hall. She had to take the shooter with the penlight first, before he had an opportunity to illuminate her as a target for his comrades. Knowing that, she had already memorized positions for the other two before she sighted on the dim profile and squeezed the trigger on her automatic rifle, taking up the slack.

The rifle bucked against her shoulder as she fired. Fighting down the muzzle, she saw the lighted profile shatter, dropping out of frame before her muzzle-flashes lit the other startled faces, turning toward her, their final glimpse of death.

She shot them both dead where they stood and felt nothing beyond relief that neither guard had managed to return her fire. Closing the space that separated her from three warm corpses, Mindel knelt and groped along the floor until she found the fallen penlight in a pool of blood. Blanking her mind to the experience, she wiped it on a dead man's jacket and stood, ready to sweep the hall in both directions, then move on to seek and find Lin Mak.

If he was still alive and present to be found.

She stabbed the thin beam to her left, then to her right. She was alone with corpses, but another hallway opened several paces distant, just beyond the three men she had slain. More sounds of battle came from that direction, telling Mindel that she'd found a path to reach the parlor and the true heart of the house.

With one last flash of light to reassure herself that no ambush was waiting in the corridor, she thrust the automatic rifle in front of her and started moving toward the flash and crack of gunfire, walking swiftly with one shoulder pressed against the wall.

MING CHO-HEI WAS ready when the first reports of gunfire sounded from the mansion. He had steeled himself against it, swallowing his fear. The strangers and his contact at the U.S. Embassy were all depending on him not to fail. He was determined not to let them down.

The automatic rifle in his lap was a surprise addition to his former one-piece arsenal. Ming hadn't argued when the tall American, Mike Belasko, purchased five rifles instead of four. Ming understood the party's pilot would remain at the apartment in Macao while they went looking for Lin Mak, and since they had been joined by no one else, he knew the fifth rifle had to be for him.

"In case you need it," the big American told him. "When we're done, do what you like with it. Go toss it in the bay, if that suits you."

Ming recognized the trust implicit in the man's gesture, all the more remarkable because he hadn't proved himself as yet, to any great extent. Ming had been grateful for the weapon, even as it frightened him.

And now, it seemed, he was about to find out what the gun could do.

Someone, either in Mak's house or among his scattered neighbors, had to have summoned the police. Ming recognized their unmarked cars, denoting special officers on call around the clock for actions that were rated sensitive. They were political police, distinct and separate from Macao's uniformed constabulary, empowered to extract confessions or use deadly force on their own initiative to keep the lid on political problems.

Ming knew them on sight and he hated them all.

Men like these had dragged his father away from home and family, long years ago. Others had manned some of the guns in Tiananmen Square, exacting reprisals under cover of the larger military operation.

And this night they served Lin Mak—or would, if Ming Cho-Hei permitted them to reach the hilltop house.

On impulse, he decided not to let them pass.

Ming had already switched off the sedan's dome light to prevent it from shining when the doors were opened. Now, as the first response car approached him, starting up the hill to Lin Mak's house, he opened the driver's door and moved into a crouch behind it, sighting down the barrel of his automatic rifle.

This for you, Father.

He fired across the point car's hood, toward eager faces framed behind the windshield. Safety glass exploded in the likeness of a frozen waterfall collapsing, and he heard one of the black-clad gunmen cry out in alarm before the car swerved hard away from him and crashed into another vehicle at curbside.

Suddenly, all hell broke loose.

Two other cars were swerving crazily behind the first, their drivers pumping brakes and twisting steering wheels, while passengers tried to discover the source of the gunfire. Ming strafed the second vehicle before the first had fully come to rest, his bullets etching zigzag lines along the driver's side. One of the black-clad officers inside the car returned fire with a submachine gun, but his aim was hampered by the swerving vehicle, and Ming did better with a burst that turned the shooter's face into a crimson mask.

Somehow, the sudden violence didn't shock Ming as he'd thought it would. He wasn't frozen into immobility or struck numb. The world didn't slow down, as in a cinematic shootout where spent cartridges and falling bodies tumbled endlessly through space. If anything, the action seemed accelerated, as if some invisible controller's hand had pressed Fast-Forward on a giant videocassette machine.

Ming saw the third car swing broadside, then start jerking through a three-point turn as the driver tried to retreat. Ming's rifle stopped him with its last few rounds, the slide locking open on an empty chamber. He fumbled through reloading while shaken gunmen leaped from the second and third cars in unison, all seeking cover.

Too many, he thought, as the magazine snapped into place and he chambered a round. Far too many.

Strangely, the thought didn't daunt him. Ming heard explosive sounds of combat from the summit of the hill and started lining up his human targets, knocking them down on the run. Some stood and fought, while others tried to hide.

As Ming shot each in turn, he saw his father's face.

LEONG CHUN-SENG was frightened and embarrassed. Crawling around like an infant was one thing, but getting lost inside the house he knew so well was simply too much. It should've been impossible, but it had happened.

Leong wasn't sure where he'd gone wrong, but he had an inkling of *when*. He'd been scrabbling his way along the corridor that connected two parallel wings of Mak's house, when another explosion had shaken the place, this one close enough that it made Leong cringe, curling up in a tight fetal ball on the floor. Gagging smoke brought him out of the curl, but Leong guessed he had to have been disoriented, maybe crawling back the way he'd come instead of moving toward the parlor, where the action was.

Granted, he'd known the sounds of combat were receding and it hadn't bothered him at first. He craved safety, if such a thing could possibly be found here,

in the midst of so much violence. Guilt and shame
soon overcame self-preservation as a driving force, but
by that time Leong Chun-Seng had lost his way and
smoke within the burning house had thickened to the
point that he could see no useful landmarks in the
corridor he occupied.

Just think!

He knew there were three corridors on each of the
mansion's three floors, each level laid out in the shape
of a giant letter H. He'd been making his way from
the north arm of that H to the south, across the shorter
crossbar, when he'd been diverted. Now, with that in
mind—praying that it was true—Leong guessed that
he was back in the administrative wing, where Mak
and others had their offices.

But what if he was wrong?

Suppose he hadn't doubled back at all, but kept on
crawling forward after the explosion. What if he was
where he meant to be, but the combatants had moved
on to fight in other parts of the house? In that case,
the kitchen and the flashlight he'd set out to find had
to be no more than thirty yards away from him, in one
direction or the other.

At least he'd managed to retain his submachine gun,
though he hadn't fired it yet. Why draw attention to
himself, perhaps get shot by his own men, when he
could find no targets in the smoke? *Someone* was firing, granted, but the noises were surreal, as if Leong
were camped outside a movie theater, with some out-
landish action film playing inside.

He had to do something soon, if he intended to survive. Before moving, he took the cell phone from his pocket, once more blindly tapping out what he believed to be the police emergency number.

"Shen-Ling Massage Parlor," an ancient voice answered.

Leong felt like screaming but feared the results of a tantrum. Pocketing the phone again, he randomly selected a direction that he hoped was south and started crawling rapidly along the wall. Leong supposed he had to have covered thirty feet before a door swung open in his path and met his skull with stunning force.

Leong rocked backward on his haunches, then slumped over on his side. Dizzy and hurting, he was conscious of the submachine gun slipping from his fingers, but he couldn't hold it. Someone kicked him, more by accident than with intent to harm, and he was conscious of a voice demanding, "Who's that? State your name!"

English? It was, and with a British accent, too.

Leong groped for his weapon, but a heavy boot came down upon one hand, grinding his knuckles. Fingers tangled in his hair and jerked Leong's head back, while a vague face loomed in close to scrutinize his own.

"You speak English?"

Leong stayed mum until he felt the blade sight of a weapon gouge soft flesh beneath his chin. "A little," he replied.

"I want Lin Mak!" his captor barked. "Where is he?"

Lie and die, or tell the truth and risk the same?

Leong chose a middle course. "Not here," he muttered. "Gone."

"Oh, yes? Gone *where,* exactly?"

Leong was rescued by a coughing fit just then, smoke triggering his gag reflex. Undaunted, the intruder hauled Leong to his feet and drove him at a rapid, stumbling pace along the corridor.

BOLAN WAS PRIMING a grenade when static crackled in his ear, McCarter's voice behind it saying, "Urgent, do you read me?"

"In a second," Bolan answered, pitching the grenade overhand through an open doorway twenty feet distant. It bounced off the jamb before dropping inside, evoking cries of alarm from the gunners crouching in what seemed to be some kind of pantry or large closet.

Bolan's adversaries scrambled for the wobbling metal egg, hands clutching and obstructing one another. Someone lost his balance, fell against the door and slammed it, costing them whatever grace they might have gained through speed. Two seconds later, detonation took the door down in a noisy puff of smoke and flame, two bodies sprawled across it like roast pig at a luau. Bolan stood waiting for the other one or two gunmen to surface, ready with his rifle, but the pantry showed no further signs of life.

"Okay, tell me," he said into his throat mike.

"I've got a prisoner," McCarter said. "He tells me Mak's bugged out."

"Where to?"

"He has a mental block on that part, at the moment."

"Do you believe him?"

Hesitation, followed by a cautious "Yeah. I think I do."

Bolan allowed himself one bitter curse, then said, "All right. Fall back. Does everybody read?"

"I'm gone," McCarter said.

"Withdrawing," Mindel announced from somewhere else, a note of disappointment in her voice.

Retreating from the house was no cakewalk. Bolan's opponents had been decimated, but enough of them were still alive and armed to make withdrawal dicey. Two of them were waiting as he left the house, crossing a patio that faced a swimming pool. They opened up with SMGs in an erratic cross fire, when the Executioner appeared, and Bolan went to ground behind a hulking red-brick barbecue, relieved that someone in the mansion's past had cultivated Western tastes.

Bullets were chipping at the brickwork, spraying puffs of mortar dust, as Bolan worked his way around to spot the snipers. One was stretched out prone beside the pool, to the Executioner's left; the other, on his right, was crouched behind a table-and-umbrella set he'd overturned for cover. It was obvious that neither one of them had much experience in firefights, if they felt secure.

The gunner by the pool was easier, so Bolan took him first. His target was reloading, reaching back to draw a fresh mag from his belt, when the soldier lined him up and walked a burst of automatic fire across his prostrate body, rolling him into the pool. A dark stain spread across the surface of the water where he slipped from sight.

And that left one.

The shooter crouched behind the table lost it when his comrade took a dive. He broke from cover, running backward toward the lawn and tree line forty yards away. It could've been a toss-up whether simple clumsiness or Bolan's next burst took him down. His legs were tangled as he fell, but he kept firing all the way, spraying the last rounds from his magazine across the wall and sloping roof of Lin Mak's house.

Bolan pumped half a dozen extra rounds into the gunman's twitching form to keep him down, then bolted for the trees himself. He reached them without incident and kept on going, following the slope downhill until he reached the wall. McCarter and Mindel were waiting for him there, standing like bookends with a sullen Chinese prisoner between them.

"This is him?" Bolan asked.

"In the flesh," McCarter said.

Bolan addressed the prisoner directly. "We want Lin Yuan Mak. You want to live. Where is he?"

The captive shrugged and ducked his head. "Don't know."

"Maybe he *doesn't* know," Mindel suggested.

"Maybe not, but he's our consolation prize," Bolan replied. "He goes with us."

"We're running out of time," McCarter said.

Bolan could hear pursuers coming through the trees. "Go over first," he told McCarter. "Silent Sam here will be right behind you."

"Right!" McCarter sprang atop the wall without apparent effort, rolling out of sight beyond it. "Set!" he called to Bolan from the other side.

"Your turn," he told the prisoner.

"Can't climb."

"I'll bet you can." Seizing the startled captive's shirt and belt, Bolan propelled him toward the summit of the eight-foot wall. The prisoner grasped hold of it to keep himself from falling, and a solid jab from Bolan's rifle sent him wallowing across.

"I'll cover you," he told Mindel, watching the trees until she cleared the wall, then following her supple form. Together, they began to run downhill, driving their prisoner in front of them until they reached the bottom of the hill.

It was a battleground, with bullet-punctured cars stalled in the intersection, bodies scattered in the street. Streetlights reflected crimson from the spreading pools of blood. Their driver, Ming Cho-Hei, appeared to be the last man standing, covering the corpses with his automatic rifle.

"You all right?" McCarter asked him.

"Better now," Ming said, flashing an enigmatic smile.

"Who are these blokes?"

"Secret police," Ming answered. "Our Gestapo."

Bolan steered their captive to the waiting car, as Ming climbed in behind the wheel. Secret police, all dead. They'd crossed a line tonight, and there could be no turning back.

Not by my hand, he told himself as the sedan began to move. Not mine.

CHAPTER NINE

They didn't go back to the flat after their raid on Lin Mak's house, since Ming Cho-Hei believed their prisoner might raise a fuss during interrogation and draw unwanted attention from the neighbors. Mindel knew what that meant, and she wasn't looking forward to the next few hours if the captive tried to tough it out.

She'd never cared for torture, though Mossad and Israeli military intelligence routinely abused prisoners suspected of terrorism, extracting confessions in defiance of the legal niceties. Mindel herself had seen two Palestinian commandos summarily executed after questioning, and she knew from after-hours conversations with various comrades that her own observations were merely the tip of the iceberg. Mindel didn't criticize her colleagues' methods; she made no complaints. But sometimes—increasingly at times like these—she asked herself, at what point in the war do we become our enemy?

Ming drove through winding, darkened streets until he reached the waterfront along Macao's northeast shoreline. Cargo ships docked here, and there were warehouses aplenty in the neighborhood. One of them stood apart, perhaps a bit more shabby and disreputable than the others. Ming pulled his sedan around back, found a midnight blot of shadow to conceal the car and parked it there.

He had a large ring filled with jangling keys, one of which fitted a padlock on a side door of the warehouse. Once inside, he threw a dead bolt, felt his way along the wall and flipped a light switch. Sudden brilliance forced Mindel to squint, but only seconds passed before she checked the nearest windows, finding they'd been painted black inside.

Ming had secured the necessary privacy for what had to happen next.

The prisoner was frightened, and with reason. He'd already watched a number of his comrades die, and now he had to wonder whether he would ever see another sunrise. Ming conveyed him to a straight-backed wooden chair that might have been prepared especially for their gathering. It stood alone, nearly dead center in the empty warehouse, lit by floodlights as if waiting for an actor to appear and launch into a Shakespearean monologue. Instead, a trembling prisoner sat in it, surrounded by armed enemies.

Ming asked their subject something in Chinese. The captive shook his head and muttered two short syllables before Ming punched him in the face and knocked him sprawling from the chair. Blood dribbled freely from his flattened nose. Mindel stood fast and gripped her rifle, as if somehow drawing strength from wood and steel.

Ming gripped his adversary by the collar of his

jacket, hauled him to his feet and dropped him back into the chair. To Mindel's ear, it seemed that he repeated his first question. This time, there was no head shake. The captive whimpered a reply, but Ming was still unsatisfied. Scowling, he slammed his fist into the subject's face a second time, driving him over backward, chair and all.

"He'll speak soon, I believe," Ming said.

"Not if you break his bloody jaw," McCarter answered.

"All we need to know is where Mak went and when he left," Bolan said.

Nodding, Ming stepped over to the prisoner, bent and flexed his shoulders, lifting man and chair upright together in a single move. Mindel wouldn't have guessed he had the strength to do it, but their guide had already surprised her more than once this night. She bit her tongue as Ming reached underneath his jacket, drew a pistol, thumbed the hammer back and pressed the muzzle hard into their captive's groin.

He didn't have to ask the question this time. Ardently, the prisoner unleashed a flood of words, with Cantonese and English mixed together. Mindel caught the words "Sumatra" and "morning," although she didn't have a prayer of making out what fell between the two.

Relaxed now, Ming stepped back, holding the pistol at his side. "He says Mak left this morning, early. He was flying to Jakarta for a meeting with an oilman from America."

"Napier," McCarter said.

Their prisoner reacted to the name, half turning in his chair, bobbing his head and speaking rapidly for several seconds more.

"That was the name he heard," Ming said. "I think it's probably the truth."

"I think so, too," Bolan replied.

"Finished with this one, then?" Ming asked.

"We're done."

"And finished in Macao?"

"It looks that way."

Ming's shoulders slumped a little as he glanced from one face to the next. "Too bad," he said. "Too bad."

Although she barely knew the man, Mindel believed she could detect sincere regret. She wondered how long he would last after tonight, if he could keep up the facade of a loyal Party member and deceive his masters in Beijing. Failing in that, she guessed his life would be a short, unhappy one.

"You want the airport now?" Ming asked.

"We'll need to make some phone calls first," Bolan said.

"Use the office telephone," Ming told him. "I swept the line this morning."

"Right. Okay."

"I'll take care of this one," Ming added, "then come back to wait for you."

He prodded their captive with his pistol—Mindel realized she'd never learned the stranger's name—and marched him toward the door through which they'd entered.

"I'll just catch that dead bolt," McCarter said, trailing after them.

"What now?" she asked Bolan, after the others had retreated out of earshot.

"I touch base with Washington," he said. "You do the same with Tel Aviv, if it's required."

"They'd rather not hear any more from me right now."

"Okay. I'll see if I can get cooperation on the ground at our next stop. As soon as Ming gets back, we'll pick up Jack and then be on our way."

"Jakarta?"

Bolan nodded, frowning as he echoed her. "Jakarta."

Washington, D.C.

BROGNOLA'S PRIVATE LINE lit up at 1:18 p.m., eleven hours—and a full day on the calendar—later than Bolan's time in Macao. He'd been expecting the call, though it could as easily have come from Phoenix Force or Able Team, embroiled with missions of their own.

But there was no mistaking Bolan's voice.

"We missed him," the Executioner stated.

Brognola felt the remnants of his lunch begin to churn. "Gave you the slip?" he asked.

"Before we landed," Bolan said. "From what we gather here, he flew out to Jakarta for a meet with an American oilman."

"Napier?"

"Sounds like it, but we can't confirm that from Macao."

"You're in pursuit, then?"

"Pretty soon. We have a few loose ends to tie up here."

"Can I help?"

"I thought you'd never ask," Bolan replied. "The language shouldn't be a problem, but we'll need a contact for munitions when we land."

"No sweat. I'll line it up."

"And transportation," Bolan added.

"You want a guide this time?"

"Not yet. It hasn't been that long since I was in the neighborhood."

"The pirate thing," Brognola said, recalling yet another bloody mission. "Right. Okay."

"If you can get a line on Global's office in Jakarta, it would be a help."

"I'll run it through the mill. Location should be simple. Maybe we'll get lucky with a floor plan."

"And the residence," Bolan said.

"Right. I'll check for on-site Global personnel at the same time."

"It couldn't hurt."

"Things are a bit erratic in that area right now."

"What else is new?" Bolan asked.

"Right."

What else, indeed? There'd been no end to chaos and bloodshed throughout the Indonesian archipelago for close to forty years, beginning with the massacre of half a million dissidents in 1965, continuing on through the civil war and genocide in East Timor. Indonesia was the kind of place where itinerant villains could lose themselves in the crowd—or find steady work, if they mouthed the right political slogans.

"When are you leaving?" Hal asked.

"A few hours," Bolan replied. "Around sunrise, our time."

"I'll get back to Grimaldi by satellite link on that info, try to catch you in flight if I can."

"Sounds good. Watch your back while you're at it. We still don't know how our players are connected."

"I'm watching," Brognola promised. "It comes with the job."

"Later, then."

Bolan severed the link, leaving the big Fed with a dial tone.

Macao

GRIMALDI FELT Bolan beside him, almost touching-close, before the tall man spoke. It was enough to spook him sometimes, even now, the way his old friend could pop up anywhere he wanted to, without a hint of warning.

"How's the fueling?" Bolan asked.

"Just wrapped it up. I've got my final preflight checklist, then the only thing we need is passengers and baggage."

"I can help you out on that. No hassles on the flight plan?"

"Nope. We're cleared through to Jakarta. All they want to see on this end are the paid-up transit fees."

"Same on the other end?"

"Smooth sailing," Grimaldi replied. "From what I understand, the government's too busy mopping up Tamils to worry much about China right now. Besides, we've got credentials up the old wazoo."

"That would explain my lower-back pain," Bolan said.

Grimaldi smiled. "The others ready?"

"Pretty much. I'll have them here within the hour, packed and ready."

"What's the word from Hal?"

"He's looking for a hardware dealer in Jakarta, hoping to touch base with you by satcom while we're traveling."

"Okay," Grimaldi said. "Look forward to it."

"I hoped we'd have this wrapped by now," Bolan admitted. "Damn thing's turning into a production of *Around the World in Eighty Days*."

"Maybe we'll nail it in Jakarta."

"Maybe part of it," the Executioner replied. "We've still got nothing on Andrastus."

"Hard to figure how a guy like that can disappear," Grimaldi said.

"He hides behind his money. No one from the inner circle wants to blow a whistle and lose his place at the trough."

"Still, this guy's like Onassis was, or Trump. You figure he's got doubles to divert the press?"

"If so, they're missing too. Hal's waiting for a rumble from the paparazzi grapevine, but it's quiet as the grave so far."

"Hey, that's a thought."

"What is?"

"Maybe his playmates took him out,' Grimaldi said. "It wouldn't be the first time rats abandoned ship and let the captain ride her down."

"We can't rule it out, but Andrastus was never in charge of the show. Take it for granted that he's got security in place, keeping a watchful eye on friends, as well as enemies. Right now he's got to wonder where the heat's been coming from, and Napier can't do much to clear that up for either of his partners."

"The divide-and-conquer ploy?" Grimaldi asked.

"It wouldn't be my first choice, and it's damn hard to control when we can't even catch a glimpse of our opponents, but it may be all we have."

"You'd better work it, then."

"I'd trade it off for one clean shot at Napier," Bolan said. "Better, ten minutes of his time."

"Maybe Jakarta," the pilot replied.

"Maybe."

"I'll keep my fingers crossed."

"Unless it interferes with keeping this thing in the air," said Bolan. Glancing at his watch, he seemed to shrug off the conversation. "I'll get the others. Back in ten."

"Okay."

Bolan vanished as silently as he'd arrived, leaving Grimaldi with the sense of awe that was a constant feature of their friendship. It was never verbalized, much less dragged out for anything resembling analysis, but it was always there. Bolan had never once,

in Grimaldi's experience, treated a comrade as infe-
rior—he wasn't wired that way—but there was still
something about him, every time they met, reminding
the man of the intrinsic difference between them.

True enough, Grimaldi was a battle-hardened,
street-wise soldier in his own right. He had skills Bolan didn't possess, most notably where flying was concerned. He'd been on board for some of Bolan's
toughest missions and had always pulled his own
weight without flinching, plus a little extra. But he still
felt like an amateur, sometimes, beside the Executioner.

And something told him that he always would.

No sweat, Grimaldi told himself. Bolan was out
there, living full-time in the zone most troops only
spent a day or two in any given year. He was the last
word in lifers, committed to an endless struggle by his
own dedication, never once counting the cost.

Grimaldi had been in the zone himself.

But he would never think of going there unless he
had a reasonable shot at coming back. No, thank you,
very much. It was a bleak life, any way you sliced it,
and he wasn't really sure it even qualified as living.

Not unless the subject's name was Bolan, in which
case it qualified as living large.

Grimaldi started running down his checklist, preparing for departure. Bolan would be back in ten, fifteen at most, with Mindel and McCarter, and he didn't
want to keep them waiting. They had places to go and
people to kill.

They were all going back to the zone.

Airborne, South China Sea

MCCARTER CRACKED his second Coke since takeoff, watching through his eastward-facing window as the vast Pacific skyline caught fire in a blaze of gold. He knew approximately where the Philippines were located but couldn't see them from five hundred miles away. Ahead, due south, Jakarta waited for them at the limit of their standard cruising distance, still more than a thousand miles of open sea and craggy islands left to go.

They were unarmed again, the weapons left behind in their temporary safehouse, marked for disposal at Ming Cho-Hei's leisure. Embarked on yet another leg of a journey that appeared to have no end in sight, McCarter took stock of the action in Macao and tried to work out what they had accomplished.

First, they'd turned the heat up under Lin Yuan Mak. Although he'd managed to escape them, they had fouled his nest and left him with a long list of questions to answer if he ever made it home to China. McCarter hoped to spare him that, for Katz's sake, but it was good to know the bastard faced official embarrassment at least, should he slip through their fingers again and go looking for shelter at home.

They'd also got another lead to Arnold Napier's whereabouts, for what it might be worth. Granted, at this point in the game, McCarter took all information they received with a prodigious grain of salt, but it was possible they'd find both men relaxed and waiting for them in Jakarta like a pair of sitting ducks.

Just barely possible.

McCarter didn't buy it, though. The mission hadn't gone that way from day one to their late departure from Macao. Each time they made a move, the enemy was one long jump ahead of them. They'd kicked some heavy ass, but it had so far been the wrong ass, more or less. They kept on skirmishing with players from the junior varsity, instead of squaring off against the pros.

Not that the second string was getting any easier.

There'd been some dicey moments in Macao, the previous night, and none of it broke even in McCarter's reckoning for losing Katz. That score was still unsettled, and would dog him everywhere he went until the men responsible were laid to rest once and for all.

And would that be an end to it? Would taking out the three prime movers nail the casket shut on Napier's plot? They hadn't even really glimpsed the fine points of it yet, although Israel was clearly earmarked for disruption, possibly destruction. And from there— what?

It was easy to surmise the broad outlines. An oilman with a billion-dollar company behind him had to have his eyes on black gold in the Middle East. The man who crippled Israel or removed it altogether as a player in the region could expect to write his own ticket with oil-rich sheikhs and warlords from Tehran to Tripoli. Andrastus and his shipping line could pick up hefty contracts for transporting shipments from the Red Sea or the Persian Gulf to…where?

China.

The People's Republic had oil of its own, an estimated twenty-four billion barrels in reserve at the turn of the new century, but it would never be enough for a nation of 1.2 billion souls and counting. The Middle Eastern states, by contrast, had closer to seven hundred billion barrels on tap. When it came to natural gas, the imbalance was even more striking, forty-odd trillion cubic feet for China, versus nearly two quadrillion cubic feet buried beneath the Middle Eastern sands.

If Napier tapped that mother lode, he could emerge from the transaction as one of the richest men on Earth. Anyone who went along for the ride would likewise bank more cash than a hard-living rock star could spend in a dozen lifetimes—and that included certain Chinese officials, led by Lin Mak, who greased the wheels of commerce from Beijing. If money weren't enough, the Reds could also congratulate themselves on finally liberating their Palestinian "brothers" from the cruel yoke of Yankee-Israeli imperialism.

It was a two-for-one shot with no losers on Napier's team—until, one afternoon in Tel Aviv, a grizzled warrior on vacation with his family had recognized familiar faces in a streetside crowd.

The rest was history, along with Katz and several dozen players from the other side. The lot of them together didn't measure up to Yakov Katzenelenbogen, in McCarter's estimation, but he wasn't finished yet.

Another crop of targets waited for him in Jakarta, and he meant to see them all plowed under if he could.

Beginning just as soon as they were on the ground.

Macao

THE NEW DAY DAWNED without promise for Ming Cho-Hei. The previous night had changed him, most profoundly and irrevocably. He couldn't decide if it was wicked of the Westerners to leave him thus, after enticing him into an armed rebellion he hadn't anticipated, or if what they'd done ranked as the single greatest favor of his life.

Driving south across the mile-long causeway that connected Taipa to the Ilha de Colôane, Ming knew the fault—if fault there was—lay not with any foreigner, but with himself. He could've driven off and left his round-eyed charges to the tender mercies of Macao's security police detachment, but he'd chosen to react instinctively and thereby crossed a line from which he feared—or was it hoped?—there could be no return.

A muffled thumping sound from the trunk of his car reminded Ming of his immediate task. Before he did anything else, before he considered whatever future still remained to him, he had to deal with Leong Chun-Seng.

And Leong had no future at all.

Ming's recent allies hadn't ordered the disposal, but he knew what had to be done. Leong simply knew too much to live. He hadn't only seen the Western visitors, but he might well have ways of reaching out to warn Lin Mak that he was now in danger.

Ming wouldn't permit him to do that.

He understood that Lin Mak was involved in something more important, far more dangerous than any of his normal duties in Macao. Ming didn't understand exactly what it was, or how much was at stake, but it appeared that he could damage the Beijing regime by helping to unravel the conspiracy.

And his last contribution to that cause would be accomplished when he'd dealt with Leong Chun-Seng.

Leaving the causeway, Ming drove south for roughly another quarter mile, then turned eastward, toward the water. A half mile short of the coast, he found a road that wound into the hills, so narrow that it had lay-bys cut into the steep banks every hundred yards or so, permitting one driver or another to pull off if two cars met, coming from opposite directions. Ming met none today, however, and proceeded at an almost risky speed into the hills.

His destination was a place he'd found by accident some years earlier. The winding road reached a dead end atop a tall hill crowned with trees. It had an eastward-facing view of the South China Sea, but was concealed from prying eyes by trees and undergrowth. Mud from the previous weekend's rain had dried without new tire tracks, telling Ming he was unlikely to be bothered there.

Reaching the place he sought, Ming parked his car and switched off the engine. Taking his pistol and his car keys, he got out and walked around behind the vehicle. Unlocking the trunk, he stepped back a long pace before the lid rose, revealing Leong's pale, worried face.

"Get out!" Ming ordered.

Leong stared at him, wide-eyed, muttering something behind his cloth gag. Ming felt foolish, remembering that Leong's hands were bound behind his back. He couldn't climb out of the trunk unaided, even if his heart was willing and his legs were steady.

Cautiously, half expecting a wild kick or head butt, Ming hauled his prisoner upright, drawing him clear of the trunk until he could stand on his own two feet, more or less. Leong was wobbly, as if he'd forgotten how to walk at some point during their hour-long drive, but it came back to him as Ming steered him toward the trees, following a discreet pace behind.

Leong had to have known that he was finished, for he bolted at the tree line, running for his life without a backward glance. It made things easier for Ming, a clean shot in the back from fifteen paces, just between the shoulder blades, and then the coup de grâce from ten or twelve inches, closing his eyes against any backsplash.

Ming put his gun away and dragged the body farther on, careful to touch only fabric, leaving no fingerprints on the body. Perhaps they could still extract DNA samples from his perspiration, where sweaty palms clutched Leong's jacket, but what of it? Without a suspect for comparison, the tests were useless.

Tire tracks? There was nothing he could do about them now. They'd be obscured with the next rain, or when the next car reached his hilltop hideaway. Ballistics didn't matter unless someone found his gun, and Ming didn't intend to give it up without a fight.

What was it they said in America? When you pry it from my cold, dead fingers.

Yes. That sounded right.

But not too soon.

There was a new day coming, for Ming and for Macao. His masters didn't know it yet, but they would be made aware of the change in the fullness of time. Meanwhile, they harbored no suspicion that their faithful servant had the strength or will to lift a hand against them. They believed he was a sheep.

Smiling, Ming drove back down the serpentine track, heading home to Macao. He needed sleep, before the advent of another day, but he wouldn't rest long.

There was too much to do, now that he had made up his mind. He would surprise them all and leave them wondering how he had passed unnoticed among them for so long.

And by the time they saw him coming, it would be too late.

Airborne, Above the Java Sea

ALMOST THERE.

They'd bypassed the green hulk of Borneo now, Bolan peering from his window without glimpsing a single wild man. Granted, there could've been a naked army capering around beneath the jungle treetops, fifteen thousand feet below them, but he still had to wonder what all the fuss was about. Somehow, real life never lived up to the advertisements.

Except, perhaps, where danger was concerned.

They were supposed to have man-eating crocodiles on Borneo, and tribes that shared the taste for human flesh. He didn't know if that was true or not, but "civilized" Java lay just ahead of them, and there were predators aplenty waiting for him in the concrete jungle of Jakarta.

Bolan hoped Lin Mak would be among them. More than that, he hoped for his first shot at Arnold Napier. If Christos Andrastus happened to be passing by at the same time, so much the better.

But he wouldn't get his hopes up.

Not just yet.

They'd had a near miss in Macao, but it was still a miss, and he was sick of running second best. Granted, it wasn't the first time he'd chased a target halfway around the world, but in the past he'd usually had a fair idea of who—or what—was waiting for him at his hellfire destination. This time, other than predicting trouble with a fair degree of certainty, Bolan kept drawing blanks.

McCarter felt the strain as much as he did, Bolan knew, and it was even worse on Mindel, since she had a private blood debt to repay. In other circumstances, Bolan might've counseled her against following Katz's killers to the Far East, but who was he to argue against vengeance? He'd begun his own long struggle with an act of retribution, and that act had led him to his present situation, hurtling through the clouds between one killing confrontation and the next.

Mindel was well trained, capable, experienced. She pulled her own weight and then some, giving the contest everything she had. He couldn't argue with her motives or her style—and yet she troubled him. It felt like waiting for the other shoe to drop.

And if it did, there might be hell to pay.

Brognola had been right about the climate of violence in Indonesia. Portions of the archipelago had been reduced to virtual anarchy during four decades of purges, revolts and oppression. Some of the killing was political, carried out between far right and left; still more was religious, between misguided Christians and Muslims. Ethnic cleansing in occupied East Timor had so far killed off nearly one-third of the island's seven hundred thousand inhabitants, with no end to the genocide in sight.

Curing Indonesia's many ills was beyond Bolan's power, but he might take advantage of the general chaos to complete his mission—if the targets could be found and isolated. As to whether that was possible, he'd simply have to wait and see. They'd know within the next few hours, one way or the other.

And if the prey eluded them once more, then what?

The Executioner would play that hand when it was dealt to him. Meanwhile, he had enough on his mind with the coming campaign against his elusive enemies.

Seated near the back of the Jetstar's passenger compartment, the soldier studied Mindel and McCarter. The Israeli seemed to be asleep, though looks could be deceiving. McCarter was using his time to skim a travel guide on Indonesia, brushing up on the geography and other basics. There'd be next to nothing in the standard tourist literature about Indonesia's endemic problems. Mass murder had a tendency to discourage group tours, after all, and Indonesia lagged in that department as it was. Most Brits and Yankees knew the country only from old movies, like *The Year of Living Dangerously,* which were likewise not inclined to start a rush of tourism.

But Indonesia did have oil, somewhere between five billion and nine billion barrels, depending on the source of published estimates. While tiny in comparison with Middle Eastern states, that crude reserve made Indonesia the second-greatest oil-producing nation in the Far East, after China.

It stood to reason that Napier and Global Petroleum would have a foot in the door, taking whatever profits could be found from the long chain of islands. The more important question now was whether they would find Napier on-site, and could they pin him down?

If so, the campaign could be over in a day.

If not, they would be looking at another chase.

Assuming they survived.

CHAPTER TEN

Jakarta

Lin Yuan Mak was asleep when the telephone rang, jarring him rudely back to consciousness from the thrall of an erotic dream. The third or fourth ring found him fumbling across the nightstand, fingers moving first to the digital alarm clock, turning it to face him.

The red numerals informed him that the hour was 4:19 a.m. He felt a sudden flash of anger, instantly replaced by dread at the realization that no one would dare to disturb him at that time of the morning unless it was a grave emergency.

More trouble, then. The certain knowledge sat upon his chest like deadweight, threatening to still his pounding heart.

At times like this, he would've much preferred to waken with a serpent in his bed than to begin his day with threats of the unknown.

Mak found the telephone receiver on the sixth or seventh ring, nearly dropping it in his awkward haste. The cord tangled on something, vexing him, but finally he freed it and brought the handset to his ears.

"Yes, hello?"

The caller was a ranking officer of the security police detachment in Macao. Mak's private secretary had
been wakened and commanded to provide a contact
number, under threat of being charged with an offense
against the public safety if he should refuse. The
caller, known to Mak as an ambitious man who had
his sights on higher office, more authority, was calling
"as a courtesy" to brief him on the details of an incident occurring some three hours earlier.

Mak listened, dumbstruck, as the story was relayed.
His home had been destroyed by an incendiary fire,
and several of his bodyguards were dead. A final count
would have to wait until the ashes cooled and could
be raked for bones. A party of security police respond-
ing to the trouble call had been ambushed and shot by
persons unknown, within two hundred yards of Lin
Mak's residence.

Did Comrade Mak have any thoughts on who might
be responsible?

He most assuredly did not.

Any idea of why he might be targeted by terrorists?

Again, no clue.

The officer, having expected nothing more, rang off
with a request that Mak submit a formal statement to
police upon returning to Macao. He readily agreed and
cradled the receiver, lifting it once more almost before
the dial tone had a chance to interrupt one conversation for the next. With his free hand, he found the
button for a bedside lamp and pushed it, blinking like
a cave dweller in the sudden glare of light.

It was his turn to call, another's turn to lurch awake in fear. He had the number memorized, of course. It was a function of Mak's personality to always be prepared, at least within the limits of predictable conditions.

He was disappointed when a male voice answered on the first ring, wide awake, and it didn't belong to Arnold Napier. Mak identified himself and told the flunky that his call was urgent, brooking no delay. Because his name was recognized by those with need to know, there was no argument.

The best part of a minute passed before Napier came on the line. He sounded damnably alert and almost jovial, Mak's second disappointment of the morning. He amended that to third, remembering to add on the destruction of his house and bodyguards.

"Good morning, Lin," Napier said. "Nothing wrong with your hotel, I hope?"

"Not the hotel," Mak answered, then described the action in Macao as it had been relayed to him. Details were sparse, but he explained the gist of it, making his apprehension plain.

Napier refrained from interrupting until the man was finished, passing thirty seconds more in silence after that before he said, "I do believe it's time we thought about a change of scene."

"You think that we're in danger here?"

"Why take the chance?"

"Where would we go?"

"I have some thoughts on that," Napier said. "For

the moment, please, just pack your things. I'll have a driver pick you up in half an hour.''

The line went dead, leaving Lin Mak confused and agitated. He supposed leaving Jakarta was the wise thing to do, but leaving for where? If he simply disappeared, his masters in Beijing would take it badly. At the very least, they'd call for an accounting, and it could be even worse. Mak could be stripped of all his power, charged with sundry crimes, even convicted in absentia. It would be totally in character for Beijing to dispatch assassins, if it was suspected that he'd turned against the Party.

Rising swiftly from his bed and moving toward the closet, Mak was more than ever thankful for his numbered bank accounts in Switzerland and the Bahamas. There was a certain irony in Mak, a lifelong Communist, depending for survival on the services of Western bankers, but he couldn't find it in himself to smile.

His Chinese bodyguards were sleeping in the room next door, relieved of duty for the evening on Napier's promise to insure security. Mak paused to question whether he should wake them, take them with him, but he decided against it. They were party loyalists to the core, when all was said and done. Dragging them along would only place him in more jeopardy, if they decided he had turned against the People's Revolution and was operating on his own.

He'd go alone, then, trusting Arnold Napier with his life. As if he had a choice.

Aboard the Aristotle, *East of Gibraltar*

ALWAYS THE TELEPHONE plagued him, making Andrastus wish he could sever all links to the outside world and simply drift away from his responsibilities. Of course, that attitude hadn't made him a billionaire and wouldn't help him stay alive when things got rough.

He'd finished with Irina in an hour and fifteen minutes. It wasn't a record, but he'd left her satisfied and smiling in the stateroom they occasionally shared for private exercise. Andrastus was returning to his own cabin and looking forward to a shower when the first mate hailed him from the head of the companionway and warned him of another scrambled call incoming from Jakarta.

It was well and good for Napier to consult him, most particularly when the news was good and meant more money in his pocket, but the news was never good these days. The past two weeks, Andrastus had become accustomed to a ceaseless litany of setbacks, losses and impending danger. Now, he knew without hearing a word of the latest message, he was about to receive more bad news.

Andrastus thanked the mate curtly and moved on to his stateroom, where one of a half-dozen telephone scramblers aboard the *Aristotle* was installed. He saw the button blinking for line one, suppressed an urge to turn it off, lifting the handset instead and forcing a cheerful tone.

"Arnold, my friend. You've solved our problem, I assume?"

Taken off guard, Napier responded, "Not exactly. There's been further difficulty, as a matter of fact."

Smiling despite the sour feeling in his gut, Andrastus said, "More trouble? I would not have thought it possible."

"It's possible, all right," Napier assured him. "In Macao, this time."

"Lin's own backyard?"

"His own damn house, if you believe it."

"At this point," Andrastus said, "I'm prepared to believe anything. Was he injured?"

"They missed him. He's down here with me."

"Down here" meaning Jakarta, in the miserable heat. Andrastus loved the sun but loathed the oppressive humidity of the tropics, avoiding them at all costs.

"Lucky for both of you," he said.

"Or not," Napier replied. "If they could slip into Macao, I'm guessing they could track him here."

"When you say 'they,' I take it that you mean—"

"We still don't have ID on any of the opposition," Napier grudgingly admitted. "I've been beating bushes from D.C. to Tel Aviv and coming up with squat."

"That's most discouraging," Andrastus said.

"Tell me about it. Anyway, we're looking for someplace to spend a little time, let things cool down and get it sorted out."

"I see." Unfortunately, it was true. Andrastus saw where this was going, and it didn't please him.

Napier waited for the invitation, dead air whispering between them, until it was clear he'd have to ask. He owed Andrastus that much, at the very least: a frank admission of his failure to this point.

"So, I was hoping, if it's not too much to ask, that we could pass a few days on your island. What's it called again?"

"Thyra."

It meant *untamed,* in Greek. Andrastus had named the island himself, after purchasing it from a bankrupt competitor. It lay midway between Crete and the southernmost point of the Cyclades, omitted from most maps of the Mediterranean. It was his private sanctuary—until now.

"Thyra, of course. You don't mind, do you, Christos?"

Andrastus scowled, hating the words before he spoke them. "Of course not. What are friends for?"

"Partners," Napier said, gently correcting him.

"Of course."

"You won't regret it, Christos."

He already did, he thought. But what he said was, "I hope not, Arnold."

"My word of honor."

"Ah. In that case…"

What? He left the comment dangling, incomplete. What could he say to a man whose word of honor counted for less than nothing?

"Excellent! We'll book a flight plan through to Athens," Napier told him, hideously cheerful in his victory. "Can you have someone meet us for the final leg?"

"Consider it accomplished."

"Marvelous. I'll see you soon."

"Too soon," Andrastus told the humming dial tone after Napier severed the long-distance link.

It meant another change of course, but that was nothing. The yacht's captain and crew took uncertainty in stride, drawing comfort from the knowledge that they earned more cash for every day they spent at sea. This deviation from their westward course would be cause for rejoicing. They were turning back for home.

But what, Andrastus wondered, would they find there?

Did the nameless enemy already know about Thyra, or would Napier show them the way?

If so, Andrastus promised himself, come hell or high water, the oilman wouldn't leave the island alive.

Jakarta

"I'M NOT SURE I understand, sir."

Half asleep and still reliving portions of a vivid nightmare, Jared Wagner wasn't sure that he could trust his ears.

"Snap out of it," Napier commanded him. "I said I'm leaving you in charge. It's just for a few days. No need to get your knickers in a twist."

"No, sir."

"Lin has a hankering to sit down with Andrastus, so we're going."

"When, sir?"

"Now. Within the hour."

Wagner squinted at the bedside clock. Even without

his contact lenses he could read the time: 4:42 a.m. Not mine to question why, he thought, grateful that he had been excluded from this literal fly-by-night adventure.

"Right," he said. "I'll get the pilots hopping, then, and—"

"It's already done. No worries. All you have to do is keep your eyes wide open while I'm gone and make sure everything runs smoothly."

"Yes, sir. In regard to that—"

"Chop-chop," Napier said. "Spit it out, son."

"If I may ask where you're going, sir, in case I need to get in touch with you for any reason?"

"Sorry, thought I told you. You remember Thyra? No? Of course, you've never been there, have you?"

"No, sir."

"Christos has a private island getaway," Napier explained. "Perfect for talking business when the walls at home have ears. If something happens—and I have no reason to believe it will—just use the satcom link to ring me up, as usual."

"Yes, sir."

"Okay. That's it, then. Go on back to sleep."

"Yes, sir."

As if he could, Wagner thought, dropping the telephone receiver back into its cradle. A person didn't drop that kind of bomb and then sign off without a fare-thee-well.

Or rather, Arnold Napier did exactly that.

Technically, it wasn't the first time Wagner was in charge. He'd been running portions of the Global empire, under supervision, for the best part of a year. He'd managed the Jakarta office well enough, but this was different. Being in charge meant literally that. He had the driver's seat, while Napier flew off to some tiny island in the Med to take a meeting, on a whim.

It should've been great news, but Wagner was already looking for the catch. He couldn't see it yet, but there was bound to be one, ready to bite him on the ass when he least expected it.

Granted, Napier was given to sudden, impulsive decisions, but to the best of Wagner's knowledge that didn't include flying off from Jakarta to Greece before dawn, when no travel was scheduled in advance. That spelled trouble to Wagner, and he worried that the unknown problem was about to become his, while Napier winged out of harm's way.

What to do?

Suck it up and perform as expected, what else?

He was playing in the big leagues now, where whiners never prospered and were soon cut from the team. Wagner hadn't invested so much time in Global Petroleum—the tedium of micromanagement, backstabbing office politics—to simply cut and run the first time he was trusted with some real responsibility.

It was his chance to shine, and if he had the opportunity to solve some problem that intimidated Arnold Napier, why, so much the better. In fact, he couldn't think of a better way to prove himself than under fire.

It still worried him, though. The uncertainty guaranteed that there'd be no more sleep for him this night.

Known threats were one thing. Every problem had a viable solution, once all angles of attack were analyzed and placed into perspective. With the unknown, though, it was impossible to be prepared.

And Wagner didn't like surprises.

Well, maybe a stripper in a birthday cake from time to time, but otherwise, no thanks.

Hang tough. Just suck it up.

Cursing, he rolled out of bed and turned off the alarm clock, set for a perfectly civilized six o'clock wake-up. Sleep was lost to him now, and there was no point putting off the start of his day, finding out what it might hold in store.

Trouble, a voice at the back of his mind muttered insistently. Nothing but trouble.

So much the better, then. How would he ever really prove himself, coasting through rosy times with nothing to do but double-check accounts and read *The Wall Street Journal*?

Adversity was the true test of mettle. Without it, a man remained unproved and unworthy.

Wagner ran the shower as hot as he could stand it, waiting until he glowed pink from head to foot, then switching it to icy cold. The combination banished any tattered shreds of sleep and left him wondering what his nightmare had been all about, why it had disturbed him so much. The images were scattered, lost, frustrating Wagner as he tried to summon them.

Good riddance.

The day ahead promised to hold sufficient challenges in store, without him brooding over phantoms.

He would take each new one as it came and do his dandiest to emerge triumphant. Failing that…then, what?

He didn't even want to think about it.

Washington, D.C.

THE SATCOM LINK WAS surprisingly clear, no more than a whisper of background static audible on Brognola's end of the line. Grimaldi picked up right away, a miracle of sorts considering the distance, and informed him they were twenty minutes from touchdown at Jakarta. The pilot piped him through from there, and Bolan picked up seconds later on what had to be an air phone, from the sound of it.

"What's up?"

"Two things," Brognola said. "First up, I've got a hardware dealer for you, operating undercover as a jeweler. Smart money says I'll bitch the name. He goes by Kusnadi Hulanapo."

"Okay, got it."

And he would, too, just like that. Bolan's memory was encyclopedic, the proverbial steel trap.

"You may want to write down the address," Brognola cautioned. It was another jawbreaker, one of those Far Eastern handles that could've been a man's long-winded name or a recipe for turtle soup. The big Fed sounded it out, then went back and spelled it for Bolan, in case they got lucky and spotted a street sign in English.

"Name of the shop?" Bolan asked.

"Kusnadi's. The quote from my source says it's 'modest in appearance, but always well stocked.'"

"That's encouraging, anyway."

"I can't confirm Napier's location," Brognola went on, "but I've IDed his new number two. Name's Jared Wagner, thirty-five years old. He's got an MBA from Stanford and the morals of an alley cat, from what I gather. Anyway, he's bent enough for Napier to promote him after Sterling Holbrook bought the farm."

"Addresses?"

"Home and office," Brognola replied. "More tongue twisters." He sounded out the street names. Bolan repeated them, nailing both cold on the first try.

"No confirmation on primary targets?" he pressed.

"Sorry, no. From what I gather, Napier's always been tight-lipped, but it's changed from a habit to an obsession the past year or so. His movements are strictly need-to-know. Flunkies get summoned to a meeting, and it's *bam!* Drop what you're doing folks, the boss is here to pat you on the back or chew you out, whatever."

"Someone always knows," Bolan replied.

"Granted. He trusts the one VP with details," Brognola said. "It used to be Holbrook, now Wagner."

"I guess we'll need to have a chat."

"Good luck. You still don't want a contact on the ground?"

"We shouldn't need one," Bolan said, "but I'll keep you in mind if it starts to go south."

"I appreciate that."

It would be too late by then, of course. Bolan knew

that. He was throwing Hal a bone, to put his mind at ease.

Fat chance.

"Okay, I'll be in touch," Bolan said. "In the meantime—"

"No news is good news," Brognola finished for him. "I know the drill."

"Later."

The line went dead before Brognola had a chance to say "I hope so."

Above the Indian Ocean

LIN MAK WAS SNORING, catching up on sleep after the early-morning roust from his hotel. Despite his evident anxiety, he'd managed to doze off while paging through a *Playboy* magazine, presumably intent on checking out the thoughtful articles.

Napier was pleased to have his guest unconscious for a while. It gave him time to think without incessant questions on security and what he planned to do when they arrived in Greece.

The aircraft was a Gulfstream III, eighty-three feet from nose to tail, with a wingspan only five feet shorter than the jet's total length. It was built to carry eight passengers and three crewmen in the lap of luxury, the contingent for this trip consisting of Napier, Lin Mak and four of Global Petroleum's top security men. The bodyguards were an international mix, including a South African, a former Spetsnaz captain, a cashiered sergeant from the British SAS and an ex-

Navy SEAL. Among them, they were fluent in nine languages and qualified with every modern weapon known to man—particularly those they carried on the plane.

There'd be no customs hassle when they got to Athens. Andrastus and Napier had enough combined influence to smooth that over, and his bodyguards were licensed to carry firearms in any case. Most governments acknowledged their deficiencies in the field of executive protection, granting broad leeway to the guardians of those with six-figure incomes and higher, as long as they paid certain fees and made an effort not to litter the streets with bodies. In security, as in all other realms of high-priced human endeavor, decorum and finance went hand in hand.

Napier had been to Thyra twice before, and he had requested it for a reason. The island was twelve square miles of sand and rock, civilized by Christos Andrastus when he built a palatial villa on its highest ground and shipped in the soil to support lush gardens, along with some strategically located trees. The place was a combination hideaway and fortress, staffed with a Cordon Bleu chef and enough hired security to staff a large maximum-security prison—or to repel invaders, if it came to that.

Which, Napier reminded himself, it just might.

Ideally, he hoped to elude his pursuers while pushing his effort to identify them, then either grease the right palms to call off the attack or hit back with all of the considerable force at his disposal. He'd been on the defensive so far, and it would stay that way until his enemies had names and faces. Only then could Napier do what he did best, applying any pressure necessary to defeat them, take them out.

Until then, the best he could do was lie low and play the part of a filthy-rich castaway.

Andrastus had been reluctant to accommodate them, and Napier couldn't fault him for that, as long as he agreed in the end. Their fates were linked to an extent, for good or ill, as long as they were partners in the present operation. If and when Napier believed his partners were no longer serving his best interests, he'd feel free to change the rules and write them out of the script. But for now, he definitely needed help and would do anything within his power to insure that neither Lin Mak nor Andrastus got cold feet.

Napier checked his Rolex watch, made allowance for the time zones they were crossing at 512 miles per hour and reckoned that they'd be stopping for fuel at Bombay in another three hours. From there, it was on to Kuwait, then across the desert where his troubles had started, to reach Athens near midnight.

Simple.

All he had to do was stay alive until then, and he'd be as safe as a diamond sitting in a jeweler's safe. No, wait—make that a brick of gold in Fort Knox. If need be, he could hide on Thyra as long as it took to resolve his embarrassing problem once and for all.

Napier wouldn't allow himself to be defeated. It was laughable, unthinkable. His wealth and power wouldn't permit it. He wouldn't contemplate defeat.

Napier took a pair of headphones from the seat

pocket in front of him and slipped them on. He plugged the cord into the armrest of his seat and spun the recessed dial to find a channel where the music pleased him. Easy listening, they called it: instrumental pap designed to substitute for sleeping pills.

It worked.

Five minutes later, he was fast asleep, dreaming of boundless power kept afloat by blood and oil.

Jakarta

THE RENTAL CAR WAS a black Toyota Camry, the four-door model, with trunk space to spare for luggage and hardware. McCarter took the wheel to start, Grimaldi riding shotgun, while Bolan and Mindel shared the back seat. They had directions to Kusnadi's jewelry shop, winding through streets with yard-long tongue-twisting names. It seemed to Bolan that the locals had to spend hours just addressing envelopes, but maybe they got used to it.

Kusnadi's was located in a downscale commercial district, a mile south of the Jakarta Fairgrounds and the American Embassy. A parking space opened up on their second pass, three doors down from the shop, and McCarter nosed the Camry into it. He fed the meter several chunky coins, and they were on their way.

Kusnadi Hulanapo was a tiny, birdlike figure swimming in a baggy shirt and trousers, brittle gray hair poking out from underneath a sort of pillbox hat. Forewarned of their arrival, he greeted Bolan and the others in passable English, bobbing his head at each introduction in a manner that only highlighted his resemblance to a scrawny bird pecking grain.

Kusnadi left a young woman in charge of the shop, Bolan detailing Jack Grimaldi to keep her company, while the proprietor led Bolan, McCarter and Mindel into the rear of his establishment. There, he opened a closet door to reveal a steep staircase, descending below street level. Kusnadi went first, the others following at intervals that placed no more than one at a time in jeopardy from an ambush below.

In fact, they found themselves alone with Kusnadi in a spacious chamber resembling a military arsenal. It was cool and dry, with weapons hanging from the walls, crated or racked in tidy rows across the floor. Bolan made out a fair variety as he moved up and down the aisles, inspecting Kusnadi's inventory.

Indonesia has no native arms industry to speak of, relying for its firepower on industrial nations of East and West alike. Since 1965 it had dealt primarily with the United States and Western Europe, that trade reflected in the range of assault rifles, submachine guns and pistols displayed in Kusnadi's basement armory. There were Kalashnikovs, of course, but they were heavily outnumbered by M-16s, Steyr AUGs, various H&K models, Beretta AR-70s, even a couple of British SA-80s. The SMGs ran toward Uzis, Sterlings and Berettas, heavy on the solid Heckler & Koch MP-5s. Side arms included Colts, Berettas, Brownings, Glocks and a lone .50-caliber Desert Eagle. Beyond those standard items there were shotguns and grenade launchers, a few sniper pieces and a tripod-mounted GE Minigun in 7.62 mm.

Bolan tried not to wonder who would want the Minigun, deciding that a country known for ethnic and political mayhem spanning half a century would find any number of takers for a weapon that spewed armor-piercing rounds at a cyclic rate of six thousand rounds per minute.

They settled on four AUGs, with eight transparent plastic magazines for each—240 rounds per weapon, and a case of 5.56 mm in reserve. For side arms, they chose Berettas threaded to accommodate suppressors, with shoulder rigs and four spare magazines apiece. Bolan passed on the grenades this time, deciding they would be too risky in a crowded urban setting, and the deal was made. Kusnadi threw in four black duffel bags, and they were on their way.

"What now?" McCarter asked, when they were back in the Toyota with the engine idling.

"Let's go have a look at Global's offices," Bolan suggested, "then swing by and see where Wagner spends his evenings."

They would have to start somewhere, and since there was no hope of tracking Arnold Napier to his hotel, apartment or whatever without guidance from the home team, Bolan thought the next-best thing was scoping out their access to the oilman's number two. Wagner could point them to the boss, but they would have to find him first, and pin him down. Bolan expected some resistance, but he also knew that any opposition could be overcome, given determination and sufficient force.

His team possessed the will, and now they had the tools. All that remained was to isolate their target and apply sufficient pressure to produce results.

With any luck, he thought, they might find Napier hanging out with Wagner, and they wouldn't have to deal with his subordinate at all, except as a secondary target. That would be the easy way, but Bolan had already hit too many obstacles in the course of this mission to expect a sudden, fortuitous breakthrough.

He fully expected to work, and work hard, for each advance they made. Why should today be any different than yesterday, or the day before that?

There was a reason why they called it war, and not a picnic. This was where a soldier paid his dues.

And there was still a chance that some of them would never make it home. Katz hadn't, after all. He never would—unless there was a place for battle-hardened warriors in the afterlife. Bolan left that to theologians, concentrating his attention on the here and now.

Sufficient unto the day was the evil thereof.

Damn right.

CHAPTER ELEVEN

It could be worse, Jared Wagner thought, wishing that he didn't hear the small voice in his head reminding him that it could be yet.

Okay, so there'd been trouble in Macao and Napier had convinced himself the unknown individuals responsible were somehow linked to those, also unknown, who'd massacred the troops of Allah's Lance in Israel, Syria and Lebanon. Granted, they had no evidence to prove it, but it was a logical conclusion. Wagner was a novice at the killing game, still undergoing his personal baptism of fire, but even he recognized that that would be stretching coincidence to the point where it merged with fantasy.

He would assume, therefore, that the unknown enemy had somehow traced Lin Mak, divined his connection to Allah's Lance and decided to strike at him in Macao. Why should that come as a surprise, after the same adversaries had challenged Napier personally a few days earlier?

The question foremost on his mind today was, what does it all mean to me?

Wagner was a realist, by no means given to fits of

altruism. He'd decided on a career in big business as a preteen, after watching Oliver Stone's *Wall Street* on some cable network. Granted, the movie was supposed to be a damning indictment of corporate corruption, but the one thing Wagner took away from it was the proclamation issued by Michael Douglas: greed is good.

Amen.

Wagner had studied, maneuvered and manipulated his way to the number-two spot in Global Petroleum, a heartbeat away from the multinational corporation's command chair, and he wasn't about to flush the whole thing now because he had a case of nerves.

On the other hand, he didn't plan to volunteer as anybody's sacrificial lamb, either. A martyr's death wouldn't improve his prospects or portfolio. His predecessor had gone that route, and all he had to show for it was a funeral plot purchased at Global's expense. And that wasn't the kind of retirement plan Wagner had in mind for himself.

Macao wasn't Jakarta. Violence in one location didn't automatically translate to bloodshed in the other. To make that leap, the enemy would first have to trace Lin Mak's travel itinerary, then cover an additional two thousand miles to stage another strike. It clearly wasn't unthinkable, especially after the leap from Lebanon to China, but it was still hypothetical, a threat unrealized.

And while he waited, Wagner had a ton of work to do.

He had already dictated nearly a dozen letters and

memos that morning, assuring various department heads and major stockholders that Global was on solid ground, its future solid and unthreatened by the recent, lamentable murder of Sterling Holbrook. There was no danger to the company at large, Wagner assured them, and stock prices—having dropped slightly over the past few days—were sure to rebound strongly with the culmination of deals even now in the works.

Wagner hadn't mentioned what those deals entailed. He hadn't named the partners who were helping Arnold Napier make his grab for the brass ring. It might've been too much for some of them to swallow—and besides, Wagner had his own unwritten rule about evidence and witnesses—don't leave any.

Wagner couldn't make up for any mistakes Napier and the other principals had made up to the present time, but he could certainly avoid making any new ones of his own. To that end, he had increased security around his home and office as soon as Napier and Lin Mak left town, drawing extra manpower from the elite force Global kept on tap in countries like Indonesia, where violence and political instability were facts of daily life.

Eight gunmen were guarding him now, as he shuffled papers and plotted his schedule for the rest of the week. Two were stationed in the office building's underground garage, two more in the lobby and four on the floor where Global's suite of offices was located. They all carried pistols, one member of each pair sporting a briefcase that contained a compact submachine gun. Wagner didn't know the make or models of their weapons, couldn't have cared less for any of the paramilitary jargon they all loved, but he was fairly confident of being covered, if and when some adversary tried to take him out.

Wagner carried no weapon himself, because he wouldn't have known what to do with it. Skeet shooting was one thing, another means of kissing well-placed ass on weekends, but he didn't plan on joining any war games.

That's what ex-commando flunkies were for.

Wagner checked his watch against the artsy sunburst wall clock, a garish monstrosity that had to have cost a small fortune but looked like something he'd have expected to find in a double-wide trailer parked on the wrong side of the tracks in some Dixie backwater. It was half an hour to quitting time, give or take a minute, and Wagner decided that he was done for the day.

It was time to relax, unwind a little, maybe even rent a little female companionship from one of the take-out services he used on a biweekly basis. It would help take the edge off his nervous frustration, let him face the following day with a new, improved attitude.

And he could put the whole damn thing on his expense account.

Reaching across his glass-topped desk, Wagner keyed the intercom and waited for his secretary to respond with a crisp "Yes, sir?"

"I'm leaving for the day," he told her. "Have security on stand-by in five minutes. They can bring the car around in front."

"Yes, sir."

He'd put in an exhausting day, albeit seldom stirring from his desk and only once emerging from his private office, to join a pair of marketing executives for lunch. There was more to being in charge than just kicking back and enjoying the perks, Wagner realized.

But the perks were definitely part of it, like telling the shooters when and where to fall in, like good little soldiers.

Smiling, Jared Wagner left his office, looking forward to the night ahead. With any luck, he would be working up a sweat before much longer, and he wouldn't have to come within a mile of the corporate gym.

MCCARTER STOOD before the office building's glass-fronted directory, pretending to study names and room numbers while Napier's security men studied him. He'd made them out as soon as he entered the lobby, a mismatched pair whose members were nonetheless obvious teammates. The glass in front of him showed both men watching from their stations on the far side of the lobby, but McCarter would've felt their gaze even if he couldn't see them.

The one on his right, closer to the bank of elevators, was the older of the pair. He wore his graying hair buzzed close enough to show tanned scalp beneath the stubble, either ignoring or deliberately emphasizing the male-pattern baldness that was overtaking him by slow degrees. He wore a lightweight, khaki-colored suit with a moderately subtle bulge beneath his left arm, a pair of steel-rimmed spectacles perched on his beak of a nose. The attaché case planted beside his right foot was a no-frills model, black imitation leather with a plastic handle, large enough to hold one of the smaller SMGs—perhaps a mini-Uzi or an MP-5 K. It could've fit two micro-Uzis, but the older gunman stood too far away from his partner to make a second stuttergun worthwhile.

The younger watchman had a sense of style, his blond hair worn long in back and covering the tops of sunburned ears. His eyes were hidden behind mirrored sunglasses, large hands clasped in front of his groin, as if to safeguard the family jewels. His suit was navy blue, jacket unbuttoned for easy access to the pistol he wore on his left hip, holstered butt forward for a cross-hand draw. That was an awkward way to go unless the shooter practiced regularly, and McCarter was prepared to give him the benefit of the doubt on that score.

The gunmen wore no corporate badges, but McCarter assumed they were part of Napier's hardforce. There'd be others he hadn't seen yet, at least two more upstairs, one or more in the garage if Napier knew what he was doing. How many guns, in all? He wouldn't find out by loitering around the lobby.

McCarter spent another moment in front of the directory, memorizing nothing. He'd known the floor number for Napier's offices—eleven—before he walked in from the street. His mission was simple reconnaissance, and there was little to be learned after he spotted the gunmen, registered dual security cameras mounted at the northwest and southeast corners of the ceiling and verified a set of service stairs beside the elevators.

In order to reach those stairs, however, McCarter would have to pass within arm's length of the older gunman, and he didn't plan on trying that just now. Raiding the office was a last resort, recognized up front as a worst-case scenario. Any action in a public building meant civilian bystanders, restricted movement and increased probability of police intervention before the raiders could accomplish anything. The office might be suitable for sniping—Bolan was checking that angle while McCarter worked close up and personal—but long-distance elimination ruled out any chance to question the target before he went down.

And before they started dropping anyone, they had to find out whether all their targets were in place. If they could tag Lin Mak and Napier in Jakarta, they would have two out of three.

Reflected in the glass, the older gunman slipped a hand inside his jacket and retrieved a compact walkie-talkie that had been clipped to his belt. He listened for a moment, volume turned down low, then spoke into the radio, a curt acknowledgment. McCarter chose that moment to glance at his watch, scowl in feigned frustration and make his way back to the street.

The gunners were in motion as he left, apparently satisfied with his departure. He dared not glance back to see if they were tracking him, but as he hit the sidewalk, turning left, he caught a peripheral glimpse of elevator doors closing behind the younger of the pair, while the man with the briefcase held his position.

Something was happening, McCarter realized as he crossed the street to the Toyota, Jack Grimaldi at the wheel, Rebecca Mindel in the shotgun seat. The Briton checked his watch for real this time, and guessed that someone had called down from upstairs, alerting the watchers that it was time to move out.

Bolan appeared on the crowded sidewalk, reaching the Camry seconds after McCarter. They slid into the back seat together, from opposite sides, closing their doors in near perfect unison.

"Something's up," McCarter said. "They're on the move, one shooter pulled out of the lobby."

"Quitting time?" Grimaldi asked.

"Could be," Bolan replied. "Let's wait a minute and find out."

It was closer to three minutes, in fact, before a white limousine nosed out of the office building's underground garage and swung around to double-park in front. No sooner was the sleek crew wagon in place than McCarter saw the older of the lobby gunmen emerge, making his way toward the car. Behind him came five more hardmen, his young cohort among them, a sixth figure moving briskly in their midst.

"It isn't Napier," Bolan said.

"Wagner?" Mindel asked.

"Looks like it."

"So, where's the boss?" McCarter asked.

"Not here, unless the bodyguards are leaving him behind," Bolan replied.

"I don't buy that," Grimaldi said.

"No way," McCarter seconded, then said to Bolan, "You want to follow him?"

The Executioner relaxed into his seat. "Looks like the only game in town," he said. "Let's roll and see where this one takes us."

Aboard the Aristotle, *West of Crete*

CHRISTOS ANDRASTUS despised living in fear. A billionaire several times over, he believed that wealth should insulate its owners from the daily trials and tribulations of the world at large. What good was money if it couldn't buy security? Lawyers, accountants, bodyguards—they all combined to form a shield around the filthy rich, protecting them from harm. Or, at the very least, it was *supposed* to work that way.

Of late, Andrastus had been disappointed in the value he was getting for his drachma. Everywhere he looked, it seemed as if security was breaking down— first in the Middle East, with Napier's "foolproof" operation; now in China, with Lin Mak. If their faceless enemies could invade Red China and tackle the state, for God's sake, where could a not-so-humble shipping magnate turn for sanctuary?

To Thyra, perhaps.

Andrastus had noticed the island quite by accident the first time, sailing past it one summer afternoon on another of his yachts. After acquiring it, he'd ordered landscaping, construction crews and military strategists to work in tandem, the end result a luxurious retreat with a capacity to withstand armed invasion. Granted, it wasn't Tarawa or Iwo Jima, but Andrastus hadn't foreseen the day when an actual military force might be fielded against him.

Not in Greece.

Not until today.

He sat and sipped ouzo, willing himself to be calm. There was still no hard evidence of an organized military move against Napier or any other cartel member, but Andrastus believed there were few—if any—assassins capable of spanning such distances, striking with such precision and destructive force, without some kind of official sanction and support. His first vote went to the Americans, impetuous as always, despite the fact that Napier's contacts had come away empty-handed from their inquiries to the FBI and CIA. There were always ways and means of getting dirty work accomplished outside the strict chain of command. Andrastus knew that well enough, from personal experience.

Reluctantly, he'd opened the yacht's arms locker and distributed weapons to all qualified crewmen. An attack at sea was unlikely, but Andrastus didn't believe in gambling where his own survival was concerned. If Napier and Lin Mak had already been targeted, it stood to reason that his own time had to be coming soon.

Coincidence on that scale was a myth.

Andrastus had even armed himself for the occasion, fastening a custom-tailored ankle holster around his left leg, adjusting quickly to the 12.5-ounce weight of the Colt Mk IV Series 80 Mustang Pocketlite pistol. If all else failed and enemies somehow got past his bodyguards, Andrastus would have six shots with which to defend himself.

And after that?

He drank more ouzo, willing himself not to worry. His security force included some of the best gunmen money could buy, seasoned killers with decades of combat behind them, veterans of grim brushfire wars throughout the Third World and Eastern Europe. Andrastus insured their loyalty with top-dollar paychecks, demanding rigorous training as part of the regimen. On another island, several miles from Thyra, he'd constructed a training facility that rivaled Fort Benning and Hereford.

Sailing past Crete, he hoped the guns wouldn't be necessary, but his soldiers would be ready if it came to killing. They were always ready, day or night, to earn the cash and other privileges that he provided. None of them had ever failed Andrastus yet.

Relaxing finally, he allowed his thoughts to drift away, across the azure sea.

If danger waited for him, he would meet it in due time.

Jakarta

THE LIMO LED THEM back to Jared Wagner's home in an affluent suburb north of downtown Jakarta. More shooters were waiting outside as the vehicle pulled to the curb, disgorging Wagner and his armed entourage on the sidewalk before a ten-story apartment house, all burnished steel and tinted glass.

"Looks like a long way to the penthouse," Mindel said to no one in particular.

"They'll have a service elevator," Bolan stated from the back seat. "We need to check it out."

"My turn," she replied without hesitation.

"You sure?"

"Positive." Waiting in the car while others did the work was tedious, frustrating. Mindel understood the risk but had enough faith in her own abilities to think that she could pull it off.

She'd come prepared, in fact, anticipating this moment. Between her feet, a plastic shopping bag held the bouquet of flowers she'd purchased from a street vendor, while Blanski and McCarter were sizing up the Global offices. She'd had the stirrings of a plan in mind, and now she saw the chance to follow through with it.

Grimaldi, driving, eyed the flowers as she pulled them from the bag and said, "Good thinking."

"Thanks."

"Where did you want to start?" he asked.

"Around this corner," she responded, pointing to the cross street flanking Wagner's building on the west. "Just drop me anywhere along the block."

"Can do."

Grimaldi turned the corner and drove far enough down the block to insure that no one loitering outside Wagner's building would notice when he braked the Camry long enough for Mindel to get out. He flashed her a smile and a thumbs-up salute, while Blanski and McCarter kept their eyes on traffic and pedestrians. Mindel took it as an encouraging sign that no one felt obliged to wish her luck.

She crossed the street, holding the flowers in her left hand, her right hand free in case she had to whip the newly purchased pistol from underneath her jacket. Her low heels made a *tick-tock* on the sidewalk as she doubled back to the main entrance of Wagner's apartment building.

There were no guards on the street outside, a hopeful sign. The doorman was a swarthy type who didn't smile at women if he wasn't being paid to do so. He was ready to ignore Mindel until she stepped in front of him, demanding his attention. If a smile could generate raw heat, hers would've melted the impassive doorman where he stood.

"Delivery for Mr. Jared Wagner," she announced, and shoved the flowers in the doorman's face.

He took a backward step, frowning, as if suspecting that the flowers might be dangerous. "You friend?" he asked at last.

"It's a delivery," she said again.

"Flowers."

"Indeed."

"Delivery use service elevator."

"Excellent. And where is that?" she asked.

He aimed a stubby index finger past the glass revolving door, across the lobby, toward a bank of elevators set into the northern wall. Despite the tinted glass, Mindel could see the elevator farthest to her right was labeled Service.

Brushing past the doorman with another smile, Mindel stepped into the revolving door and let it carry her through half a circuit to the air-conditioned lobby. One foot on the carpet and she had the gunmen spotted, two on station at the far east wall. They tried to pass for visitors, inconspicuous in their side-by-side easy chairs, newspapers open for browsing, but it didn't wash.

Mindel was conscious of the soldiers watching as she crossed the lobby with long, purposeful strides. She went directly to the service elevator, as if she'd made the journey a thousand times before and knew exactly where to go. She pressed the elevator's button, let the gunmen study her without acknowledging their presence while she waited for the door to open. When it did, she stepped inside and pressed a button for the seventh floor, still perfectly aloof as the door closed again and killed her lobby view.

The elevator wasn't one of those that signaled which floors it was visiting, as it rode up and down the shaft, but Mindel took no chances. She imagined one of the gorillas in the lobby reaching for a two-way radio, alerting his penthouse compatriots to a potential problem. They'd be waiting on the ninth floor, she imagined, but her failure to appear would put their minds at ease, give them a reason to relax their guard a bit.

Meanwhile...

She got off on the seventh floor and dropped the

flowers in a wastebasket that stood beside the elevator doorway. Checking both directions, she picked out the stairs a few yards to her left and went that way, relieved to find the access door unlocked. She checked the knob from both sides, to be sure, before she let the door close at her back.

Taking her time, avoiding all unnecessary noise, she climbed four flights to reach the penthouse level, pausing at the final door. It had no window, but she pressed her ear against the panel, listening. No voices audible beyond, which could mean anything or nothing.

It was time to take a chance.

She drew the black Beretta, held it with the safety off and turned the doorknob slowly, silently. With agonizing slowness, Mindel cracked the door a half-inch, then an inch. The slice of hallway visible from where she stood was empty, quiet as a grave.

Holding her breath, she pulled the door open and risked a glance around it, down the corridor—and froze as she heard voices coming toward her, just beyond her line of sight.

Kuwait City

''HOW MUCH LONGER?'' Lin Mak demanded, shifting restlessly in his seat.

''Not long,'' Napier assured him for the second time within ten minutes. He wished Mak would read a magazine or go to sleep—do anything, in fact, but make his pitiful anxiety so obvious.

In fact, Napier wished that he'd left the Chinese

diplomat behind, to fret and worry in Jakarta, but it hadn't been an option. Not this time.

But soon, perhaps.

Napier imagined that Mak's stock was selling pretty cheap at home right now. After the bloody business in Macao, his disappearance from the scene and failure to contact authorities after the fact, the man had to be skating on the proverbial thin ice. One false step—or a helpful shove at an opportune moment—and he'd be history.

But who would take his place?

Better to wait, Napier decided, until the deal was finalized. Then, with connections completed, signed contracts in hand, he could freely cut Mak loose and watch him drift. If he escaped to Switzerland or ultimately stood before a Chinese firing squad, what difference would it make? By that time, some other official would've stepped into the vacuum, tickled pink to cut a deal with Global Petroleum.

It was a fact of life, whether he plied his trade in the East or the West. Self-interest always triumphed. Avarice always won out in the end.

People were only human, after all.

Mak swiveled in his seat, seemed on the verge of repeating his monotonous question, but he saw the look on Napier's face and reconsidered, scowling through his northward-facing window. With a telescope, he could've seen Iraq from where they sat, but as it was, his view was limited to blacktop runways and a portion of the airport terminal. Refueling had to be almost finished now, but still the minutes dragged, seeming to last forever.

Almost there, Napier thought. One more hop would put them on the ground in Athens, where Andrastus would have soldiers waiting to protect them, see them safely on their way to Thyra. There, with any luck, they would for all intents and purposes cease to exist.

Wagner alone knew where Napier was going, from Jakarta. Napier trusted him—his greed, if nothing else—to keep his mouth shut on that score. And just in case he faltered, or fell into dangerous hands by some chance, Napier had spoken privately with Wagner's chief bodyguard, receiving strict assurances that there would be no repetition of the Sterling Holbrook sideshow.

Not this time.

Napier left his seat and moved aft, to the Gulfstream's galley, where a well-stocked bar was located. He poured himself a double shot of single-malt Irish whiskey, Old Bushmills, and drank it down in two swallows, enjoying the fire it lit inside him. The tension in his stomach melted, uncoiling like a watch spring winding down.

Outside, he heard the fuel hose disengage, technicians completing their last-minute work on the Gulfstream. Napier was back in his seat as the pilots returned from their walking tour of inspection, satisfied that nothing had been overlooked, no crucial operation slighted. They'd be airborne in a few more moments, winging westward toward the Mediterranean and sanctuary.

Flying over all that oil.

And much of it would soon be his. Napier had suffered setbacks, granted, but his master plan was still on track. As soon as his men took delivery of the black-market nuclear device, he would be ready for the last stage of the operation. Delivery of that package, and the firestorm that would follow, were not matters that concerned him now.

He left that part of it to destiny and concentrated on the details readily within his grasp.

Lin Mak, for one, and how to keep him pacified until the smoke cleared and the black gold started flowing. By the time Mak realized he was expendable, it would already be too late for him to save himself.

Fait accompli.

Napier smiled as the Gulfstream began to taxi toward takeoff.

The French, he thought with private satisfaction, always had a word for everything.

Jakarta

"HERE SHE COMES," McCarter said. "No tails, as far as I can see."

Bolan watched Mindel cross the street, Grimaldi slowing on his latest pass and waiting for her to catch up. He watched for any movement on the sidewalk that would indicate pursuit, but she was in the clear.

A moment later, she was in the shotgun seat and Grimaldi had the Camry in motion, checking side mirrors and rearview as he joined the flow of traffic once again. Mindel turned in her seat, including all of them as she began to speak.

"It's as we thought," she said. "Two watchers in the lobby, two more in the hall outside the penthouse suite."

"You got that far?" McCarter asked.

"Barely. Enough to look around a bit before the goons came by."

"They didn't see you, then?" Bolan asked.

"Only in the lobby," she replied. "They didn't try to follow when I went upstairs."

"Hardware?"

"Concealed side arms," she said. "One of the lobby watchers had a briefcase standing by his chair. I take for granted it held something larger than a pistol."

"Same thing as the office building," McCarter said. "They're consistent, anyway."

"The two outside the penthouse didn't carry any luggage," she went on, "but they'd have backup close at hand. We can assume the in-house crew has more artillery."

"You used the service elevator?" Bolan asked.

"Up to the seventh floor. I took the stairs from there."

"No lookouts in the stairwell?"

"Not from seven upward. Maybe lower, or perhaps they were between shifts. It surprised me, too."

"We'll have to play that part of it by ear," the Executioner declared. He didn't like loose ends, but they were sometimes unavoidable.

"How many guns is that?" Grimaldi asked.

"Six in the limousine," McCarter said, "and two more waiting on the street. We can assume he leaves a team upstairs to keep the home fires burning while he's at the office."

"Figure ten or twelve, minimum," Bolan calculated.

"And still no sign of Napier," Mindel said.

"Nothing to indicate he might be chilling in the penthouse?" Grimaldi asked.

"No. It's hard for me to picture him and Wagner sharing digs, like college roommates."

"So, where is he, then?" McCarter asked.

"That's what we need to ask his number two," Bolan replied.

"Sooner the better, then, I say." McCarter's tone was brusque. "This shouldn't be a bloody marathon."

"It's what it is," Bolan remarked. "We can't do anything before nightfall."

"Suppose he has a date," Grimaldi said. "Then what?"

"We'll tag along," Bolan suggested. "See if maybe we can go Dutch treat."

"Rich buggers never take the check, if they can help it," McCarter groused.

"Payday's coming," Bolan promised him. "Our friend upstairs just doesn't know it yet."

"We've got some time to kill," Grimaldi said. "Three hours, anyway, before it's dark. Suggestions?"

"Whatever we do," Bolan said, "we need to keep an eye on Wagner until showtime. That's job one."

"There's a restaurant a half block down from the apartment house," McCarter said. "We'll probably get ptomaine, but it makes a decent vantage point."

"Parking?"

"Looked like they had a lot in back."

"Suits me," Grimaldi said. "Who else is hungry?"

Bolan's stomach growled in answer to the question, but he covered it by shifting in his seat and saying, "I could eat."

"Me, too," Mindel said.

"Right, then. It's unanimous," Grimaldi stated. "I'm on the case."

"Just watch the bloody speed limit," McCarter chimed in from the rear.

"Relax, old chap. It's in the bag."

They drove around the block once more, Bolan surveilling Wagner's building as they passed. No sentries were apparent from the street, but he supposed the pair Mindel had seen were still on duty in the lobby. Getting past them was the first challenge his team would have to face. Whatever happened after that would be determined, in large part, by whether they succeeded in avoiding violent clashes at the outset of their penetration.

But once they were inside, he knew, they could expect a warm reception from the enemy. Red-hot would be more like it, he supposed, and that could cut both ways.

Grimaldi found the restaurant and turned into an

alley west of it. The parking lot was small but nearly empty. He had room to turn and back into an open slot, ready to exit on a moment's notice.

"Leaving the hardware in the car?" Grimaldi asked, when they were parked and he had switched the engine off.

"I think the duffel bags might raise some eyebrows," Bolan said.

"Okay. No carjackers around this neighborhood, I guess."

The parking lot was boxed in on three sides, no exit other than the alleyway by which they'd entered. Bolan calculated that they wouldn't find a safer place to park it in Jakarta, short of hiring someone to stand watch while they were in the restaurant. His first concern now was the possibility that Wagner might decide to exit while they occupied a window table, watching him depart but unable to overtake his car before he slipped away.

Another gamble, right.

His stomach growled again, and Bolan took the hint, trailing the others toward the sidewalk and the restaurant. They had three hours and change to kill, before they made their move.

And then, he knew, the killing in Jakarta would begin.

CHAPTER TWELVE

Rebecca Mindel felt overdressed for a killing. Her suit was too stylish, altogether too sophisticated for battle, and while the short skirt would be suitable for running or kicking an adversary in the groin, her high-heeled pumps would never take the place of combat boots or simple running shoes. Her knee-length raincoat was appropriate, given the weather in Jakarta, but its main function was concealment of the Steyr assault rifle she carried slung beneath her right arm, clutched against her side.

She crossed the street with long strides, spike heels clicking on the rain-slick pavement. Mindel knew she might have to ditch the shoes when the shooting started, but for the moment they were part of her cover. They emphasized her shapely legs, naturally drawing male eyes away from her face, and she had untied her hair to let it fall around her shoulders, further shielding her profile. Mindel didn't know if the same two guards would be working the lobby, but if so, she hoped to slip past them without being recognized from her afternoon reconnaissance mission.

If that failed, and they tried to intercept her, she

would have to kill them both. She would use the sound-suppressed Beretta nestled in her large handbag, if possible, or even take them hand to hand. If all else failed, and strictly as a last resort, she would unleash the Steyr AUG.

But that would mean she'd failed in her part of the plan, and Mindel wasn't ready to concede defeat.

Not yet.

She stood outside Wagner's apartment building for a moment, glancing back toward the alley where Blanski and McCarter waited for their turns to crack the enemy's stronghold. Mindel couldn't see them from where she stood, but she knew they'd be there.

Watching.

Mindel dismissed them from her mind and pushed through the revolving door, her second visit to the apartment house lobby in five hours. It was still early evening, by tropical standards, but she was relieved to see two unfamiliar lookouts in the lobby. Both tracked her as she moved with purpose toward the bank of public elevators opposite the door, their gaze like fingers roaming over Mindel's body, probing where the cold eyes came to rest.

She was afraid they'd spot a telltale bulge beneath her raincoat or tumble to the fact that her oversize handbag didn't match the stylish outfit. Either way, they'd try to stop her or alert their friends upstairs that trouble was approaching.

Mindel ignored them, hiding behind the easy arrogance that some attractive women hold in reserve for use as a weapon or as a defense mechanism. She knew they were watching her, trying to decide if she was danger on the hoof, but neither of them moved to intercept her before she reached the elevators. One of the cars stood open, waiting for her, and she entered it without hesitation, turning back to face the lobby for a moment as she pressed the eighth floor's button.

The door slid shut in front of her, cutting off Mindel's view of the lobby. She imagined the two lookouts reaching for cell phones or two-way radios, warning their comrades on the penthouse level to stand ready.

Be my guest, she thought, slipping her right hand into the slit pocket of her raincoat, its lining cut to let her reach the AUG's pistol grip. If they stopped the elevator on another floor or had a shooter waiting for her on eight, she'd be ready.

Mindel checked the watch on her left wrist, imagining the other members of her team as they moved into their positions. She wished them luck and hoped they wouldn't be cut off before the time appointed for their rendezvous. If she was forced to sweep the penthouse by herself…

She put that deadly prospect out of mind as the elevator cleared seven and slowed on its way to the eighth-floor stop. Standing to one side of the door, taking advantage of the small car's minimal cover, she was ready to return fire if a welcoming committee met her there.

The door hissed open and she was alone. Checking the hallway left and right, Mindel exited the car and moved directly to the door that granted access to the stairs. It was another point of vulnerability, but she pushed through boldly, following the Steyr, and met no opposition. Two flights of stairs rose above her to the ninth floor and their target, seemingly unguarded.

Mindel stepped out of her shoes, picked them up with her left hand and started to climb.

As EXPECTED, the back door to Wagner's apartment building was guarded. One man had the duty, standing to one side of the doorway and its naked light bulb mounted on the wall overhead, aswarm with flying insects in the tropical night. It was a lousy job, but someone had to do it for the boss's sake.

All right, then.

McCarter had closed to within fifty feet of his target, taking advantage of the trash cans and garbage bins that made the alley a poor man's obstacle course. He had rats for company, some of the largest he'd ever seen, and their scuttling movements helped cover McCarter's advance as he paced off the distance, keeping to the shadows, the Beretta in his fist muzzle-heavy with its fat suppressor.

He could try a shot from fifty feet, but forty would be better, and thirty better still. Closing the gap, McCarter watched his man in profile, silhouetted with the light behind him, shadows of the moths and other insects dancing on the wall behind him.

Closer.

When two reeking garbage bins lay between them, the sentry lit a cigarette and blew a plume of smoke into the night. McCarter found his target through the drifting cloud and waited while the guard glanced to his right, checking the east end of the alley, turning back when he saw nothing to alarm him. McCarter took him with a clean shot through the temple, rushing forward as the man collapsed, in case a second bullet was required.

It wasn't.

The back door to Wagner's apartment house was locked, as expected. McCarter could have picked the simple pin lock, but he had neither the time nor the proper equipment to beat the dead bolt by stealth. He took a semiauto pistol from the corpse and slipped it into his waistband for backup, then started turning out the sentry's pockets, looking for a key.

The rear guard had to have a way inside the building, in case he received an emergency summons on the cell phone clipped to his belt. The telephone would be pointless if a runner had to come and fetch him from his post, McCarter reasoned.

The key was in a pocket of the lightweight vest the man had worn to hide his shoulder rig and pistol from casual passersby, if the alley got any foot traffic. McCarter tried the key and found it fit both locks. He paused long enough to drag his man behind the nearest garbage bin, then went back and slipped inside the apartment house, taking time to lock the door again behind him. He didn't know what time the shifts changed, but every second McCarter could buy for his team by restoring the scene to a normal appearance was worth the effort.

The service elevator waited for him, unguarded. It

was roughly three times the size of a normal passenger car, designed to accommodate cleaning equipment and furniture deliveries. McCarter had the spacious car to himself as he punched the button for the ninth floor.

BOLAN ENTERED the apartment building's lobby three minutes after Mindel disappeared through the tall revolving door. He made a point of pausing just inside and checking out the lobby, dismissing the twenty-something clerk behind the information desk and lingering deliberately as he locked eyes with the sentries stationed there, one after the other.

They were instantly alert, suspicious, just the way he wanted them. He knew they were watching as he crossed the lobby, heading toward the elevators, and he could practically feel them leap from their chairs as he veered off course at the last minute, bypassing the cars and ducking through the door marked Stairs.

Bolan double-timed up the stairs to reach the second-floor landing ahead of his pursuers. He wasn't sure if both would follow, or if one had standing orders to remain behind and watch the lobby, come what may. He wanted both of them, hoped he could neutralize the team before the upstairs action started, but Bolan was a realist.

He'd take what he could get.

Below him, the metal door slammed shut behind his two pursuers. Bolan held the sound-suppressed Beretta steady in a two-handed grip, sighting down the slide toward the point where they'd have to appear if they followed him upstairs. He tracked them on the first flight by their footsteps, giving them credit for having sense enough to keep their mouths shut, anyway.

The silence in the stairwell had to have spooked them, for the shooters broke formation coming up the second flight. One should've hung back, covering the man in front of him, but they were anxious to catch up with Bolan on the stairs and find out what he wanted in the building. It was too late to hide as the Executioner stepped into view, the Beretta seeming impossibly huge from below with the suppressor attached, its muzzle yawning at the first man on the stairs.

Bolan didn't give the gunner time to think about it, much less use the pistol he clutched in his fist. Squeezing off a round from less than twenty feet, the soldier drilled the shooter's forehead above the left eyebrow, spraying his partner with gore. The dead man tumbled backward, colliding with the other and nearly taking him down, before the second gunman sidestepped and shoved him away with a muffled cry of disgust.

Number Two was quick, but not quick enough. He raised his handgun on the rebound, seeking targets with the one eye that wasn't smeared with blood. The gun looked like a Smith & Wesson Magnum, possibly a .41 or .44. Bolan didn't need that kind of racket in the stairwell yet, maybe alerting Wagner's bodyguards upstairs. He triggered two quick rounds and sent the second shooter tumbling downstairs after his companion, landing in a heap, the two of them resembling someone's cast-off laundry.

Bolan waited for a few more seconds, making sure

no one else from the lobby was trailing the others, before he resumed jogging upward, taking the steps two and three at a time. By the time he reached the fifth floor, Bolan's thigh and calf muscles were burning, but he held the pace until he reached the seventh landing, slowing on his last approach to eight.

Rebecca Mindel had him covered as he started up the last flight, lowering her pistol when she recognized him. Bolan covered the distance between them, glancing upward at the last two flights before they reached the ninth and final floor.

"Did they follow you?" she asked him.

"They tried."

"We're clear, then."

"For the moment. If the gang upstairs phones down, it could get hot."

"We shouldn't keep them waiting."

Shoulder to shoulder, they mounted the stairs, moving with special care as they approached the door emblazoned with a yellow number 9. Mindel glanced at her watch, frowning.

"Another forty seconds."

"Time enough," he said, and reached for the doorknob with his left hand.

"THAT'S RIGHT. Like that. Right there."

The hooker had her face in Jared Wagner's lap, doing her very best to please him for the second time since she'd arrived at the apartment. He appreciated zeal from his subordinates and didn't bother to persuade himself that she felt anything for him beyond an urge to make him happy and insure repeat business.

So far, so good.

It was the third time Wagner had employed this particular girl, an Amerasian in her late teens, provided by a service exclusive and expensive enough to provide attractive companions with minimal risk of disease. Wagner called her Leila, because the name appealed to him and he couldn't wrap his Yankee tongue around the jawbreaker name she was born with.

Speaking of tongues…

Wagner was on his way to liftoff when a sudden racket brutally distracted him. Gunfire? At first, he thought one of the stupid bodyguards was watching Schwarzenegger on the DVD again, cranking up the volume, but then he heard his people scrambling for the door, grabbing their weapons on the way.

"Oh, shit!"

Leila recoiled as Wagner vaulted upright on the mattress, groping for the bedside lamp. He was about to flick it on, then reconsidered, understanding that the light would only make him a better target for—

For whom?

Instead of switching on the lamp, Wagner reached past it, dragging open the top drawer of his nightstand and reaching inside for the small pistol he kept there. He had never fired a shot in anger and never expected to do so, but in these troubled times it didn't hurt to keep a little hardware handy, just in case.

Leila saw the gun and recoiled, scooting back on her haunches to the far side of Wagner's king-size bed.

She pulled the satin sheets around herself, as if for modesty, though Wagner would've guessed she didn't have a bashful bone in her curvaceous body.

If she thought black satin would repel a bullet, he decided, she was dumber than he'd thought.

Wagner was rolling out of bed and reaching for his clothes, gunfire still echoing along the hall outside his flat, when Eric Dempsey barged into the bedroom, brandishing a submachine gun, and slammed the door behind him. Dempsey was in charge of Wagner's bodyguards, the one man most responsible for seeing that he stayed alive in situations just like this.

"I need you on the floor, sir," he commanded, reversing their usual roles now that they had been propelled into his narrow realm of expertise. "Right now!"

He didn't spare a glance or second thought for Leila, huddled on the bed. No one was paying Dempsey to protect a teenage hooker, and he plainly didn't care what happened to her one way or another. That was fine with Wagner, who would miss her for about five minutes if she stopped a bullet, knowing that he could replace her with a phone call any time he felt the need.

Assuming he was still alive to place the call, that was.

"Who is it, Eric?" he demanded.

"Damned if I know," Dempsey said, dropping the normal "sir" in his excitement. "We've got two, three shooters in the hallway. They got past the boys downstairs, somehow, and we've got two men down outside, so far.''

"For Christ's sake get me out of here!" Wagner demanded.

"We're cut off from both the elevator and the stairs," Dempsey replied. "Unless we get some reinforcements in behind them, we've got nowhere left to run.''

Wagner swallowed a rush of panic. "Do something, goddammit!"

Dempsey turned on him, leveling the submachine gun.

"I intend to," he replied.

THE SHOOTING STARTED as Blanski opened the stairwell's door. Mindel flinched at the first explosive sound of it, surprised and instantly embarrassed by her own reaction. Blanski, for his part, dropped into a crouch and lunged through the doorway, Beretta in hand.

Mindel went with her Steyr AUG. All bets were off now, with weapons blasting in the ninth-floor hallway, and she saw no further need for stealth. The rifle offered superior firepower, penetration and stopping power—everything she needed for room-to-room fighting against a superior force.

But as she followed Blanski through the doorway, smelling cordite in the air, Mindel saw that the opposing force had been reduced by two within a few short seconds. McCarter was advancing from the west end of the passage, the direction of the service ele-

vator, tracking with his AUG and watching out for
targets on his way. Two men she'd never seen before
lay dead or dying in his wake, and slamming doors
along the hallway told her more had gone to ground.

How many more?

She wouldn't know until they'd rooted out the gunners and disposed of them, and how long would that
take? More time than they possessed, perhaps, unless
McCarter and Blanski had some short cut in mind for
finding and extracting Jared Wagner.

Even as the thought took form, a gunman craned
out of a doorway on McCarter's right and triggered
two quick pistol shots, both misses. As the shooter
retreated, the Briton stitched a line of tidy holes across
the wall that hid him, 5.56 mm bullets drilling fiber-
board and plaster as if they were paper. A cry of an-
guish from the other side told Mindel that he'd scored
a hit.

Blanski was firing, too, his 9 mm rounds drilling a
door some ten or fifteen feet downrange. Too late in
closing it, one of the opposition fell against the inside
of the door, his prostrate body blocking it, one lifeless
arm protruding from the gap.

Mindel knew there were four apartments on that
floor, all rented to Global Petroleum, reserved for its
executives to use while working in or visiting Jakarta.
At the moment, it appeared that Jared Wagner was the
only VIP in residence, although his bodyguards had
access to the other flats.

How many? Mindel asked herself again.

She lost the train of thought as a door swung open

on her right, the stubby muzzle of an automatic weapon thrust into the hallway. It was following McCarter, but the gunman never had a chance to fire. Mindel fired without aiming, her bullets slicing through the wall and spewing plaster dust on impact. Her barely seen target lurched backward, triggering a short burst as he fell, his bullets peppering the ceiling.

They were in the middle of a shooting gallery. It wasn't quite a trap, since their arrival hadn't been anticipated and the guards weren't truly on alert, but the cross fire could still prove deadly if they didn't clear the rooms to either side.

Where's Wagner?

A woman's scream answered the question, or at least provided something in the nature of a clue. Mindel supposed the bodyguards would be denied that kind of recreation while on duty, meaning that the woman had to be Wagner's—unless her assumptions were totally wrong and the shooting had startled a maid or housekeeper.

At this hour? No way.

Blanski was up and running toward the body-jammed doorway from which the scream had emanated. Mindel followed close behind him as he hit the door full force and drove it back, despite the dead-weight blocking it. A bullet took a bite out of the doorjamb, near his face, Blanski returning fire with his Beretta, switching to the Steyr as he cleared the threshold.

Mindel was right behind him as a gunman rose behind the nearby sofa, lining up another shot. She fired with Blanski, short but well-placed bursts that spun their human target like a dervish, spattering the wall behind him with a crimson Rorschach pattern.

From the bedroom to their right, more screaming, cut short by a rattle of machine-gun fire. Mindel was closer and she didn't hesitate, rushing the door and kicking it barefoot with force enough to snap the simple lock.

"WHAT ARE YOU doing, Eric?"

"Following my orders," Dempsey said. The muzzle of his weapon didn't waver. It was locked on Jared Wagner's naked chest.

"Whose orders, dammit? Spell it out!"

"Whose do you think?"

Wagner was desperate to buy more time. He held his pistol out of Dempsey's view, beneath the tangled sheet, trying to thumb the hammer back without a telltale sound.

"You don't mean Napier?" he demanded.

"Who else?"

"But why?"

"Simple. It pissed him off when Holbrook spilled his guts to strangers, and he doesn't want an instant replay. I was told to make sure you weren't captured. Get it?"

"I can pay you," Wagner said. "Give me a figure."

"Sure." The gunman sneered. "You want to write a check or put that on your Visa card?"

"Try cash."

"And have the chief put out a contract on me when

he hears I muffed a simple job? No thanks. It's check-out time.''

Leila screamed as Dempsey raised the submachine gun, scrambling out from underneath the satin sheets in all her naked glory. Cursing, Dempsey swung his piece around and stitched her with a short burst to that perfect chest, driving her back against the wall with a pathetic, stunned expression on her face.

Wagner seized the opportunity, triggering two quick shots from his pistol. The first missed Dempsey by at least a foot, the second furrowing his side, an inch or so above his belt line. Dempsey howled, recoiling, holding down the trigger of his SMG as it swung back toward Wagner, spraying death around the bedroom.

Wagner dived headlong to the floor, his feet tangled in bedding as he fell, landing painfully on his left shoulder. He clung to the pistol right-handed, firing a wild round to keep Dempsey off balance, even though he couldn't see his target now.

Bullets flayed the sheets and mattress, blasting feathers from his pillows, as Dempsey returned fire in a rage. Seconds later, Wagner heard the bedroom door burst open, fearing Napier's reinforcements come to finish Dempsey's work, but another automatic weapon joined the chorus, firing two short bursts that silenced Dempsey's gun.

Wagner lay where he was, his shoulder throbbing, afraid to stir and thereby give himself away. It didn't matter, as a woman whom he'd never seen before stepped into view, sighting down the barrel of a fu-turistic rifle toward his face.

"The pistol," she commanded. "Lose it!"

Wagner wasn't suicidal, so he did as he was told. The woman came around to kick the weapon out of reach, beneath the bed, and Wagner saw a man behind her, armed with the same kind of weapon. He'd never seen either one of them before, but they hadn't shot him yet, which was a bonus in the circumstances.

"Who the hell are you?" he asked.

"Your ticket out of here," the man replied, "unless you'd rather take your chances with the hired help."

Wagner thought about it, picturing the sneer on Dempsey's face, his finger tightening around the trigger, seconds away from turning Wagner's brain into wallpaper.

"Screw that," he said. "Let's hit the road."

"You'll want to grab some clothes," the woman said, unflinching in the face of Wagner's nudity.

"Oh, right." He staggered to his feet and moved off toward the bedroom closet.

"Only clothes," she warned him, following along behind. "And make it fast."

BOLAN WATCHED the suite while Mindel covered Wagner, making sure that he took nothing from the bedroom closet but sufficient clothes to cover him for their escape. She nagged and prodded him, urging the frightened oil executive to greater speed, while Wagner sought to make himself a sympathetic figure in her eyes.

"Relax," he pleaded. "I'm cooperating here, all

right? You think I'd cover for a man who tried to have me killed?''

"Meaning your boss?" Mindel asked pointedly.

"Damn right! He told that thug you shot to take me out if things got rough."

"Nice friends you have."

"My point exactly," Wagner said. "They're obviously not my friends, so you don't have to treat me like an enemy."

"Convince me later," Mindel snapped. "Right now, put on your shoes and let's get out of here."

"I'm hurrying, okay?"

Two shooters came in from the hallway, one checking the suite while his partner hung back at the door, firing an Uzi burst into the hall outside. McCarter's answer cut a zigzag track across the wall and sent the shooter in the doorway reeling for cover, a curse on his lips.

Bolan took his best shot from the bedroom, taking down the Uzi bearer with a 3-round burst that swept him off his feet and left him draped across a stylish sofa, crimson stains marking the plush upholstery. The shooter's sidekick dropped behind an ornate coffee table, tipping it for cover, but the wood veneer provided no safety from Bolan's 5.56 mm rounds as he strafed the table, left to right. A squeal from cover marked the hit, and Bolan marked his target's passing by the fading shivers of a foot protruding from behind the table.

"Time to move," he told the others. "Ready or not, before we get more company."

Wagner started to protest, hopping on one foot with a Gucci loafer in his other hand, but Mindel shoved him toward the bedroom doorway, driving him before her while Bolan scanned the suite beyond. They passed four sentries, two eliminated when they entered, and the two latecomers who had fared no better. Pausing at the bullet-punctured door, Bolan took note of deathly silence in the outer hall and hailed McCarter from the foyer.

"Three to go," he said. "We're coming out."

"Come ahead," McCarter answered. "The sooner, the better."

Bolan counted half a dozen corpses in the hallway, crumpled where they'd fallen under fire. There was no more active opposition at the moment, but he knew that didn't rule out reinforcements from some other quarter, or police arriving to surround the building while they were upstairs.

"Which way?" McCarter asked.

"The elevator's faster," Bolan said. "Let's take the chance."

The service elevator could turn out to be their coffin, Bolan knew, but every second counted now, and hustling their prisoner down eighteen flights of stairs was no way to save time. For that matter, a firefight in the stairwell would be no significant improvement on an elevator ambush, especially if they were dueling with police and Bolan was forbidden by his private code from firing back.

They hurried to the service elevator, Wagner prodded by Mindel's AUG all the way. He got his second shoe on in the elevator, nearly toppling over as the car lurched between floors. It seemed a long ride down but lasted only seconds, Bolan and his warriors snapping fresh magazines into their weapons, ready for anything when they hit the ground floor.

An empty hallway yawned before them, mocking their preparedness. Emerging from the elevator, Bolan heard excited voices emanating from the general direction of the lobby, turning toward the back door and the alley as Mindel and McCarter left the car, Wagner sandwiched between them.

"Hurry up!" Bolan told them. "We're all out of time."

GRIMALDI HAD the Camry parked in back of the apartment building, ten feet from the service entrance, sitting at the wheel with a Beretta in his lap. He had the lights off, engine running, all four doors unlocked. The pistol sprang to hand when the door burst open, pale light spilling into the alley, figures racing from the building to the car. Grimaldi counted four, recognized three of them and held his fire.

Mindel piled into the back seat, half dragging the hostage behind her, McCarter bringing up the rear and making it a sandwich. Bolan had no sooner dropped into the shotgun seat than the Stony Man pilot floored the accelerator, burning rubber out of there.

A wail of sirens greeted them as they left the alley, swinging left onto a street with one of those tongue-twisting names Grimaldi couldn't pronounce. He flicked on the lights, slowed their pace to something in the neighborhood of legal and relaxed as flashing lights bore down on them from the direction they were headed. Two, three, four police cars raced toward the scene, more sirens wailing in the distance as the first four cruisers passed him by.

Grimaldi turned right at the next light, drove two blocks, then turned left to resume his former course. They merged flawlessly with traffic, Grimaldi minding his speed, going with the flow.

"Is this the guy?" he asked Bolan.

"One of them, anyway."

"Where are we taking him?"

"Someplace with privacy," McCarter said.

"Hey, people," the hostage said, "I already told you I'm cooperating. Nobody screws Jared Wagner twice."

"You'll want to save your breath," Bolan advised him.

"Not a problem, chief," Wagner said. "We're all friends here, right?"

"Not even close," the Executioner replied.

"I'm thinking waterfront," Grimaldi offered. "Something in a nice, dark warehouse."

"Fine by me," Bolan said.

"No argument from this kid," Wagner echoed from the back seat. "Anything you want, it's cool. In fact—"

"Shut up!" McCarter and Mindel ordered, speaking in unison.

"Hey, I'm just saying—"

The sound of a slap silenced Wagner, evoking a

frown from Grimaldi. He didn't trust any prisoner who came on too friendly from the get-go, working overtime to please his captors. Grimaldi wasn't sure what Wagner meant about Bolan's team saving his life, but any sudden change of heart—much less from one so highly placed among the opposition—smelled to him like rotten fish.

Grimaldi took them north, away from downtown, toward the waterfront. Jakarta was western Java's largest port, no shortage of docks and warehouses to choose from. The trick would be finding someplace where crew didn't work around the clock, sufficient privacy and darkness to let Bolan and McCarter work their prisoner. With any luck, they wouldn't have to squeeze him much. But if it came to that…

Grimaldi knew the stakes and what the game had already cost Stony Man. The life of one conspirator meant nothing, in comparison. Grimaldi would pull the trigger himself, if it came to that. But he hoped they wouldn't have to squeeze the guy too much.

Killing was one thing, in the line of duty. He'd done plenty of it, from the air and on the ground, but the interrogations always left Grimaldi feeling queasy, interfering with his dreams.

He watched the hostage in his rearview mirror, willing him a message. *Make it easy on yourself. Give me a break.*

Judging from the expression he could see on Wagner's face, the guy seemed to think he was home free. Grimaldi thought their prisoner might have a rude surprise in store.

Frowning, Grimaldi focused on the road in front of him. His mission was to find a place. Whatever happened after that was up to Wagner and the others.

Not my fault, Grimaldi thought, and wished that he could make himself believe.

CHAPTER THIRTEEN

The warehouse had that long-abandoned look that featured dust, cobwebs and windblown trash collected at the base of walls outside, with rust and mildew taking over the interior. It was the kind of place that Jared Wagner might have purchased for a low bid in his early days with Global Petroleum, when he was still a field representative, before he moved upstairs to the executive suites.

This night, he thought, it was the kind of place where he might die and not be found for days or weeks, while rats gnawed on his bones.

That prospect made him queasy, nearly turned his legs to rubber, but he swallowed the panic and tried to focus on something constructive. The trick to surviving a hostile takeover in business, he'd learned, was to refrain from any obvious resistance and to make himself seem indispensable. The first part had been easily accomplished by Wagner's surrender in his apartment—although, admittedly, the fact that he'd had two machine guns pointed at his face might make him seem like a less than enthusiastic convert.

As far as indispensability went, his captors plainly

wanted something, or they would've killed him in his
bedroom. All he had to do was work out what they
wanted and do everything within his power to supply
it, while suggesting—subtly, mind you—that nobody
else on Earth could provide the same quality service
at any price.

Simple…unless they really didn't want him alive,
after all, but were planning to protract his death, making it slow and painful for some reason best known to
themselves.

When he was seated on a dusty folding chair, hands
cuffed behind his back, Wagner took another stab at
conversation. "We could save some time," he said,
"if you'd explain exactly what you want and let me
help you."

"You're the helpful type, are you?" one of the
three men asked him, British accent noticeable.

"It's like I told you in the car," Wagner replied.
"When Global's goon squad tries to take me out, that
severs any ties between the company and me. You
want to burn them for whatever reason, I'll chip in for
matches."

"Just like that," the tallest of the three men said.

"Hell, yes! How many chances should I give them?
Dempsey was about to blow my frigging brains out
when your girlfriend stopped him. What I want is to
keep breathing. That's job one. So ask me anything.
I'll answer if I can, and point you in the right direction
if you're chasing information I don't have."

"This Dempsey didn't work for you?" the tall man

asked. Wagner decided he was probably the leader of the team.

"He worked for Global, just like me. Of course, I thought he was supposed to be my bodyguard. Nobody mentioned that his goons were set to clip me at the first sign of trouble."

"And that order came from Arnold Napier?" the woman asked.

"So I'm told. Always the last to know," Wagner remarked, hoping his boyish smile still held at least a vestige of its fabled charm.

"Why would Napier want you dead?" the leader asked him.

"My predecessor bought the farm last week," Wagner replied. "I'm guessing you may know more about that than I do. Am I right? Never mind. Before he shuffled off this mortal coil, I'm told he passed along some information that the company held near and dear. Dempsey and friends were an insurance policy, assigned to make sure I didn't repeat that mistake."

"But now you want to talk." The Brit sounded skeptical.

"Why not? They condemned me without giving me a chance to prove myself. If I'm paying for the sin regardless, I may as well commit it. Right?"

"Out with it, then," the woman said.

Wagner shrugged, feeling the handcuffs pinch his wrists. "What is it that you want to know, exactly? Bottom line, what saves my life?"

"Napier," the leader of the snatch squad said. "We want him, and we're tired of playing catch-up."

"Then you won't be pleased to hear you've missed him by about nine hours," Wagner said. "Right now, my guess would be that he's cruising over the eastern Mediterranean, sipping a cold glass of champagne."

"Where's he off to?" the Brit asked.

"A little vacation with two of his partners. You know about them, I suppose?" Wagner managed a smile. "I'm betting you had something to do with the big noise in Macao."

"Is Lin Mak with him?" the leader asked urgently.

"Should be," Wagner replied, "unless they had a spat and Mr. Napier put him out to walk at twenty thousand feet."

"They're going to see Andrastus," the woman told her male companions. It wasn't a question.

"Bingo. Seems like you folks don't really need me after all. If you could ditch the cuffs and drop me at the airport, I'll be out of here before you can say 'American Express.'"

"Not so fast," the leader replied. "We still need to know where they're meeting. And I mean exactly where."

"Didn't I mention that?"

"It must've slipped your mind," the Brit replied.

"Sorry." Wagner put on a penitent face. "I must've been distracted by the guns and chains. Andrastus has a private island. You're astounded, right? Greek billionaire, an island hideaway. Who'd ever think of that?"

"Location," said the Italian-looking guy who

hadn't spoken since they left the car. "I'll need coordinates."

"Can't help you there," Wagner answered. "I'm
not among his thousand closest friends, so I don't rate
an invitation. I can tell you that it's Greek, which
ought to narrow down the field, and that he calls it
Thyra." Wagner spelled it for them and dredged up
another smile.

"We'll need to check this out," the leader told his
troops, ignoring Wagner in his chair.

Not good.

Wagner spoke up, saying, "And when it checks
out—which it will, because I'm telling you God's honest truth—we're cool, right? I mean, right?"

"We need to talk this over," the leader said.

"Right," the Brit agreed.

The woman turned to Wagner with her gun and
said, "Don't wander off, all right?"

"That's cute. Why don't I wait for you right here?"

As if he had a freaking choice.

Keeping his fingers crossed behind his back, he settled in to wait.

THEY HUDDLED in a corner of the warehouse, out of
earshot from their hostage tethered to his chair.
McCarter spoke up first, keeping his voice low
pitched. "I wouldn't trust this character as far as I can
throw him," he observed.

"Give me an option," Bolan stated.

"We have to check it out," Grimaldi said. "Someone in Washington should have the lowdown on Andrastus and his island.''

"I'll make the call," Bolan replied. He didn't need to ask which "someone" Grimaldi had in mind.

"I'll need to make a call, as well," Mindel remarked. "Greece puts us back within the region where my people may wish to be kept informed."

"They're still your people, then?" McCarter asked. "I thought they cut you loose for playing with the bad boys."

"I suppose we'll see."

"Do keep us posted, will you, love? Inquiring minds, and all that rot."

"Let's say it checks," Bolan remarked. "We've still got Wagner on our hands."

"I can't see giving him a pass," Grimaldi said.

"No way," McCarter echoed.

"No," Mindel agreed.

"I hate to ice him if he's played it straight," Bolan said.

"He's a part of it, the same as Napier and the rest," Mindel reminded him.

"Late in the game, though, if he just replaced Holbrook last week."

"He knows too much to be a novice," Grimaldi said.

"What if we could find another way to take him out of circulation?" Bolan asked.

McCarter frowned. "Such as?"

"I'm working on it."

"No free walk," the former SAS commando repeated.

"Not an option," Bolan confirmed.

"I'll abstain, then, for now."

"Same here," Grimaldi said.

Mindel appeared reluctant, no doubt thinking of her uncle, but at last she said, "All right."

"I'll find out if his story hangs together. We can go from there," Bolan suggested.

Nods around the circle sent him off to find the warehouse loading dock, where he could use the satellite uplink without a metal roof to interfere with any signals. Mindel would be reaching out to Tel Aviv at the same time, he guessed, albeit with some trepidation on her part.

Bolan found the open air he wanted, propping the warehouse door open behind him. He palmed his cell phone, pressed a button to enable the scrambler and tapped out a long string of digits, counting off thirty-four seconds before another phone rang in Washington, halfway around the world.

"Hello?"

"It's me," he told Brognola.

"What's the word?"

He ran it down in brief, naming Wagner and summarizing his comments, requesting the big Fed's suggestions for nonlethal disposition if his story checked, with coordinates for the supposed Greek island of Thyra.

"I never heard of it," Brognola said at last, "but if

there's such a place, they'll have it filed and indexed at the Farm.''

"And Wagner?''

"That's no problem. We can always take him off your hands. What did you have in mind?''

"He needs to do some time,'' Bolan replied.

"That means a statement and a plea,'' Brognola said. "You think he'll go for it?''

"He's had a look at the alternative.''

"Your call, then. If he tries to weasel out—''

"I'll handle it myself,'' the Executioner promised.

"Suits me,'' Brognola said. "I'll reach out to the embassy and put the wheels in motion. Can you give me half an hour on this other thing?''

"No problem.''

"Right, then. Let me call the Bear, and I'll have something for you when you call me back in thirty minutes.''

"That's affirmative.''

Aaron "the Bear'' Kurtzman was top man with computers and intelligence collection on the team at Stony Man Farm. If Thyra existed, he would be able to track it down and report the coordinates to Brognola in Washington, D.C. From there, it would be Bolan's task to find the place and deal with any adversaries seeking shelter there.

He checked his watch and grimaced. Half an hour wasn't long, but waiting stretched it thin and made the time slow to a crawl. Bolan considered going back inside, to tell the others what was happening, then shrugged off the notion. Calling upon his hunter's patience, he sat on a discarded crate and waited for the time to pass.

THERE WAS NO QUESTION of a landline this time, but Mindel called Tel Aviv anyway, half expecting to be disconnected when she asked for Gideon Herzhaft. Instead, after a wait lasting no longer than the average four-course meal, she heard his gruff voice on the line.

"Rebecca. Should I ask where you're calling from?"

"You'll be more interested in where I go from here," she said.

"Will I?"

She almost smiled as she replied, "I guarantee it."

"I suppose you'd better tell me, then."

"We're on our way to Greece."

"So, it's the shipper, then."

They had to talk around the subject, since her cell phone had no built-in scrambler. "Yes," she answered simply.

"That's in our backyard," Herzhaft remarked.

"It's why I'm calling you, to let you know."

"That's very thoughtful." If he meant to be sarcastic, Herzhaft needed lessons. "Can you tell me where you'll be, exactly?"

"No," she lied unhesitatingly. "Not yet."

"As soon as possible," he prodded her.

"Of course."

"Perhaps, since you'll be nearly home, you'd reconsider the arrangements that you've made."

She blinked at that. Oblique or otherwise, there was

only one possible interpretation to Herzhaft's remark. He was asking her to desert Blanski and McCarter, to give them up in effect and cast her lot entirely with Mossad once more.

"That would be premature, in my opinion," she replied.

"I'm sure you know what's best, Rebecca, but delaying the decision could be hazardous."

And now a threat. She bristled at his tone, but kept most of the anger from her own voice as she answered, "You'll recall that I was ordered to resolve this matter on my own."

"In China," Herzhaft countered, "not in Greece."

"It's all the same to me."

"You're making a mistake," he said.

"I'll live with that."

"Will you?" he asked her pointedly.

"I'm going now," she said. "I'll call back if I need your help."

"Don't wait too long," Herzhaft counseled. "The offer isn't good indefinitely."

Instead of replying, she broke the connection, embarrassed to find that her hands were trembling. She had defied Herzhaft and the Mossad, perhaps for the last time. If he was in a spiteful mood, Herzhaft was capable of making life difficult for Mindel and her companions, staking out the major airports in Greece and shadowing them to their final destination. What would he do after that? Was a covert strike force on tap to swoop down and eliminate Israel's enemies, as in the past? Or would Herzhaft let Rebecca take the risks again, as he had throughout the rest of the mission so far?

She didn't know the answer to those questions, and it troubled her. Despite the treatment she'd received from her superiors since Uncle Yakov's disappearance and subsequent death, Mindel still felt as if she owed a debt of loyalty to Mossad. Her patience wasn't infinite, however, and she had grown weary of the attitude displayed by Herzhaft and his masters, pleased to use Mindel and her companions until they were slaughtered, only then willing to risk a more substantive involvement.

Folding the little telephone, she returned it to her pocket, shifting the Steyr AUG on its shoulder strap. How, she wondered, would Washington wish to deal with a scheming traitor like Jared Wagner? Granted, he was a mere upstart compared to Napier, Andrastus and Lin Mak, but his designs on Israel had been equally destructive. By Mindel's reasoning, he earned no special dispensation simply for arriving late at the scene of the crime. If Blanski's chief in the United States decided to release Wagner, she'd find a way to stop it—to stop *him.*

That much, Rebecca Mindel promised to herself.

There would be no free pass for anyone who plotted genocide against her people and her homeland.

Never again.

It was the motto that commandos fighting for the Wrath of God had carried into battle when they hunted Nazi fugitives, and later Arab terrorists responsible for atrocities like the Lod airport massacre and the Munich Olympics slaughter. Some in Israel and abroad suggested that the time for nonviolence had arrived, and that forgiveness should become the order of the day. Mindel had very nearly joined their ranks, and not so long ago.

But that had been before her uncle was assassinated, before she learned that a cabal of wealthy men plotted the destruction of her homeland for personal profit. Mindel could no more turn her back on that knowledge than she could forsake her own flesh and blood in time of need.

Israel was her birthplace, her home. For better or worse, her destiny was intertwined with that of the tiny, beleaguered nation where she had first drawn breath.

Her uncle had known that feeling. He had died because of it, defending his homeland.

Mindel, in turn, could do no less.

BROGNOLA WAS READY and waiting when his private phone line rang again, thirty-four minutes after his last conversation with Bolan. He'd finished early with the calls to the State Department and Stony Man Farm, wishing he still smoked cigars as he counted the minutes to Bolan's callback. He almost leaped at the phone when it finally rang, but restrained himself with an effort.

"Brognola."

"It's me."

"I have news of your subjects, beyond what you asked for," the big Fed declared.

"Go ahead."

"We owe this to our friends in the U.K. They've been sitting on a Ukrainian arms dealer, operating out of London and Paris for the past six months or so. Sometime last night, they got a flash that he was taking orders for a suitcase nuke, the dirty kind, with delivery scheduled for this afternoon in Bratislava. Long story short, they teamed up with Austrian authorities and bagged it coming across the border at 5:00 a.m., with three arrests. The delivery boys aren't talking, but their bill of lading for 'machine parts' shows delivery scheduled to a paper front for Global Petroleum."

"Napier." Bolan pronounced the name as if it were a curse.

"That's the consensus," Brognola replied. "From Austria, they could've trucked it down through Italy and ferried it across to Syria or Lebanon, maybe right into Tel Aviv if they were feeling nervy."

"Take out the capital," Bolan said, "and overrun the rest while everybody's still in shock."

"It's your basic twenty-first-century nightmare," Brognola acknowledged. "And Israel's probably the most vulnerable target on Earth, in terms of size and location."

"Is Tel Aviv aware?"

"London's been burning up the lines. They knew before we did, or I'd have tried to tip you earlier."

"Call it a setback for the Global team," Bolan said. "We should move on them before they have a chance to activate a backup plan."

"In which case, you'll be wanting those coordinates for Thyra."

"I'm all ears."

"It's north of Crete and northwest of Kárpathos," Brognola explained, then read the map coordinates he'd written on a scratch pad, dictated by Aaron Kurtzman from the data room at Stony Man. Bolan repeated the numbers from memory, one pass all he needed to lock them in tight.

"Any background or sitrep?" the soldier inquired.

"A bit," Brognola said. "Andrastus bought the island nine years ago from another shipping tycoon he drove under. He's done some construction since then, described to the Greek tax collectors as residential improvements, but no one's bothered to inspect the place as far as we can tell. Andrastus has enough friends in the government that no one tries to twist his arm for details. It's his home away from home, and paparazzi are discouraged. Over the years, Greek authorities have filed missing-person reports on three tabloid types who went looking for stories on Thyra without invitations. Officially, they were all lost at sea."

"And unofficially?" Bolan asked.

"No one seems to care," Brognola said. "For all we know, there could be others, but they didn't make a splash."

"Call it a hardsite, then."

"Sounds like it. We've got nothing on defenses, though. You'd be going in blind."

"We may not have a choice."

"Just so you know. Andrastus prefers retired special-forces personnel for his security team. He uses everything from Navy SEALs to Spetznaz on the team. At last count, he had two hundred employees authorized to carry firearms in Greece and abroad.''

''That's some security,'' Bolan remarked.

''I doubt they're all on Thyra,'' Brognola went on, ''but since we can't pin any of them down, you ought to be prepared.''

''I'll keep it in mind. Any chance of an eye in the sky?''

''I'll see what I can do,'' Brognola said.

''Okay. What's the word on our guest?''

''If you've got a mind to, you can drop him at the embassy in downtown Jakarta. They'll have papers waiting for him, in the nature of a plea bargain. Should he refuse the deal for any reason, they've agreed to sit on him for forty-eight hours, lose his passport and file or whatever, but after that they'll have to let him go. The way it stands right now, there's no case against him if he decides not to play ball.''

''I'll make him an offer,'' Bolan said. Switching gears, he added, ''We'll need a connection for hardware and transport in Athens. Someone reliable, who won't mind losing a boat if this thing falls apart.''

''Call me psychic,'' Brognola said. ''I already made some calls. You have a pencil handy?''

''Hit me,'' Bolan answered.

''First, the hardware. Try a pawnbroker named Anatol Spaneas.'' Hal read off an Athens address. ''If he doesn't stock the tools you need, Farris Mylonas should be able to accommodate you.'' Yet another address was offered, giving Bolan time to write it down, in case he didn't trust his steel-trap memory.

"And transportation?" he asked.

"Cletis Panopoulos," Brognola replied. "He runs a dealership—Callisto's—out of the marina, with a sideline doing contract work for Langley. I'm advised his product won't come cheap, but he'll forget about police reports in the event of loss or damage."

"Fair enough."

"You sure this is the way you want to go?" the big Fed asked.

"I don't see any other way," Bolan replied. "Do you?"

"Guess not. If I can help in any way—"

"I'll let you know."

"Okay, then. Watch your back."

"I always do."

MCCARTER HAD grown tired of watching Jared Wagner squirm and fidget in his chair. Granted, the handcuffs were uncomfortable, but the leader of Phoenix Force felt no sympathy for the man who was willing to sell out his country and participate in genocide to fatten his own stock portfolio. He supposed Wagner hadn't been involved in Katz's death, per se, but McCarter was willing to snuff him on general principles, to help restore some balance in the deadly game they played.

Mindel had worn a sour face when she returned from talking to her boss, not offering to share whatever might be preying on her mind. McCarter let it go and waited thirty minutes more for Bolan to return, hearing the soldier's footsteps echo through the warehouse as he came back from the loading dock.

"We're set," Bolan announced without preamble. "I've got coordinates for Thyra that should let us plot it on a map, in case it's not on any we can find in Athens. Also, sources for equipment and a boat to get us there."

"I guess we can't fly in?" Grimaldi asked.

"Fly, yes," Bolan replied. "Land, no. We take for granted that the place is fortified and staffed with shooters who know what they're doing."

"How many?" McCarter asked.

"That's unknown," Bolan said. "Andrastus has a couple of hundred professionals on his payroll, but I'd be surprised to find more than half of them hanging around on the island."

"Only half?" McCarter smiled. "That's encouraging."

"The good news is, we ought to find all three of our primary targets waiting for us when we get there."

"*If* we get there, don't you mean?"

It was Bolan's turn to smile. "Call it the power of positive thinking."

"My people won't help," Mindel said, her expression a toss-up between anger and disgust. "They're 'interested,' but not enough to get involved."

"It's just as well," Bolan replied. "They'd want to run the show if they pitched in."

"Too many cooks," Grimaldi said.

"We could've used the reinforcements, though," McCarter added.

"I'm thinking we could go another way," Grimaldi suggested. "As long as the target area's restricted to hostile personnel, why not just hit them from the air and take the whole place down that way? It's quicker than a boat ride, and you don't risk losing anybody on the beach."

"We need target confirmation," Bolan answered. "There's no way to get that from the air."

"Too bad." Grimaldi's frown was eloquent.

"We're off to Athens, then?" McCarter asked.

"ASAP," Bolan replied.

"So, what about our friend?"

"He has a choice to make," the Executioner replied, moving to stand before their captive.

Wagner risked a smile, trying to keep up his facade of optimism in the face of danger. "Are we all set now? I wouldn't mind a change of scene."

"Be careful what you wish for, mate," McCarter cautioned him.

"I've talked to Washington," Bolan said. "There's an offer on the table, but you don't have lots of time to think about it."

"Spell it out."

"We drop you at the U.S. Embassy. They're waiting for you as we speak. You make a full and detailed statement, names and pertinent specifics, *A* to *Z*. They'll look at your cooperation when it comes to sentencing, but you'll do time."

"That's not the sweetest deal I ever heard," Wagner replied.

"It could be when you think of the alternatives."

The oilman frowned. "Which are?"

"We settle it right here, right now."

"I see your point. This kind of bargain might be shaky on appeal, though. Have you thought of that?"

"First thing," Bolan assured him. "And you could be right. The thing you have to ask yourself is, do you really want to hit the streets again, too soon?"

Still frowning, Wagner asked, "That would be bad, because...?"

"For one thing, Napier and his pals may think you sold them out, and if we miss a few—hell, even *one*—they're bound to nurse a grudge. Then, there's the disappointment factor."

"Care to spell that out?"

"The four of us," Bolan said, indicating his companions with a glance to either side, "would all be deeply disappointed if you tried to weasel out of your arrangement with the state. The chances are, we'd feel obliged to look you up and register our disappointment personally."

"I get your drift," the hostage said.

"So, it's your call."

Wagner sat up a little straighter in his chair and flashed a brittle smile. "Let's go," he said. "I wouldn't want to keep them waiting at the embassy."

BOLAN WALKED a half block back to the waiting Camry after leaving Jared Wagner at the U.S. Embassy gates, in care of two well-armed Marines. Grimaldi had the wheel, McCarter riding shotgun, as Bolan slid into the back seat with Mindel and they pulled away from the curb.

"I still think this bit has snafu written all over it," McCarter said. "Five minutes talking legalese across a shiny desk, and friend Jared will have a lawyer rushing over to complain about the violation of his civil liberties."

"Could be," Bolan admitted.

"And that doesn't bother you?"

"I told him what would happen if he blew the deal," Bolan replied.

"Suppose he thinks you're bluffing?" Grimaldi asked.

"Then he'd be dead wrong."

McCarter could've mentioned that locating Jared Wagner might be hopeless when he had the whole wide world to hide in, but he let it go. Instead, he asked, "So what about this island, anyway?"

"We've got no intel to speak of," Bolan admitted, "but I'm hoping for some details when we're closer to the target. Our transport connection should know something about islands in the region, if he's working with the Company."

"Location's only half of it," McCarter said. "I'd feel much better if I knew how many shooters we'd be meeting with when we go ashore."

"Hal's trying to arrange an overflight, but it may not be feasible. Anyway, with modern construction you can't count slit trenches or privies and try to extrapolate troop strength.''

"It's better than nothing," McCarter insisted.

"Let's hope he can pull it off, then."

"I still say an air strike's the clean way to go," Grimaldi said.

Bolan had considered the pilot's proposal, but he'd already experienced too many near misses with Arnold Napier and Lin Mak. Even if they razed the island and sank it beneath the Mediterranean's whitecaps, he'd never be sure of a clean sweep unless he saw the targets for himself.

Unless he saw them dead.

He owed that much to Katz, at least: the certainty that he'd not only been avenged, but that his killers hadn't wriggled through the net to fight again another day.

"We'll hold that in reserve," he told Grimaldi. "Just in case."

There was no need to say in case of *what*. He didn't have to spell it out for Mindel or McCarter. Even if they managed to obtain a head count on the fortress island's personnel, there would be questions that no aerial photography could answer. Were fences electrified or not? Had the beaches and footpaths been mined or otherwise booby-trapped? Were security cameras or motion detectors in place on the island? How well were the defenders armed, and were they adept in the use of their weapons?

Bolan had a partial answer to the last question, at least. According to Brognola, Christos Andrastus had hired the best security he could get, favoring ex-military personnel from various elite forces. That meant rugged types, proficient with all kinds of military hardware and skilled in hand-to-hand combat, though some might never have served in actual combat situations. Either way, they would be tough, well paid and highly motivated to succeed.

Which meant they'd also be bad news.

"How long to get us airborne?" Bolan asked Grimaldi.

"Between fuel and flight plans, say an hour and a half, with any luck. It could be longer."

"Right. We need to ditch the hardware first, then head back to the airport. I don't want to stall this any longer than we have to."

"Napier could be checking in with Wagner any time," McCarter said. "If something gets his wind up, he could run again and we won't have a clue where to start looking for him."

"Same thing if we'd iced him," Bolan answered. "It's a gamble, either way."

"Suppose we miss again?" McCarter prodded.

"We keep trying," Bolan said. "I don't know any other way to play the game."

That was the hell of it, he thought. They'd traveled halfway around the world and back again, pursuing enemies who slipped away from them like phantoms in the dark of night, and there was still no guarantee the men they hunted would be waiting for them when they reached their destination. Bolan felt as if he'd stepped onto a treadmill that was running of its own volition now, compelling him to match its pace.

In which case, there was only one thing left to do.

He would pick up the pace and challenge the machine, run it into the ground and see which lasted longer—cogs and gears or flesh and grim determination.

And before he reached the end, he meant to have the enemy within his grasp.

CHAPTER FOURTEEN

Thyra

There was a sense of homecoming Christos Andrastus felt whenever he returned to Thyra's solitude, which he experienced nowhere else on Earth. It wasn't his native soil, in fact—his birthplace was a mountain village north of Athens—but the first time he'd set foot on Thyra, Andrastus had been captivated by its stark beauty, the isolation that set him apart from the outside world. The island's owner had refused to sell, prompting Andrastus to initiate a cutthroat war of attrition, eventually driving his competitor into bankruptcy, claiming Thyra—and the loser's fleet of tankers—as his prize.

The island never failed to soothe him—or, to be precise, it hadn't failed before today. This evening, as he waited to receive his self-invited guests, Andrastus felt a stirring of uneasiness that spoiled the sunset for him, making him regret the day he'd shared the secret of this place with Arnold Napier.

Live and learn, Andrastus thought, but how could he have known their partnership would come to this?

The plan had always been risky, of course, but Napier had minimized the danger, while Andrastus had let wishful thinking carry him away.

Repent at leisure?

No.

Andrastus refused to let the others spoil Thyra for him, as they'd ruined everything else. He wasn't sure they could still salvage anything from the original master plan, though Napier feigned confidence and spoke of impending victory. His latest gambit was the most dangerous yet, but at least it had some prospect of succeeding.

And if it failed...what then?

A clean sweep, Andrastus decided. He would save himself, his empire, at any cost to the others. Napier had virtually ceased consulting him on strategy. Why should he telegraph his moves at this point in the game and thereby jeopardize whatever hope he had of saving something from the ruins?

Napier and Lin Mak had run to him for help, but now Andrastus thought it might be time to help himself. If there were any further troubles, if the latest plan fell through and left them dangling...well, it was a long flight from Jakarta to the Med, and there were often storms at sea. If he declared that some disaster had befallen his two visitors, who was there in the world to contradict him?

No one.

Andrastus was a man of action, relegated by Napier to an advisory role that ill suited him. He looked forward to seizing the initiative once more. It was almost enough to make him hope that something *would* go wrong with Napier's backup plan.

That was madness, of course. Smooth sailing was the best kind, always. If Napier's latest effort carried their scheme to successful fruition, so much the better. But if it failed, it would be his last effort.

Oh, yes.

Andrastus checked his diamond-studded Rolex watch, confirming that his yacht should be returning soon, with Napier and Lin Mak on board. A phone call from the airport had confirmed their arrival in Athens. Customs would have slowed them a little, but there were seldom any untoward delays for the filthy rich. Another half hour or so, and the yacht should be visible, steaming toward Thyra on a southwesterly course.

Andrastus hoped that Napier would come bearing good news for a change. He was fed up with the incessant litany of disaster that had become routine of late. What good was wealth and power if a mogul couldn't shape events to suit himself and make his own life easier?

Andrastus heard his houseman coming, crepe-soled shoes whispering on tile. He waited, facing westward through a giant picture window toward the fading sunset, darkness settling in the corners of the room around him. He would have to turn on the lights soon, to hold the night at bay.

"Excuse me, sir," the houseman said.

"What is it, Niko?"

"The radio, sir. Twenty minutes to arrival."

"Thank you."

"Yes, sir."

Andrastus slipped a lightweight jacket on, considered taking a pistol along, then decided against it. Two bodyguards were waiting for him on the patio as he left the house, falling in step behind him as Andrastus led the way to the pier. It was a minor show of force, but he wanted Napier and Lin Mak to know who ruled Thyra from the moment they set foot ashore. If there was any doubt in their minds, any sneaking suspicion that they called the shots on this island, Andrastus would swiftly disabuse them of such notions.

And he would especially enjoy the look on Napier's face when he saw the strapping young men with their weapons on display.

It was two hundred yards from the house to the pier, but Andrastus enjoyed the excursion. He felt better already, now that his mind was made up, thinking, step into my parlor, said the spider to the fly.

NAPIER COULD SEE Andrastus waiting on the pier while they were still a quarter mile from shore. The pier was lit by floodlights, in anticipation of the *Aristotle*'s landing, making human figures clearly visible despite the hour and descent of darkness on the Med. Behind the Greek, two flankers stood at ease, light glinting from the polished barrels of their automatic weapons.

So.

He couldn't blame Andrastus for being prepared, but Napier wished there'd been a way for him to bring along more than the slim quartet of bodyguards that had accompanied him from Jakarta. Here, they'd be outnumbered and outgunned if anything went wrong—and given the course of recent events, what were the odds of something going right?

Stow that, he warned himself. Negative thinking was a trap, self-perpetuating, that could undermine any man's best efforts. He'd suffered a run of bad luck, it was true—they all had, in fact—but luck came in cycles, and Napier's was past due for a change. As soon as he had confirmation that the nuke was on its way from Austria to Israel—stashed in one of Global's tankers, putting in at Tel Aviv for some emergency repair work—Napier could relax.

They'd all be winners when the smoke cleared, laughing all the way to the bank.

And in the meantime, it couldn't hurt to have a few extra shooters on standby, just in case.

Lin Mak joined him on deck as the yacht slowed, finally stopping dead in the water. They were still some distance offshore, but the great yacht could go no farther without danger of running aground. They would transfer to a motor launch for the run to the pier, one last dash across open water before Napier set foot on dry land again.

It was a smooth transition, Napier enjoying the smaller boat's speed, though Lin Mak was clearly on the verge of being seasick. Napier tried to ignore him, concentrating on the pier and their welcoming committee. Up close, he could see that Andrastus had chosen his bodyguards well. Aside from the fact that one was Teutonic in appearance, the other inky black, they could've been bookends. Both men were sculpted from the same hard stock, grim faces under close-cropped hair, athletic bodies straining at their clothes as if intent on shedding them for combat. Both regarded Napier, seated in the launch, as if he were nothing but a target in their sights.

Disembarking from the launch was more difficult than boarding or leaving the yacht. It rode the swells lightly, trying to shift out from under his feet as Napier rose, moving toward the starboard gunwale. One of the shooters stepped forward, offering a hand, and Napier noted that it was his left, leaving the gun hand free for action if the need arose.

Professionals.

The oilman didn't know if he should feel relieved or ill at ease. He settled for a pose of studied relaxation, hoping that his men would pick it up and follow his example.

Andrastus, beaming, moved to greet them, momentarily outnumbered by Napier's retinue. It didn't seem to faze him as he shook Napier's hand, then Lin Mak's. "What word of the delivery?" he asked at last. "Are we on track?"

"I'll need to make a call to check," Napier replied. "I didn't want to use the radio."

"Of course, by all means. Come with me, my friends. I have secure lines in the house."

And what else? Napier wondered as he trailed Andrastus back along the pier. He glimpsed the stylish bunker that the Greek called home, a boxlike shape against the fading gray of twilight, bleeding into velvet night.

A man could disappear on Thyra and no one might ever find him. So could six men, if it came to that. Napier decided he would have to watch his step around Andrastus and make sure he gave his host no cause to take offense.

It was a long swim back to Athens, and the sharks that worried Napier most were right there with him, on dry land.

LIN MAK'S ROOM WAS larger and more luxurious than the hotel suite he had lately vacated in Jakarta, but the trappings of wealth failed to put his troubled mind at ease. He worried that it might already be too late to salvage his position with the Chinese government, imagining the glee of his rivals when he couldn't be found to explain bloodshed at his residence in Macao.

Mak wondered if a formal warrant had yet been issued for his arrest. There were subtler ways to achieve the same end, but he knew several high-ranking party members who would revel in his humiliation and do anything within their power to bring him down. Mak had given them the perfect opportunity this time, and the hell of it was that he couldn't even call home to check his own status, since the inevitable order to return—and his inability to obey it—would only make his situation that much worse.

Mak wished the scene at home had been his only worry. If that were the case, he could simply fall back on one of his three alternative identities and disappear, set for a modestly luxurious life in hiding with the money he'd already banked from Global Petroleum. Unfortunately, that wasn't the case. This night, Mak thought he had as much to fear from his own allies than from rivals or police in the People's Republic of China.

In fact, he had begun to question whether he would ever leave Andrastus's island alive.

Mak tried to tell himself that he was simply being paranoid, but a part of his mind refused to accept that bromide. He knew that Napier's gunmen were capable of sudden, unpredictable violence, but they weren't his only concern at the moment. Mak had noted Napier's shifting glances as they came ashore, watching the riflemen who flanked Andrastus and the others stationed all around the house, inside and out. And for the first time in their criminal association, he considered that the Greek might pose a greater threat than Napier, in the present circumstances.

Andrastus had several times voiced his reserve about certain moves Napier made, suggesting that the oilman's strategy was too risky, a potential danger to them all. He'd never pressed the point, but now that their plans were disrupted, Napier and Lin Mak in flight for their lives, Mak wondered if Andrastus might decide to cut his losses and dispose of them. Where better to make his move, after all, than on the fortress island he owned and controlled, safe from the prying eyes of journalists and the police? Who was there in the outside world to testify that Mak or Napier had ever set foot on Thyra in the first place? They could vanish, weighted bodies dumped into the Mediterranean, and their passing would remain a mystery for all time.

Mak poured himself a glass of whiskey from the wet bar that stood against one wall of his suite and drained the strong liquor in two deep swallows. His eyes blurred for a moment, brimming with startled tears, before the whiskey lit a reassuring fire inside him, calming his razor-taut nerves.

But not entirely.

Mak could drink himself into a stupor, and the same doubts would remain when he awoke—*if* he awoke. He simply didn't trust his partners as he had when they began their venture, and he guessed that trust was gone forever. Napier's strange incompetence in dealing with their nameless enemies the past two weeks brought grim, unwelcome thoughts of treachery to mind, and Mak was unable to shake them.

Like any ranking member of the Chinese Communist Party, Mak knew about betrayal firsthand. Treachery was second nature in Beijing, for all the talk of selfless sacrifice. He hadn't reached his present station without walking over those who'd been his friends and comrades. He expected no less from his partners in the present outlaw venture, but that didn't mean he had to take it lying down.

Escape from Thyra might be difficult, even impossible, but he could still take certain steps to help himself, beginning with the acquisition of a weapon.

Doggedly determined now, Lin Mak began to search his rooms, seeking any humble object that

might put him on an equal footing with the friends
whom he increasingly regarded as potential enemies.

Athens

BOLAN WAS DOZING when Grimaldi's voice roused
him and blew away the tattered remnants of his
dreams. It took a beat for him to understand that Jack
was speaking from the cockpit, on the Jetstar's intercom, announcing their approach to Athens.

Finally.

The long flight had been tedious, the refueling stops
uneventful.

Bolan checked his window as they banked into their
final approach. The Aegean Sea was pristine blue,
speckled with islands, none of them the one he sought.
They still had work to do, risks to face and equipment
to procure, before they made the next leg of their journey over open water.

Would it be the last lap? And if so, who would
prevail?

Bolan wasn't clairvoyant, and he knew that over-
confidence could be a fighting man's worst enemy. It
bred negligence, laziness and careless mistakes—any
one of which could get a soldier killed without warning. Napier's team was on the defensive, but they were
flush with cash, defending familiar turf. Andrastus had
professional soldiers on his security team, and Bolan
would've been surprised if the shipping tycoon
didn't also have well-placed friends in the Greek government.

It all spelled trouble for the visiting team, especially if they announced their intentions and gave the defenders warning of their approach. Bolan needed stealth now more than ever and he hoped Brognola's reaching out hadn't set any ripples in motion around Athens, however inadvertently.

The last thing they needed was to step off the Jetstar and into the clinging strands of a deadly spider web.

Nice and easy, he thought, as the plane continued banking, putting the early-morning sun in his eyes. Bolan turned away from the glare and glanced around the cabin. Mindel and McCarter were both awake now, peering out their windows at the sea and rocky islands down below. They ranked among the best soldiers he'd ever fought beside, and Bolan hoped he wasn't leading both of them to an untimely death.

"We have a green light on approach," Grimaldi told them, from the cockpit. "See you on the ground in ten."

Bolan's seat belt was already fastened, buckled while he slept as a hedge against any surprise turbulence. He leaned back in his seat now, closed his eyes and tried to picture Arnold Napier's face, the expression it would register when he confronted death.

Take nothing for granted, the voice in his head cautioned Bolan. That was his cautious side, warning the gung-ho warrior not to get carried away and forget that his adversaries still had a small arsenal of tricks concealed up their custom-tailored sleeves.

They could still stop him dead.

And that was the problem, of course. In real life,

the good guys didn't always win. Evil had triumphed on more than a few occasions, in the course of human affairs, and Bolan sometimes had the feeling that he was fighting a losing battle, shoveling sand in the face of a flood he could never repulse.

Do your best, then. One step at a time.

Beginning in Athens, right.

He was tracking his enemy down to the end of the line, one step at a time.

CHAPTER FIFTEEN

Athens

Bolan started by treating the city as enemy turf. He harbored no grudge against Athens or its people— quite the opposite, in fact—but he had to assume that Christos Andrastus was so well established in Greece, so wealthy and influential that he had to know everyone who mattered. A local boy made good, with billions of discretionary dollars in his bank account, could pull most any string he wanted to, in Greece or any other country on the planet. It was just the way things worked, regardless of the setting or the political system involved.

So they would have to watch their step in Athens, trusting Brognola's contacts only to a certain point, forever conscious that Andrastus or his people might be lurking in the shadows, watching and waiting for an enemy to be revealed. To come this far and walk into an ambush would be the last straw.

Grimaldi drove the rented car, a Nissan Maxima, with Bolan riding shotgun, Mindel and McCarter in the back. They found the address Brognola had given them for Anatol Spaneas, driving twice around the block to check for watchers on the street outside the pawnshop. No one seemed to have the place staked out, but Bolan knew there could be sentries tucked away in any of the other shops along the street, in upstairs windows, even crouching on rooftops, and he would never spot them from the car.

"Looks clear to me," Grimaldi said on their second pass, "but I wouldn't want to guarantee it."

Bolan understood his hesitancy, felt the same himself, but if they didn't risk the move, their play was stalled before they even started.

"Right," he said. "Let's try it."

Grimaldi made another circuit of the block and found a place to park the Nissan, two doors west of the pawnshop. He waited another moment before switching off the engine, then said, "You want me to come in?"

"Better wait here," Bolan replied, "in case we need to bail out in a hurry."

"Okay." Grimaldi was reluctant, but he'd go along with the program.

Crossing the sidewalk, McCarter and Mindel falling in step behind him, Bolan remained alert for any pedestrians who showed a bit too much interest in his party, any passing motorists who stared too long or lifted a microphone to their lips. An electric chime sounded as they entered the pawnshop.

A white-haired man of sixty-something years came to meet them from the rear of the shop. He was all smiles, behind a mustache and eyebrows so thick they looked fake, like theatrical appliances for the title character in *The Wizard of Oz.*

The pawnbroker sized them up at a glance and greeted them in English. "Good morning, gentlemen and lady. How may I be serving you?"

"Mr. Spaneas?" Bolan asked him.

The smile flickered enough to note surprise, then came back at full strength. "That is me," he confirmed. "You are American, I see."

"I was referred to you by friends in Washington," Bolan declared. "They tell me you're the man to see for special hunting gear."

The smile flickered again, losing wattage. "I may see your identification, perhaps?" Spaneas asked.

"Of course."

Bolan showed him the Mike Belasko passport, waiting while Spaneas looked it over and returned it. When he was satisfied, the pawnbroker called a young man from the shop's backroom and spoke to him in rapid-fire Greek, leaving him in charge of the shop while Spaneas led Bolan's party to a storeroom in back, then up a short flight of stairs to the shop's second floor. He jangled keys and found the one he wanted on a bulky ring, admitting them to a room that smelled of fresh paint and gun oil.

"My special stock," Spaneas said. "I have a catalog if you require something larger, but there may be a delay before delivery."

Eyeing the racks of small arms and their crated ammunition, Bolan shook his head and told Spaneas, "This should cover it."

Greece has no native weapons industry. Its military forces buy their arms primarily from Germany and the United States, while other weapons find their way across the border via black-market channels. The pawnbroker's stock was a mixed bag, therefore, his assault rifles including M-16s, Kalashnikovs, Israeli Galils and German HKs. Submachine guns ran the gamut from Uzis and MP-5s to British Sterlings and a Daewoo K1A from South Korea. The pistols included Berettas and Glocks in various calibers, Walther P-88s, vintage Colt semiautos and the freak of the lot, a Russian four-barreled SPP-1, designed to fire darts underwater.

Bolan bypassed the exotic models, consulting briefly with Mindel and McCarter before they made their selections. They chose four AKSU assault rifles, shortened versions of the Russian AK-74, backed up with silencer-equipped Beretta side arms. Ammunition and spare magazines filled out the order, along with a mixed bag of fragmentation and incendiary grenades. Duffel bags held the lot, and Bolan slipped one of the Berettas under his windbreaker before they left the shop.

Better.

Whatever happened next, at least they would be able to defend themselves. And with a little luck, they might survive the night.

Thyra

THE CONVERSATION with his contact in Vienna left Arnold Napier with a headache throbbing in the space behind his eyes. He felt an urge to scream and punch the walls, but such displays would do more harm than good.

Could it get any worse?

Maybe. If he displayed weakness in front of his two partners, it just might be a great deal worse.

Fatal, perhaps.

Napier steeled himself against the inevitable reaction, knowing that he couldn't keep the latest news from Andrastus or Lin Mak. They were bound to find out sooner or later, and if he delivered the tidings himself, at least he had a long-shot chance at spin control.

Dear God, how did it come to this?

He found them in the game room, sipping single malt whiskey and idling over a game of billiards. Lin Mak played poorly, distracted and unfocused, but Andrastus didn't seem to mind. Both men looked up from the table as Napier entered, Andrastus raising his glass in a mock salute.

"What word, then," he asked, "of Plan B?"

Napier crossed to the wet bar, poured himself a double whiskey and drank it straight down before answering. He felt the others watching him, their silence eloquent with concern.

"The shipment was seized," he informed them, "in Austria."

Andrastus blinked at him, his face going blank. He didn't seem to understand the message. "Seized? What do you mean? Seized by whom?"

"The police, I assume. Maybe the military. I'm not sure," Napier admitted. "The point is, it's gone."

"Gone?" Andrastus echoed. "What do you mean, it's gone?"

"I've told you," Napier said. "The shipment was intercepted on the border crossing into Austria. It's been confiscated. If you're asking where they'd take a contraband nuclear weapon, I haven't the faintest fucking idea. All right? Are we clear?"

He regretted the outburst immediately, even though it made him feel better, releasing some of the tension that festered inside him, making Napier feel vaguely dizzy and nauseous.

Lin Mak was the first to recover. "Can they trace it?" he asked.

"Given time, I assume so," Napier answered. "They've taken the transport crew into custody. Ukrainians, they'll be. God knows if they'll talk or how much they know about the supplier. They'll talk eventually. Everyone does. The bill of lading leads back to a paper front, but breaking it down is only a matter of time and manpower. It's bad. Let's say that, for a start."

"That strikes me as an understatement," Andrastus stated. "Would 'disastrous' not be a better choice of words? Perhaps 'catastrophic'?"

Napier fanned the air with his empty glass. "There's no need to overreact," he said.

"Overreact?" Andrastus gaped at him. "Perhaps you think we ought to celebrate?"

"I didn't say—"

"What *are* you saying, Arnold?" Lin Mak challenged him. "More importantly, what are you *doing* to salvage the situation?"

"I've just found out about the problem," Napier replied, "but since you ask, I've taken steps to dismantle the receiving office in Bratislava. The authorities will find nothing of consequence, if and when they go looking."

"Nothing of consequence, Arnold?" The Greek's tone was mocking. "They have the weapon, for God's sake!"

"Better that than us, don't you think?" Napier softened his voice, cringing inwardly as he added, "But there's another problem, too, I'm afraid."

"Saints preserve us." Andrastus dropped his cue onto the billiard table, staring at Napier in frank disbelief. "What now?"

"I called Jakarta with a heads-up on what's happened," Napier said, "and it seems my number two went missing last night. There's been trouble at the company apartments. Several members of the security team were killed."

Mak muttered something in Chinese that didn't sound friendly.

Andrastus turned on Napier, scowling. "So, they followed you from Macao to Jakarta," he accused. "And why not from there to my doorstep? The two of you will lead these bastards to me yet!"

Napier was on the verge of lashing back when a sudden thought occurred to him. It pleased him to see Andrastus taken aback by the smile on his face. "Let's hope so," he said.

"Are you mad?" the Greek challenged.

"On the contrary," Napier told him. "I'm thinking more clearly than ever. You have faith in your soldiers, I take it?"

"Of course!"

"Then relax and hope for the best, Christos. If the bastards somehow manage to trail us, we can finish it once and for all."

Athens

CLETIS PANOPOULOS knew trouble when he saw it, and the four strangers approaching him along the dock had danger written all over them. It was nothing obvious—indeed, he supposed most who saw them would take the quartet for simple tourists—but Panopoulos knew better. Their faces were hard behind sunglasses and casual smiles, the woman a part of the group, no more softness about her than the men.

They were killers, Panopoulos decided, but he didn't think they'd come to murder him. Rather, he guessed they were about to put good money in his pocket.

Panopolous watched one of his salesmen greet the foursome, then turn and point toward the office, a small frown of disappointment on his face. No one liked losing a commission, but these four had asked for the old man himself. Panopoulos could sense such things. He had an eye for trouble and a nose for profit, tempered by an understanding that the two things often went together, hand in hand.

He left the office, meeting them outside, near the dock where the best of his smaller boats were tied. They'd come for transportation, obviously, and he guessed they'd want something average size or slightly smaller, merging speed and comfort with evasive capability.

"Good evening," he hailed them, slipping naturally into English. "Welcome to Callisto's!"

The tallest of the three men spoke for all of them. "We're looking for a boat that will accommodate the four of us," he said. "Something in a small cabin cruiser to take us around for a couple of days. A friend in the States mentioned you."

"May I ask the friend's name?"

"Mr. Langley," the stranger replied.

Panopoulos held on to his smile through sheer willpower and years of practice. He'd heard nothing from his American contacts for nearly a year, but he dared not refuse. Money had been offered and accepted, promises exchanged. A man was only as good as his word.

"Of course." He beamed, all mock enthusiasm. "We're old friends. What sort of travel did you have in mind?"

"We're island hopping," the American replied, keeping it deliberately vague.

"Sleeping on board?"

"I doubt it, but it's possible."

"Sport fishing?" Panopoulos asked facetiously, in the spirit of keeping up appearances.

"Just some cruising."

"To rent or own?" The crux of it, now, was the money.

The tall man glanced at his companions, who regarded him silently in return. The woman shrugged.

"We'll only need it for a day or two," their spokesman repeated, "but I want to be on the safe side, in case we hit a squall and take some damage."

Panopoulos knew what that meant. Twice before, he'd had boats returned by friends of Mr. Langley with suspicious damage. One had been pocked with obvious bullet holes, the other scarred along the bow and to port, as if it had rammed some larger craft. Panopoulos had cashed his bonus checks in each case and refrained from asking questions.

"In that case," he said, "perhaps a deposit against the purchase price would be agreeable, refunded in part if you decide against the purchase and return the boat undamaged within...shall we say three days?"

"Sounds good," the American said, without silently polling his comrades this time. "What have you got in stock?"

"The perfect choice, I think," Panopoulos replied.

He led them to the berth where a four-year-old Bénéteau Antares 620 was moored. "Twenty feet overall," he said, launching into the sales pitch, "with a two-foot draft. Ninety horsepower at full throttle over open water. A small galley and head belowdecks, with sleeping accommodations for three. Her cruising range is eight hundred kilometers."

Panopolous watched them do the arithmetic silently,

each to himself. After a moment, the leader asked, "How much?"

"She rents by the day for two hundred U.S. dollars," Panopoulos said, fudging it. They looked like money, and the Company had deep pockets. "For a security deposit, refundable on safe return, less rental fees and fuel, shall we say twenty thousand U.S.?"

For an instant, the dealer thought he'd blown it by asking too much. He cringed inwardly at the thought of having to apologize, bargain himself down in effect, if they declined the price. He couldn't afford to offend Mr. Langley, after all.

Panopoulos was on the verge of speaking, withdrawing the quote, when the tall America produced a fat wad of greenbacks from his pocket and started peeling off hundred-dollar bills.

"Twenty it is," he said.

Panopoulus couldn't help smiling now, cheeks stretched to their limit and beyond. "I hope you will enjoy your cruise, my friends," he said. "Greece welcomes you."

"We'll see," the grim American replied.

Thyra

CHRISTOS ANDRASTUS lit a long cigar, his ninth of the day, and waited for the nicotine to do its work, combining with the ouzo he'd consumed to soothe his nerves. All things considered, it was no small task. He could have used a tranquilizer, but he wanted a clear head.

There was so much to think about, so many preparations to be made.

Napier had failed. That much was clear to him beyond the shadow of a doubt. For all his plans and speeches, all the hollow reassurances, the CEO of Global Petroleum was a beaten man. Not broken yet—he still had money and resources, after all; his mind still spewed out strategies, each one more far-fetched than the last—but he was on his way. The morning's announcement of the losses in Jakarta would mean heavy losses on the stock market. If the reports went further and associated Global with some sort of terrorist activity, indictments were sure to follow. Napier would become a fugitive in his own homeland, condemned to roam the world or find a third-rate nation that would shelter him.

No.

It wouldn't come to that, Andrastus told himself, because he wouldn't let it happen. Pressed too closely, Napier might decide to make a deal with the authorities, sell out his partners for immunity or a reduction of his punishment. As for Lin Mak, who could predict what he might say or do to keep the Chinese execution squads at bay?

There was a moral to this story, he decided. For decades, Andrastus had trusted no one but himself, dealing with subordinates and rivals alike from an attitude of natural suspicion, assuming that every man envied his wealth and wished him ill. It was a jaundiced view of life, granted, but it had kept him reasonably safe and he had prospered. After letting down his guard with Napier and Lin Mak, though, Andrastus had been swept along by a tide of events beyond his control, reduced to the status of a hanger-on while Napier called the shots.

No more.

His mind made up, Andrastus had only to speak with his chief of security and the arrangements would be made. Tomorrow after breakfast should be soon enough. He would give Napier one last night to scheme and come up with a plan to save himself, to salvage their design. If no such brainstorm visited the oilman overnight, he would be dead before the stroke of noon, buried at sea with Lin Mak to keep him company.

Good riddance.

After they were gone, Andrastus would still have some minor housecleaning to do, shredding some documents, eliminating sundry inconvenient witnesses, but that could wait. Without Napier and Mak, nothing of substance linked him to the plan that had gone sour. If and when the Greek authorities were moved to question him, he would acknowledge doing business on occasion with the CEO of Global Petroleum, but he wasn't accountable for Napier's madness or his movements. Who on Earth could say Christos Andrastus was responsible for any scheme hatched in America, halfway around the world?

No one.

At last he felt relaxed enough to sleep. A long, hot shower finished off the transformation, sluicing his worries away, leaving Andrastus clean and at peace.

Let the others cringe from nightmares, tossing in their beds.

They had brought the trouble upon themselves.

An innocent man had nothing to fear, as long as his money held out.

BOLAN STOOD at the boat's starboard rail, beside the wheelhouse, scanning the dark Mediterranean for running lights, watching the sky for aircraft. He and McCarter were concerned about an ambush at sea, but there'd been no reasonable alternative to an amphibious landing on Thyra. Dropping in by parachute would have placed them even more at risk, with no ready means of withdrawal, and even the sleepiest sentries would've been roused by a helicopter flying in to drop a strike team on the island.

This way, at least, he thought they had a fighting chance. They would approach without lights, the wind in their faces, and kill the engines far enough from shore to keep from tipping their hand. The run to the beach would be grueling, all three paddling like mad in the dark, expecting searchlights and muzzle-flashes at any moment, but if their luck held out a little longer, they would have dry land beneath their feet again and he could go to work.

The Executioner could do what he did best.

Bolan had faith in his compatriots and in himself. He trusted Jack to follow orders and hightail it out of there if they went down, get word to Hal from Athens that the play had fallen through. What happened after that was someone else's worry. He could safely leave that task to other minds and other ready hands.

The Med was calm this night, without a cloud to interrupt his view of moon and stars. Out here, away from land, there were no artificial lights to dim the heavenly display. If not for the cruiser's laboring engine, he could have imagined himself a seafarer from ages long past, perhaps viewing this bit of the world before any other living man. If he unrolled one of the sailing charts from those days, he would find it decorated with great coiling serpents, above the legend Here Be Monsters.

That much, at least, was still true. There were monsters ahead, waiting at their destination, more deadly than any reptile ever imagined by superstitious sailors of old. The human predators were always worse—more calculating and malicious, killing their own kind for sport or profit, slaying even when they didn't need the meat to keep themselves alive.

Napier and his cronies had conspired to kill thousands, perhaps millions, and for what? Among them, they already had more cash than any normal person could spend in a hundred lifetimes. What malignant soul-rot possessed them to plot genocide in pursuit of more money, more glitter and gloss?

Bolan knew his enemies, but at a deeper level he supposed that he would never truly understand them. Some of those he'd opposed in the past fought for power, land or a philosophy that promised great rewards in some elusive afterlife for those who spilled sufficient blood on Earth. He understood the predators who acted out of hunger, for revenge or jealousy, to sate some dark, aberrant hunger within themselves. Even sexual sadists had a motive he could comprehend, however twisted it might be.

But when the filthy rich conspired to kill for cash alone, money they'd never even live to spend, it made him wonder whether they were truly mad, or if they stood outside the human species somehow, touched by avarice beyond what any normal mind could comprehend.

How much was too much?

This night, Arnold Napier and his coconspirators would learn the answer to that question, but it wouldn't do them any good.

Not in this life.

Mindel appeared beside him, leaning on the rail, a sea breeze running invisible fingers through her hair. "How much longer?" she asked him.

"A couple of hours, I think."

"It's too easy."

"We aren't ashore yet."

"I keep thinking we'll miss them again, miss them forever. I dream of chasing them around the world until we're all in wheelchairs."

"Don't count on it," Bolan replied.

"You think they'll be there, then?"

"I'm not out here to get a tan," he said.

That made her smile for something like two seconds. "I think Uncle Yakov was a lucky man," she said, "to have such friends."

"It didn't do him any good, though," Bolan answered.

"Is that what you think? That he'd say you've failed him?"

Bolan shrugged. "We're always playing catch-up. If I had a crystal ball, we could cancel the game."

"It's never done," she informed him. "We don't even see it all. We never will."

"Philosophy?" he asked her, smiling.

"Just a little." She returned the smile.

"Don't let it get you sidetracked, when we hit the beach."

"I won't," she said. "All business then."

All business, right. And bloody business it would be.

The Executioner could hardly wait.

CHAPTER SIXTEEN

Thyra

The inflatable boat was jet-black and powered by raw muscle, Bolan and McCarter plying its stubby oars while Mindel covered their approach to the island. Nothing stirred on the shingle of beach they'd selected for landing, but there could still be sentries prowling on the bluff above, watching their approach over gun sights and letting them close the range for an easier kill. Each passing second, each stroke of the paddles, brought them closer to the do-or-die moment of contact.

Bolan concentrated on the beach and its white curl of surf, trusting Mindel to cover them if someone ashore started shooting. In that event, retreat to the cruiser would be nearly as dangerous as forging ahead. He'd leave that call until the moment it was inescapable, if anything went wrong.

But nothing did.

They beached the rubber boat and dragged it well clear of the surf, against the sheer face of the bluff, and moored it to a tent peg driven deep. Among them, they were carrying the only gear they had, nothing abandoned at the LZ but the boat itself.

Brognola's satellite photos had made the choice for them, revealing not only the beach but a path from the sand to the crest of the bluff, a steep hike that made them walk hunched forward, muscles burning in their calves and thighs before they made it halfway to the top. It was another point where snipers could've picked them off or pinned them down with virtual impunity, but the defenders missed their chance again.

Dumb luck, or were they finally about to catch a break?

Bolan, on point, slowed his pace to an aching crawl as he neared the high ground. If there were sentries anywhere within a hundred yards, they stood a decent chance of spotting him as he crested the rise. Even black-clad as he was, hands and face darkened with war paint, he would still be a difficult target to miss at close range.

The others hung back as directed, waiting for him to go over the top. When no one greeted him with gunfire, Bolan bellied down and covered the plateau for his companions. In moments they lay prone beside him, one at either hand.

They lay together, charting darkness, listening for any sounds of an approaching enemy. The night wind tickled evergreens along the island's wooded spine, but Bolan didn't reckon it was loud enough to cover the advance of troops.

"All right," he said at last. "Let's go."

They'd planned it out while they were still at sea, using Brognola's photos. They would stay together through the woods, until they were within two hundred yards of the house. From there they would separate, encircling the residence as best they could to approach it from three sides. Triangulated fire should keep the home team hopping.

Bolan hoped it also would make up for any advantage he surrendered by splitting his small force. Above all else, he hoped it wouldn't get the others killed.

The woods were dark and fragrant, their aroma yielding to a man-made smell as Bolan's team drew closer to their destination. The soldier pegged the smell as broiled meat, a draft from the commodore's kitchen. If Andrastus and his guests had eaten well, they might be slower on their feet than usual—whatever usual might be.

One decent shot, the warrior told himself. That's all he needed.

He'd half expected floodlights blazing all around the house, but it was nearly dark, the muted light from curtained windows barely leaking through, as if Andrastus had decided too much light would place his visitors at risk.

Nice try, but no cigar.

"It's time," he told the others. "Any questions now, before we separate?"

Both shook their heads, emphatic negatives.

"Okay. Five minutes, starting…now!"

He stood and watched them vanish into darkness,

Mindel to his left, McCarter to the right. Five minutes wasn't long to wait, after they'd come this far.

Not long at all.

MCCARTER PUSHED his limits, moving through the trees as he circled the house counterclockwise. He stayed within the tree line, but kept the sprawling structure in view, watching for guards along the way. He'd expected more in the way of defense, and his relief felt hollow, as if something about the layout was too simple, too good to be true.

Where were the shooters?

McCarter reviewed the bare-bones statistics on Thyra. The island was shaped like a teardrop, with the broad end—and the Greek's exotic villa—to the east. It was a mile and change in length, from east to west, and some three-quarters of a mile across its widest point, north to south. A small army could maneuver within its confines, and Christos Andrastus employed such an army.

So, where were they now?

More stats, all hypothetical this time. Andrastus had about two hundred shooters on his payroll, if Brognola's information was correct. McCarter guessed that some of them would be dispersed to other stations of his empire, taking care of business. How many for Thyra, then? He couldn't guess, but only a fraction of the total number would be on duty at any given time, the rest held in reserve for an emergency.

Like this one, bloody right.

But if they did the job the way it should be done,

the home team would be taken by surprise, some of them neutralized before they could respond effectively. As for the rest...

One of them stood before him suddenly, a shadow with the glint of metal where an automatic rifle had been slung across one shoulder. Frozen in midstride, McCarter waited for the sentry to sound an alarm, bring others crashing through the trees. It took three agonizing heartbeats for him to decide that he was looking at the shadow-figure's back, and that the gunman hadn't noticed him.

Not yet.

Still time to save it, then, if he was smooth enough.

It seemed to take forever, drawing the Beretta from its holster on his hip. It was muzzle-heavy with the fat suppressor, prompting him to brace it in both hands. McCarter had his mark lined up, a clean shot at the back of the gunner's head, when his target surprised him and stepped out of sight behind a tree to his left.

Bloody hell!

McCarter moved forward, closing the gap. One step, then another. He was afraid to blink, eyes locked on the tree where his mark had disappeared.

Third step.

He felt the twig before he heard it snap, grimacing in anticipation of the sound. It was more of a crunch than a snap, but it carried the five or six yards to the target. Around him, McCarter heard the woods go deathly still.

The shooter stepped back into view, and he was facing toward McCarter now. The glint of metal had been transferred from his shoulder to his hands, the rifle angling toward a target he had yet to recognize.

McCarter hit him with a double tap before the shooter found his mark. Two classic head shots, putting out the lights, but something fired between dying synapses as he fell, the autorifle spitting out a 3-round burst before it kicked free of his lifeless hands.

Dammit!

There would be no five minutes now. His time was up, raised voices in the darkness driving home that point, in case McCarter wasn't clear about it.

"Shit!"

He veered off course and cut a path through ferns and low shrubs, toward the house.

NAPIER WAS SIPPING claret when the burst of gunfire sent a tremor through his body and the wine spilled down his chin, staining his shirt with mock bloodstains. He set the glass down and thrust his trembling hand into a pocket, safely out of sight.

Lin Mak stood frozen at the bar, a bottle tilted toward his waiting glass. "Was that gunfire?"

"It wasn't thunder," Napier said. He made a beeline for the door, was reaching for it when a member of the house staff opened it and poked his head into the game room. Napier snapped at him, "Where's Christos?"

The mercenary eyeballed him with thinly veiled disdain. "If you'll follow me, gentlemen, Mr. Andrastus is waiting."

Napier's bodyguards moved in around him. Four to

one, he liked the odds so far. "I asked you where he is!"

"And I'm prepared to show you, sir, unless you'd rather stand and argue. Frankly, I'm not sure we have much time."

"Time for what?" Napier demanded.

"To keep you alive, sir. Of course, if you'd rather stay here…"

"Lead the way," Napier said.

As the shooter retreated, he told his own men, "Watch that bastard. This could be a trick."

Mak left the bar and rushed to join him as they left the room, two bodyguards in front of them, with two more bringing up the rear. The Asian seemed about to speak, but Napier cut him off, raising a finger to his lips. He strained for any further sounds of gunfire and heard nothing from the night outside. Napier was on the verge of hoping it had been a fluke, the product of a nervous trigger finger, when all hell broke loose.

It sounded as if half a dozen automatic weapons had begun to fire in unison. The sounds were muffled and distorted, but it seemed to Napier that they came from all around him, not just from the south side of the house, where the initial shots had echoed moments earlier.

His bodyguards drew weapons without waiting for the order. They were pros, and knew when it was time to shift from words to action. Napier was encouraged by the hardware in their hands, but he lost the feeling in a hurry when he thought about the odds against them. Andrastus had close to fifty armed men on the island, outnumbering Napier's team by more than ten to one.

So, why were they shooting outside? he asked himself, frowning at the illogic of it. No ruse was required if Andrastus had decided to take them out. Quite the opposite, in fact, since the gunfire put Napier's men on alert, when it would've been easier to lull them with a false sense of security and take them by surprise.

Napier was still grappling with that riddle when their escort brought them to a door, knocked twice and entered without waiting for a summons. Napier urged his shooters through the doorway, following close on their heels. He found Andrastus standing in a room that resembled an arsenal, cradling a semiautomatic shotgun in his arms.

"Christos, what the hell—"

"We have intruders, I'm afraid," the Greek interrupted him. "I see your men are ready. Good. If you need anything before you go, please help yourselves— but quickly, if you will. There may be little time."

"That's twice I've heard that," Napier said. "I don't know what you've got in mind, but—"

"I was thinking of survival," Andrastus told him. "You presumably have no objection on that score?"

"You told me we were safe here, Christos!"

"Safe!" The tardy echo from Lin Mak was pitiful.

Andrastus scanned their faces with his clear gray eyes, a thin smile turning up the corners of his mouth. "Unfortunately," he replied, "it seems I was mistaken."

THE TROOPS WERE in a hurry, rushing through the forest, chasing sounds of gunfire. It was only natural for them to overlook the woman dressed in black, her face darkened by cosmetics, crouching in the shadows off to one side of the trail. They could've been forgiven for the oversight, but there was no forgiveness in the cards this night.

Rebecca Mindel let them pass her by, then shot them from behind. Two short bursts from her Kalashnikov dropped the runners sprawling on their faces. There was nothing fair about it, but she wouldn't lose five minutes' sleep over the dead. They'd chosen sides and paid the price for their mistake, while others waited for the chance to try their hand.

Mindel moved out, tracking the sounds of combat, wondering if Blanski or McCarter had run afoul of the Greek's private army. She hoped they were both still alive, but whatever befell them, she had work to do.

More lights were coming on around the house, blazing under the eaves and along flagstone walks, through the garden and over the large swimming pool. The glare picked out soldiers in silhouette, sprinting here and there to their duty stations, communicating by hand signals in lieu of spoken words. Mindel admired their efficiency, in the abstract, but it wouldn't stop her from killing them if they gave her half a chance.

Rapid firing away to her right marked the point where Blanski should have been. He was catching hell from the sound of it, and giving as good as he got. The storm of fire drew several defenders away from their stations, rushing to join in the action, and Mindel took advantage of the gap in their line, working closer to the house.

She pushed off from the tree line, jogging across the neatly manicured lawn, cutting glances to left and right as she ran. She was halfway to the patio and pool before anyone seemed to notice, and then a shout went up from a lookout posted near a utility shed, some fifty feet beyond the pool.

He rose, still shouting for assistance, shouldering his weapon as Mindel dropped into a crouch. Her stubby AKSU had the same range as its parent AK-74, but the much shorter barrel made long-distance accuracy a challenge. Mindel took the extra second to frame her target in the rifle's sights before she squeezed the trigger, stitching him with half a dozen rounds from close to ninety feet away.

The impact pitched him over backward, rattling the shed, leaving broad crimson smears on beige paint as the dead man surrendered to gravity, slithering down to the turf. It bought her time, but not enough to dawdle, as his backup caught the drift of what was happening and moved to close the trap. A couple of the stragglers running off toward Blanski's stretch of the perimeter turned back, cursing, to find a target they could see.

Choices.

She could retreat and seek cover in the woods, or press on over open ground to reach the house. It was no choice at all, to Mindel's mind. Running and firing from the hip, cursing her enemies in Hebrew as she

charged, Mindel advanced on her objective—on the
men who'd killed her uncle and could never wash the
bloodstains from their hands.

CHRISTOS ANDRASTUS let his houseman lead the way,
followed by half a dozen mercenaries, six more bringing up the rear behind his party of seven. The Greek's
first impulse had been to kill Napier's bodyguards
while the oilman watched, then fling Napier and Lin
Mak into the night, let them live or die on their own,
but his rational mind had won out, reminding him that
his partners might still be useful as bargaining chips.
Alive, perhaps they could be traded for his own safe
passage. Dead...

Well, there was always time for that.

His predecessor on the island had been paranoid—
with good reason, as it turned out—and one of his
architectural surprises was an escape tunnel leading
from the house to a separate garage. Cars were unnecessary on Thyra, where a healthy man could walk
the island's length in twenty minutes, but the garage
housed a variety of smaller vehicles, including three
electric carts for hauling luggage from the pier up to
the house. More importantly, the garage was located
downhill from the house and a hundred yards distant,
invisible from the villa proper and outside the perimeter of gunfire now circling his home.

If Andrastus could make it that far, with his escort
intact, he had a chance of reaching the *Aristotle* and
sailing away from Thyra before his enemies noticed.
Napier and Mak were welcome to come along for the

ride, but they'd be disembarking before he reached Athens, along with their gunmen.

He would give them to the Med.

Bon appétit!

They reached the kitchen pantry, with its special cupboard slotted in among the others. Andrastus nodded to his houseman, watching Napier's face as the cupboard was opened, a secret catch released, and the entire wall of shelves swung outward to reveal a narrow staircase leading downward into darkness. At the touch of a switch, fluorescent lights flared to illuminate the staircase and the tunnel mouth below.

"You're kidding, right?" Napier asked.

"Hardly," Andrastus said. "It's our way out, to safety. If you'd rather stay and fight, of course, I'll understand."

"No, thank you!" Mak replied.

"Where does this go?" Napier demanded, still suspicious.

"It will take us, indirectly, to the *Aristotle*."

"Indirectly?"

"Tunneling between the house and harbor proved too difficult, I'm told. We're wasting precious time, Arnold."

"So we just sail away?"

"A simple cruise," Andrastus said. "We can return after my people deal with the intruders."

"If they do."

"Have faith, my friend. And hurry, if you please."

"You first," Napier replied.

"Of course."

Andrastus let his houseman lead the way, then followed him downstairs, the shotgun heavy in his hands. Behind him followed Mak and Napier, with their armed contingent, mercenaries bringing up the rear to cut off any last-minute retreat.

They reached the bottom of the stairs and stood before the tunnel's mouth. Even with lights, it still remained an uninviting place—a serpent's yawning throat.

"I don't like tunnels," Napier groused.

"By all means, go back to the game room, then," Andrastus said, "and make yourself at home."

"You said this place was safe!"

Andrastus let the final trace of warmth bleed from his voice. "It always has been in the past. I'm forced to ask myself how we were found. Perhaps you left a trail, my friend? Perhaps you're not as careful and efficient as you claim to be?"

"Now, wait a min—"

Andrastus cut him off. "You have a choice to make, Arnold. Accompany me or stay behind. In either case, make up your mind. I won't stand here and argue while your enemies draw closer every minute."

"*My* enemies? Listen, Chris—"

"Stay or go. Decide now."

Napier glared at him, furious, struggling to control his rage. "Let's go, dammit!" he said at last. "Lead on."

"A wise choice," Andrastus said as he turned and stepped into the tunnel's mouth.

LIN MAK DIDN'T like tunnels, either, but he had seen the futility of arguing with Andrastus about their escape route, the folly of remaining behind while gunfire raked the house and grounds. In spirit, he was already aboard the *Aristotle,* though he'd never seen the yacht and had to draw details from his imagination.

Anything, he realized, was better than remaining in this shooting gallery where every passing moment brought him closer to untimely death.

If he survived the night, Mak vowed, he would have nothing more to do with Napier or Andrastus. He would slip away from them at the first opportunity and fly to Switzerland, where he had ample cash and travel papers in three different names. Asia was lost to him, but that still left five continents, a world in which to lose himself and spend the rest of his life in reasonable comfort without dreading every telephone call, each knock on the door.

They might hunt him at first, the Chinese or his two erstwhile partners, but Mak had faith in his ability to throw the trackers off his scent. The trick would be escaping from Thyra, then ditching Napier and the Greek before they could draw him into another mad scheme. He hoped that it wasn't too late already, but he couldn't concentrate on that.

Not yet.

Mak needed all of his resolve and courage to survive the next few hours.

The dirt and concrete overhead muted sounds of gunfire as they passed beneath the battlefield, but Lin Mak still flinched when an explosion sent its shock waves rippling through the earth. Another followed seconds later, closer still.

"Grenades?" Napier asked, speaking to his nearest bodyguard.

"Sounds like it, sir."

"Jesus!"

"We're almost there," Andrastus said without a backward glance.

"I hope so. Christ, I didn't know you were one of the freaking mole people!"

"You surprise me, Arnold."

"Oh, yeah? How's that?"

"So high-strung," Andrastus said. "So nervous all the time. I'm amazed you've come this far in business."

"High-strung, my ass! Let these wild men chase *you* for a couple of weeks, and we'll see how calm *you* are."

"I trust that won't be necessary," the Greek replied. "We should be able to resolve this matter tonight, once and for all."

Mak wasn't sure he liked the sound of that, the way Andrastus said it, but he kept his mouth shut. They had almost reached the downward sloping tunnel's end, he saw now. Up ahead, another short staircase led to a door around eye-level. He imagined fresh air in his nostrils, hoping that it wouldn't smell of cordite.

"Here we are," Andrastus announced, as they reached the foot of the staircase.

"Where's 'here'?" Napier asked him.

"Have patience, my friend. It won't be long now."

Mak hoped Napier wouldn't ask, "*What* won't be long?" He feared Andrastus might answer and spoil any chance of survival Mak cherished. If they could just climb out of the tunnel and find—

Find what?

He didn't know what to expect, but the Greek's houseman was mounting the stairs now, pistol in hand, and opening the door. He checked whatever lay beyond, stepping across the silent threshold, then came back and waved for the others to follow.

Moments later, Mak found himself standing inside some sort of garage. In place of normal cars, however, the rectangular building was filled wall-to-wall with motorcycles, four-wheel all-terrain vehicles, and several larger vehicles resembling golf carts.

Napier surveyed their choice of getaway machines and shook his head. "What this? We're going golfing now?"

"Mind your manners, Arnold," the Greek scolded him. "You know there's no golf course on Thyra."

"Mind my— Why, you—"

Grim-faced now, Andrastus racked the shotgun's slide and turned to face Napier. The oilman's bodyguards surged forward, cocking weapons of their own. Another heartbeat found them ringed by more guns, ready to explode. Mak closed his eyes and wished he knew a simple prayer.

"Is this the way you want to end it, Arnold?" Andrastus asked. "I'd have thought you were intelligent enough to save yourself, at least."

"What are we doing, then?"

"I've answered that already. We'll be going to the *Aristotle*."

"What, on these things?"

"Yes, unless you'd rather walk."

"I'm getting fed up with being surprised, Christos. That's the bottom line."

"Then let us hope the enemies you've led to my doorstep will stop surprising you." Napier had no response to that, glaring past Lin Mak until Andrastus waved them toward the nearest golf cart. Putting on a brittle smile, the Greek said, "Gentlemen, please take your seats."

AROUND THE TIME guns started going off, Grimaldi decided he couldn't sit offshore and watch the party from a distance. He'd already scoped the north side of the island through a pair of field glasses that had been left aboard the rented cruiser, picking out the yacht anchored in a sort of harbor there. It sat a hundred yards offshore and something like a half mile from the house atop the island's highest ground.

There was a risk involved, of course, and Bolan would be pissed off at his deviation from the plan. There'd be hell to pay if he blew it, but Grimaldi liked the odds. No lights at all were showing on the yacht, which told him that the crew had either gone ashore or was sacked out for the night. Smart money said the crewmen would've used a launch to go ashore, after the passengers off-loaded and they finished their last-minute chores.

Perfect.

It would've helped to have some LAW rockets aboard the cruiser, maybe a grenade launcher, but Grimaldi thought he could make do with his AKSU and a couple of thermite grenades he'd squirreled away from their purchase in Athens, anticipating a possible need to torch the rented boat when they were finished with it. Now, he thought, the incendiaries might be put to better use.

Grimaldi hadn't spent much time at sea, but the cruiser's controls were rudimentary. He'd had plenty of practice on the trip out from Athens, getting used to the console before he had to manage under fire, with friends depending on him. As he turned for shore now, all that really troubled him was the possibility of an armed watchman dozing on board the yacht, or the greater likelihood of his being spotted by lookouts ashore.

In either case, he guessed it wouldn't matter now that battle had been joined on Thyra and the feces had most definitely hit the fan.

Grimaldi whistled as he steered the cruiser toward his target, a tune out of nowhere, cutting it off when he recognized the theme song from *Gilligan's Island*. He wasn't superstitious—no more than any other pilot, at least—but there was such a thing as tempting fate.

And at the moment, Grimaldi needed all the luck he could get.

Pulling into the small cove, he throttled back and brought the cruiser slowly in beside the yacht. He left some twenty feet between the vessels, eyeballing the decks for any sign of movement now, but all the action seemed to be ashore, where grenade blasts had joined the staccato sounds of gunfire. If there was anyone aboard the yacht, Grimaldi reasoned, they'd have been awake and topside by now, checking out the fireworks.

He cocked the AKSU and left its safety off, slinging the short rifle over his shoulder for easy access. Grimaldi left the cruiser idling in neutral and palmed the two thermite grenades as he left the wheelhouse, stepping up to the boat's starboard railing. The ghostly white yacht—*Aristotle,* he saw from its name on the bow—rode silently at anchor, almost close enough to touch.

He pulled the first grenade's pin and flicked it over the side, cocking his arm for a pitch toward the pleasure craft's stern. That's where the fuel would be, he reasoned, or close enough. Once the thermite got started, it would burn through decks and bulkheads as if they were cardboard, until it found sea water and turned it to steam.

"Fire in the hole!" Grimaldi told the night, and tossed the grenade.

BOLAN WAS pinned down, still forty yards out from the house. He lay behind a tree, hugging the turf, while interlocking fire from three or four automatic weapons chewed up the soil and undergrowth about him, sprinkling him with leaves and shredded bark.

The home team had reacted more cohesively than he'd expected when the shooting started from McCarter's section of the line. He'd shown himself, emerging from the trees and moving toward the villa, but the mercs had come from nowhere, nearly tagging him before he scuttled back to cover under fire.

Whatever happened in the next few minutes, Bolan thought the Greek had got his money's worth.

At one level, it seemed a shame to kill such men, but they had chosen sides—the wrong one, in this case—and they were standing in his way. Because there was no way around them, he would have to take them down, unless one of them caught a lucky break and tagged him first.

Risking a glance around the tree, Bolan drew fire and jerked back, swiping mulch and sawdust from his eyes. Too close. But if he couldn't even spot his targets, how could he return fire and reduce their numbers?

Shake them up. That was how.

He carried the grenades clipped to his belt, around in back, to spare unnecessary bruising if he had to belly down, like now. Bolan ignored the frags and chose one of the thermite canisters. It wasn't made for antipersonnel work, but he knew he wouldn't have a chance to drop it on his enemies precisely. Shrapnel from a frag grenade was limited in range, and much of it flew upward when the charge exploded in an open space, like the expansive lawn in front of him. White phosphorus, by contrast, gave off smoke and heat; its flash was certain to distract his adversaries for a moment, even if it didn't singe their flesh.

He yanked the pin and made a sidearm pitch, lobbing the canister some forty feet in front of him and toward the house. He counted seconds, got to *six* before it blew and someone started screaming near ground zero, shrieking from the very pit of Hell.

Dumb luck, he thought, and rolled out to his left, around the east side of the tree. Somehow he'd caught one of the shooters in the open, maybe rushing up to take him by surprise, the tables turned when the white-hot flash enveloped him. The guy was dancing now, a crazy reel across the lawn, beating at flames an ocean wouldn't quench. Thermite would burn in water, underground, in outer space. It was the Devil's breath, and there was no escape.

Bolan let the flaming scarecrow run, seeking his comrades. One of them was kneeling on the grass, some thirty feet away, gaping in horror as his sidekick stumbled past. Before he could recover his composure, Bolan hit him with a 3-round burst and put him down for good.

That left one more, at least. Bolan spied him off to the right, dodging through a haze of chemical smoke, making a run for the tree line. The Executioner led the runner, craning for the shot, and cut his legs from under him with a burst of 5.45 mm rounds. The gunman fell across his line of fire, twitching as Bolan stroked the AKSU's trigger one more time to finish it.

He rose, preparing to advance across the smoking lawn, but froze there, as an unfamiliar sound came from his flank. What was that?

Turning toward the noise, he saw a four-wheeled ATV burst into view, swerving along a paved track through the trees, running downhill, in the direction of the shoreline. Two more came behind it, gunmen in the saddle, and behind the ATVs a pair of golf carts, their electric motors purring.

Bolan saw a Chinese face turned toward the house, toward him, before the first cart vanished on its downhill run. Lin Mak?

Who else?

Cursing, the Executioner ran after the retreating vehicles. He barked into his headset, telling Mindel and McCarter what had happened, no idea if either one could hear him or if they were even still alive.

He ran into the night, chasing the sound of engines toward the sea.

CHAPTER SEVENTEEN

"Heads up! Our targets are running on wheels toward the bay!" Bolan announced. "I'm in pursuit!"

McCarter cursed, slamming a fresh magazine into his Kalashnikov's receiver and jacking the slide. Huddled behind a massive poolside barbecue constructed out of brick and black wrought iron, he wondered what he was supposed to do next.

How many of their targets were escaping? All of them? Should he fall back and join the chase? More to the point, *could* he withdraw, while three or four opponents sprayed his precarious cover with gunfire?

He began by assuming that Bolan knew what he was saying. If Bolan had glimpsed only one of their primary targets in flight, he'd have used the mark's name and no plural description.

All three, then. Bloody hell!

A continued assault on the house was pointless, but that didn't change McCarter's situation. Before he could retreat and join the chase, he'd have to take out those who'd pinned him down with streams of interlocking fire.

They were using submachine guns, all 9 mm by the

sound of them, at least two firing from inside the house, while another lay behind a kind of cabana, belly down on the pavement and sniping at McCarter across the deep end of the swimming pool. Engaging any one of them meant exposing himself to another, unless...

When in doubt, go all out.

McCarter calculated distance while he unclipped a thermite grenade from his belt. Call it twenty feet from his position to the glass doors facing on the patio, where two or more of his enemies had gone to ground. They posed the greater threat, with concentrated firepower, and McCarter also recognized that his incendiary device would have a greater impact on the house than on bare concrete and tile.

He hefted the grenade, rehearsing the pitch mentally before he pulled the pin and lobbed the canister overhand toward the house. It didn't have to land directly on his targets, or even penetrate the house, but the closer it came to his marks, the more effective it would be.

McCarter heard someone shout a warning before the grenade went off with a crump and a whoosh, spewing smoke and white-hot coals that stuck and burned on impact, searing flesh, fabric, plaster—any substance known to man, in short.

The screaming started instantly, along with warning shouts in Greek that he took to mean, "Fire! Save your ass!" McCarter rolled out to the right of the barbecue, tracking voices with his Kalashnikov, keeping the brickwork between himself and the cabana gunner.

Peering through the smoke, he saw that one of his adversaries had taken a thermite hit, rolling on the floor and bashing at his torso with both hands, while the other was up and retreating to safety.

McCarter helped the second shooter reach his final destination with a short burst to the spine that punched him through the pall of smoke and out of sight. He crab-walked back to see how the cabana shooter liked the fireworks, ducking as another burst of Parabellum stingers rattled past his face.

Dammit! The bastard hadn't budged.

All right, then. If it worked once, he would try the same again.

This time, McCarter palmed a frag grenade and drew the pin, holding the safety spoon firmly in place. Again, it didn't matter if the egg was dead on target, but he had to get it past the swimming pool and reasonably close to the cabana, or the effort would be wasted. Fifty feet was no great challenge, but he would be pitching blind, from cover, and he had to pin the distance down or risk meeting a storm of deadly fire when he emerged to finish it.

He made the toss, hoping he'd got it right, waiting for the blast and storm of shrapnel to pass before he broke cover, rushing the cabana in a sprint. The shooter from the home team wasn't wounded, but he'd ducked long enough to keep from getting stung. Returning to his vantage point, he blinked to find his target closing fast and tried to use his Uzi SMG.

Too late.

McCarter stitched him with a rising burst that laid

the shooter on his back, awash in blood. McCarter fell
back, running across the patio and into the trees, seeking a shortcut that would take him to Thyra's harbor.

THE GOLF CART VEERED around a corner, nearly pitching Lin Mak from his seat. He clutched the cushion
underneath him, hands like talons threatening to rip
the vinyl upholstery. Beside him, Napier sat hunched
forward on the small bench seat. His bodyguards were
in the next cart back, electric motor whirring as it
raced along behind them.

They had covered roughly half the distance from
the garage to the beach, a trio of mercenaries leading
the procession on their snorting ATVs. Christos Andrastus sat beside the driver of Mak's cart, the shotgun
braced across his lap. Behind them, sounds of battle
raged around the villa, gunfire and explosions wreak-
ing havoc with the night.

"Security!" Napier jeered at their host. "You call
this security?"

Andrastus answered without turning in his seat. "I
call it your responsibility, and I grow tired of your
complaints."

"Oh, really?"

Mak placed a hand on Napier's rigid arm. The oilman turned on him, livid, but seemed to think better
of his next comment when Mak shook his head, a
silent warning.

Not now, he thought, desperately. Not here.

They were in enough danger already, without forcing a quarrel and spilling blood among themselves.

The argument would better be resolved some other time, when they weren't at imminent risk of being shot or blown to smithereens.

"How long before we reach the pier?" Mak asked, hoping he could distract Andrastus.

"We are almost there."

And so they were. The Greek had barely spoken when their paved track left the trees and leveled off to parallel a beach. Mak craned his neck to see ahead and recognized the dock where they had landed only hours earlier. Offshore, the *Aristotle* waited for them, dark and silent, with a smaller craft positioned off her port side, amidships.

"Christos!" Mak pointed, leaning forward as their cart sped toward the pier. "Shouldn't the other boat come in and...and..."

"Pick us up," Mak meant to say, but then he saw the motor launch they'd used to come ashore, still moored against the pier. Before he fully understood, Andrastus had begun to rage in Greek, raising his shotgun and aiming off across the harbor.

Napier recoiled from that anger. "Christos, what the hell?"

Andrastus fired a shotgun blast, Mak gaping in shock as a fireball erupted near the *Aristotle*'s stern. He was amazed the shot could reach that far, much less do so much damage to the mighty vessel.

A second explosion rocked the yacht an instant later, no shot from Andrastus this time. The *Aristotle*'s stern was all ablaze now, flames reflected on the water for a hundred yards around. Andrastus muttered something coarse, then slapped his driver's arm and pointed toward the pier, urging him to greater speed.

"I'm driving as fast as this damn thing will go!" the driver snapped, his head swiveling as he searched for enemies on the beach, or at the tree line above them.

They reached the pier seconds later, as the great yacht shuddered with yet another explosion. This one seemed to emanate from somewhere deep belowdecks, the vessel listing to port and settling deeper in the water. From his seat in the cart, Mak saw the smaller boat swinging clear of the stricken yacht, some of their enemies pulling away as the Greek's mercenaries opened fire from shore.

"Enough!" Andrastus bawled, moving among them and slapping their guns down. "They're out of range!"

"Okay," Napier demanded, "what's Plan B?"

"To stay alive," Andrastus answered, "and avoid our enemies ashore until more transport can be summoned."

"What about the launch?"

"Be my guest," the Greek said. "It has fuel enough for ten or twelve miles, then you drift."

"I'll take my chances, Christos."

"Yes, my friend, you will." The mercenaries closed ranks with Andrastus as he spoke, blocking Napier and his four men from the pier. "But you will take them here, with us."

BOLAN KNEW he couldn't outrun speeding ATVs, and while it might've been a toss-up with the golf carts over a limited distance, they had a lead he couldn't close by sticking to the paved road they were following. Instead, after some fifty yards, he took a chance and veered off through the trees, crashing down the slope toward where he knew the Med lay waiting for him, dark and still.

It was a gamble, since he didn't know this part of the terrain and none of it was clearly visible on the satellite photos he'd studied, the sloping ground concealed under treetops, hidden from a prying eye outside the stratosphere. For all he knew there could be trip wires, gullies, muddy slopes waiting to spill him weaponless, with broken bones, down to the beach.

And still he ran, trusting the pull of gravity to give him extra speed. Sprinting downhill was always faster, if a runner didn't twist a knee or snap his ankle, trip on something in the undergrowth and crack his skull against a tree or stone. It wasn't skiing, granted, but he made good time, angling across the slope as he descended, making for the pier that had to be the jumping-off point for his targets' flight by water.

When he was halfway down the wooded slope, a series of explosions echoed from somewhere in front of him. The house was at his back and well above him, telling Bolan that the blasts had emanated from somewhere at sea, north of the island. He immediately thought of Jack Grimaldi on the cruiser, wondering if a patrol boat had surprised him after all, or if he'd run too close to shore and met disaster from a lookout with some weapon that could reach him from the beach.

When he was near the bottom of the slope, Bolan saw firelight through the trees, reflecting on the harbor's glassy surface. From the tree line he could see the source, a once great vessel now engulfed in flame for nearly half its length and plainly sinking. Water boiled around the stern, as if the hull was breached and flooding her belowdecks, but it couldn't quench the fire topside.

Even from a distance, Bolan recognized the smell and glare of thermite, and he glimpsed the cruiser nosing out of firelight, into darkness there, beyond the breakwater.

Grimaldi, right—but he wasn't the victim in this piece. He was the player who exceeded his directions and, at least this time, might well have saved the day.

Three hundred yards downrange, he saw the carts and ATVs parked on the grass and sand around the pier. He didn't bother counting heads. However many of his enemies were there, Bolan would have to take them all. If Mindel and McCarter couldn't help him, then he'd try it on his own.

As if in answer to the thought, a voice came through the earpiece of his headset. "On my way," McCarter grated, fairly panting with exertion. "Have you caught them yet?"

"They're at the pier," Bolan said. "Jack scuttled their ride."

"Good job! I'm there in five, if you can leave me some."

"No promises," Bolan responded, as he started down the beach.

It troubled him that they'd heard nothing more from Mindel, but he didn't chase the thought to its extreme conclusion. There could be any number of reasons for her continued silence, besides death or a crippling wound. Bolan refused to write her off so easily, but neither could he count on her for help right now, when their primary targets stood before him and he found himself alone. Even McCarter's five minutes might put him on the scene too late, if Napier and the others had a backup plan in place.

But they were arguing among themselves. He saw it now, drawing encouragement from the delay that let him close the gap between them. It would be too much to hope they'd shoot each other while he watched, but if they only stalled a little longer, he could reach them and—

Too late.

A small, frustrated sound breached Bolan's throat as his quarry began piling back into their vehicles, engines revving in the night.

Desperate, refusing to be left behind, he found more speed somewhere inside himself, sprinting through dappled moonlight toward the pier.

ANDRASTUS WATCHED Napier recoil from him. The oilman glared, saying, "So this is how you treat your partners?"

"Those who bring the devil to my doorstep and then try to run away, perhaps," the Greek replied. "You're fortunate I care enough to save you from yourself."

"Don't do me any favors, Christos," Napier answered.

"We have a chance to stay alive," Andrastus said, "but not at sea with three or four men drifting in a boat, where they already have a vessel waiting. Stop and think! I know a man on Crete, a helicopter pilot. He will come for us if I ask him."

"And how'd you plan to do that?" Napier challenged. "Shout across the ocean?"

Andrastus smiled and slipped the cell phone from his pocket. "You surprise me, Arnold. I assumed you'd be familiar with the marvels of technology."

Napier relaxed a little, but not much. "All right, so make your call. But can we do it on the move? I don't like standing here, where any bastard with a piece can pick us off."

He had a point. Andrastus nodded toward the carts and watched his men fan out, still watching Napier's bodyguards in case they tried to rush the launch. To Napier's credit, he turned back and climbed into the golf cart that had brought them to the pier, Lin Mak reluctantly seated beside him.

"Follow the beach due west," Andrastus told his driver. "Give me time to make the call."

The cart lurched into motion for a jerky start, rear wheels digging briefly at the sand, then they were moving. Andrastus let the shotgun rest across his lap, glancing back at the *Aristotle*'s flaming hulk as he punched the number into his cell phone and listened to it ring three, four, five times before a sleepy male voice answered in Greek.

Andrastus identified himself and began to issue curt instructions, silencing the other party's questions with a sharp command for silence and attention. He was nearly finished when the golf cart's driver, to his left, cried out and slumped forward over the steering wheel.

Andrastus heard the shots a second later, coming from behind him. Still clutching the cell phone, he spun in his seat, quick enough to spot a gunman sprinting after them along the beach. Muzzle-flashes from his weapon marked the runner's progress, all the more impressive as the golf cart drifted to a halt.

Andrastus shouted after his bodyguards, pulling away on their ATVs, engines revving. How could they miss the sound of riflefire? Andrastus triggered two quick shotgun blasts that brought them back, making U-turns on the beach and narrowly avoiding collisions with one another, like members of some inept motorcycle drill team.

"Get back there and stop that bastard!" he raged at them, sending them back the way they'd come, eastward. He didn't know if they could do the job or not, but at least they could slow down his enemies, give Andrastus a chance to—

Do what?

Run away!

He used the shotgun as a lever, shoving his flunky out of the cart and scooting across to the driver's seat. Calling over his shoulder to Napier and Mak, he said, "Hang on! We're not done yet!"

It crossed his mind that they were deadweight now, slowing the cart, but then Andrastus thought of them as shields, a fleshy wall to block his adversary's aim, and he felt better about taking them along for the ride. The second cart fell in behind him, racing west along the beach through darkness, looking for a place to hide.

IT WAS A FLUKE that saved Rebecca Mindel's life but cut her off from the remainder of her team. The bullet missed her face by fractions of an inch, came close enough to warm her cheek in passing, causing her to recoil and return fire, a long burst from her AKSU making the sniper dance before he collapsed in a lifeless heap.

Before the surprise exchange, she'd heard Blanski calling for backup. "Heads up! Our targets are running on wheels toward the bay! I'm in pursuit!" Now, when Mindel tried to answer him, she found a snapped-off sprig of wire and plastic where her microphone had been a moment earlier.

"Dammit!"

She left the dead man where he'd fallen and the house in flames, retreating toward the island's northern shoreline. It struck her as bad business, leaving sentries still alive around the house, but they were pawns and strictly low priority. If Napier and the other VIPs were slipping through the net, her place was with the other members of her team, to stop their quarry from escaping one more time.

It seemed a long run to the beach, though it was downhill nearly all the way, no farther than a quarter mile. She had to watch her step, afraid of crippling injuries, and twice froze in her tracks to listen hard for any sign that she had been pursued. When there was none, she ran on through the trees and darkness.

The sounds of combat kept Mindel on course. A series of explosions, sounding far-off in the distance, told her battle had been joined. Moments later, gunfire echoed from the beach, joined by the ratchet sounds of off-road vehicles as she drew closer to the tree line. Finally, as Mindel cleared the last twenty yards, she could see muzzle-flashes, bobbing headlight beams and the reflected glow of fire on water.

What?

Dismissing it, she burst through the tree line in time to see four all-terrain vehicles roar past her, weaving zigzag patterns on the sand as they raced toward a lone figure standing away to her right.

Blanski?

She knew it had to be, and her next action was automatic. Swiveling to track the ATVs, Mindel triggered a burst from her Kalashnikov that spilled the nearest rider from his saddle. The four-wheeled vehicle ignored his passing and ran on without him, albeit losing speed and swerving toward the surf without a sentient hand to guide it.

The remaining hunters missed her entry to the battle, so intent were they on riding down their target. All of them were firing at Blanski now, the black-clad warrior answering in kind as he dodged toward the tree line and cover.

Mindel stepped farther out onto the sand and raised her weapon, sighting down the barrel after her retreating enemies. The next nearest was rising from his seat, firing at Blanski with a stubby SMG—an MP-5 K or a mini-Uzi, she supposed. Bracing the AKSU's folding stock against her shoulder, Mindel triggered a burst that ripped into her target's shoulder and sent his weapon cartwheeling across the sand, while he slumped across the ATV's handlebars.

Still the shooter hung on, fighting for control of his vehicle and grappling it to a halt on the sand. Slumping to his left, he dropped from the saddle and put the ATV between them, shielding himself for a moment while he tried to draw a pistol left-handed.

Mindel didn't give him time to get there. Holding down the AKSU's trigger, she drilled the fuel tank and sent gasoline splashing across the hot engine, onto the sand. It might have flared spontaneously, but she wasn't taking any chances. Another burst threw sparks from the ATV's engine block and the gas went up in a rolling fireball, the remainder in the tank detonating like an incendiary grenade.

She heard the wounded gunner screaming, vaulting to his feet and headed for the surf in a clumsy, shambling run. Mindel used the last half-dozen rounds in her weapon to drop him short of the water, then ditched the empty magazine and fed a fresh one into the receiver.

She faced eastward, in time to see Bolan finish the last of the mounted assassins. The tall man moved to join her, Mindel staying where she was and glancing backward, to the west, where a pair of golf carts were fast receding out of range.

"The VIPs are all aboard there," Bolan told her, as he closed the gap. "We have to catch them."

Sudden crashing from the tree line brought them both around, twin weapons tracking toward the source of sound. They recognized McCarter almost simultaneously, muzzles lifting as he crossed the beach to join them. ⬤

"Bloody hell!" he said. "Don't tell me that I've missed the show."

"Not yet," Bolan replied. "The last act's on the road."

McCarter flashed a grin. "All right! What are we waiting for?"

NAPIER GLANCED BACK fearfully along the beach and saw muzzle-flashes blinking as the last of the ATV riders went down. Fuming, he turned back to Andrastus, himself busy steering the golf cart.

"There goes your strike force, shot to hell," he told the Greek. "Next bright idea?"

"We still have men and guns," Andrastus said over his shoulder. "You give up too easily."

"Give up? In case you hadn't noticed, we just got our asses kicked back there!"

"The helicopter's on its way," Andrastus answered. "We're to meet it at the west end of the island."

"Great! That's if we're still alive, I take it?"

"You can go your own way anytime, Arnold." Andrastus sneered. "I can't slow down for you, of course. Feel free to jump!"

"Just hurry up, goddammit!"

"We're at top speed now. Sit back and close your mouth, or I *will* stop!"

The bastard sounded like he meant it, so Napier shut up. He felt Lin Mak watching him but wouldn't meet his Chinese partner's gaze. Napier had no more slick solutions up his sleeve, and while he hated finding himself at the Greek's mercy, there was no other way off his island of death.

He swiveled in his seat again and looked back toward the pier, then past it to the latest killing ground. Two of the ATVs were moving, and at first it gave him hope, making him think he'd misinterpreted the images his eyes had picked out from the shadows and confusion on the beach. Maybe the Greek's security detachment had been victorious, after all!

That desperate hope vanished as the ATVs came racing after them, running swift and straight along the beach. When the rider in front started shooting at them, automatic fire crackling across his handlebars, Napier knew they were in trouble.

"They're chasing us on your own goddamn bikes!" he told Andrastus. Only sheer will kept him from punching the Greek in the back of his head.

Disbelieving, Andrastus looked back and blinked at their pursuers, then faced forward and bent over the golf cart's steering wheel, as if his posture could gain them extra speed.

Two of Napier's gunmen in the second golf cart were already returning fire, dueling with the ATV riders. Napier leaned across the back of his own cart and shouted to his men, "A hundred thousand dollars to

the man who takes them out! A hundred thousand
each!"

At that, the driver of the second card slammed on
the brakes and grabbed his own weapon, stepping
down from his seat to the sand and turning to face the
enemy. Around him, the others piled out and did likewise, forming a skirmish line across the beach.

"What have you done?" Mak asked him, wild-
eyed.

"Just what it looks like, old son," Napier answered.
"I've bought us some time."

At least he hoped that was the case, but with Andrastus at the wheel he wasn't sure. Their cart seemed
incapable of doing better than twenty or twenty-five
miles per hour, while the ATVs were capable of twice
that speed.

Heedless of the shotgun now, he poked Andrastus
in the ribs and told him, "Hurry up, for Christ's sake!
We don't have all night!"

BOLAN HAD ONE of the ATVs to himself, while Mindel
rode double with McCarter, hunched forward on the
buddy seat and firing past him as they chased their
quarry westward, with the glassy sea off to their right,
dark forest looming on the left. Bolan himself
squeezed off a short one-handed burst but wasn't
happy with the AKSU's kick and concentrated on his
steering as they closed the gap.

He ducked when gunners in the second cart began
returning fire, then switched off his headlight to make
their job harder. Beside him, McCarter did likewise,

while Mindel kept firing short bursts for effect. She hadn't scored yet, as far as Bolan could tell, when the second cart wavered, then lurched to a halt, its passengers hopping out with weapons in hand.

Here we go.

Deprived of options, Bolan braced his Kalashnikov across the ATV's handlebars and started down the beach, McCarter joining in as they raced toward the enemy picket line. Muzzle-flashes winked their Morse code of death as he sped toward the waiting gunmen, bullets zipping past him in the darkness, close enough to pluck his sleeve and whisper in his ear.

Sixty yards. Fifty. Forty.

At thirty and counting, the skirmish line broke, two of the shooters crumpling where they stood, two others breaking for the trees, while the last leaped back into the golf cart and gunned it for safety.

Too late.

Bolan veered toward the tree line and the runners, while McCarter and Mindel rode up on the cart driver's blind side and shot him to tatters, leaving him dead at the wheel. Bolan's targets had given up fighting, but he strafed them anyway, dropping one on the sand, catching the second with a lucky shot just as he reached the trees. Dead or merely wounded, the runner pitched forward into shadow and was gone.

As he swung back from the trees, rejoining the second ATV, Bolan registered the chill sensation of cold liquid splashing his thigh. Not blood, then. A downward glance showed him the clean hole where a bullet had pierced his fuel tank, gasoline jetting out in a simulated arterial spray. Bolan used his teeth to tear a strip of fabric from his sleeve, throttling back while he wadded it up in one hand and wedged it as a makeshift plug into the bullet hole.

It was all he could do, but the ATV's fuel gauge was edging toward empty. He didn't know what kind of mileage the vehicle got, but guessed there was ten or fifteen minutes' worth of fuel left in the tank, at the outside.

So be it.

If he ran dry on the beach, he would continue the pursuit on foot. His quarry wouldn't get away this time because the Executioner sat back and threw his hands up in defeat.

Still driving flat-out at maximum speed, Bolan racked his brain for details of Brognola's satellite photos. He knew that less than half of Thyra's northern coastline featured beaches, the rest a line of rocky crags where breakers threw themselves against sea-scoured stone around the clock. And while he couldn't see the far end of the beach yet, lost in darkness up ahead, he knew his adversaries had to be running out of road.

Encouraged by the thought, he fired another burst at the retreating golf cart, then cranked up the throttle on his ATV to gain more ground. Ahead of him, the cart's driver appeared to panic, swerving toward the tree line for security.

It was a serious mistake.

The cart lost speed and traction all at once, sand spurting from beneath its fat rear tires. The driver tried to gun it and the cart tipped over, not so much rolling as toppling clumsily onto one side, like one of those funny cars driven by clowns in a circus. Bolan slowed as its three occupants scrambled clear, one of them squeezing off a shotgun blast in his general direction.

He couldn't tell if the others were packing, but Bolan took it for granted. Better safe than gut-shot by an "unarmed" man. He gunned the ATV and kicked free of its saddle at the same time, leaving the four-wheeler to roll on without him, losing most of its momentum before it collided with the capsized golf cart.

That provoked another shotgun blast, then Bolan saw his targets scatter, one breaking for the woods, one toward the surf, the third sprinting on down the beach. Afoot, he took the nearest of the three, noting the shotgun in his target's hands. Behind him, Mindel hastily dismounted and pursued the runner who seemed bent on hiding in the sea, McCarter racing on after the third man.

Bolan's adversary triggered two more shotgun charges on his short run to the trees, missing with both, then dropped his empty weapon, drawing something from his belt that could've been a side arm. The Executioner knelt and tracked him with the AKSU, leading just enough to make it count, and cut his target down with half a dozen rounds.

He found Christos Andrastus stretched out on the sand, a cell phone clutched in his right fist. He had no other weapon and the phone was useless to him now, a small voice squawking in Greek from the earpiece until Bolan pried it from the dead man's fingers, spoke two words into the telephone, then pitched it toward the trees.

"Too late."

He didn't know whom Andrastus was trying to reach or what kind of help he'd been seeking, but the Greek was out of business now.

Behind Bolan, a rattle of gunfire from the surf made him turn. He saw Rebecca Mindel wading back to shore, knee-deep in foam, reloading her Kalashnikov.

"Lin Mak," she said, as he approached her. "I guess he thought he could swim back to China."

"How's that working out for him?" Bolan asked.

"Not so well."

They both faced westward, marking the taillights of McCarter's ATV no more than a hundred yards distant. Bolan was already moving in that direction when a high-pitched wail reached his ears, carried on a breeze that smelled of salt and kelp.

They found McCarter thirty yards beyond the ATV, standing atop a bluff that faced the sea. He peered down into thrashing darkness, where the breakers hissed and fumed on jagged rocks.

"Where's Napier?" Bolan asked him.

"Crazy bugger went over the side," McCarter said.

It was a drop of forty feet or so, from where they stood. Bolan leaned over, staring into the void, marking the place where waves drew phosphorescent patterns on the rocks. For just a moment, he imagined a pale face uplifted on the swell, then dashed against the cliff and sucked away. It didn't reappear, and after counting off two minutes he drew back.

He had counted on seeing the oilman dead, but there was nothing to be done about it now. They could drag the sea until doomsday and still find no vestige of Arnold Napier.

Perhaps it was better that way.

"We finished here?" he asked his two companions.

"Suits me," McCarter said.

"Yes," Mindel replied.

Relieved, he keyed his microphone and spoke into the night. "Floater, do you read me?"

"Five by five," Grimaldi answered. "Where and when?"

He cocked an eyebrow at McCarter and Mindel. "The pier?"

"Okay."

"Why not?"

"We could have company along the way," Bolan reminded them.

McCarter grinned and said, "That's their problem."

"The pier," he told Grimaldi, "if you're finished bombing yachts."

Bolan could almost hear Grimaldi smiling as his old friend said, "I'm on my way."

EPILOGUE

Jerusalem

The bus stopped at the summit of Mount Herzel to disgorge its passengers. Every seat had been filled for the ride from downtown Jerusalem, the passengers riding in reverent near silence to their destination. Those who spoke at all did so in whispers, as if fearing to disturb their fellow travelers.

From the bus stop, it was a ten-minute walk over sunbaked pavement to Yad Vashem, the Israeli memorial complex dedicated to Holocaust martyrs and heroes. Bolan made the walk that morning with Rebecca Mindel, David McCarter and Jack Grimaldi, the four of them taking their time while others hurried on to make their guided tour of the facility.

Bolan and his three companions were here on a private errand. They needed no tour guide to show them around or remind them of how they should feel.

Two days had passed since they scourged the island of Thyra with fire, and reports of the event had waffled through a 180-degree rotation, helped along with strategic news leaks from the States and Tel Aviv. Initially, it was reported that Christos Andrastus and a group of unknown guests had been attacked by terrorists and massacred on Thyra, but later accounts suggested the Greek and his visitors had been engaged in some criminal conspiracy—the details left deliberately vague—when competitors from a rival syndicate had crashed the party and wreaked havoc with the home team.

At the moment, while Bolan and his friends approached the solemn Hall of Remembrance, Greek police were scouring Thyra for survivors and evidence of a far-reaching plot that imperiled Greek security and her relationship with Israel. Various employees of the Andrastus shipping empire were already in custody, along with certain executives of Global Petroleum arrested in New York, Jakarta and Cairo.

No mention of a nuclear device or global terrorism reached the press. Charges could always be finessed as the legal proceedings dragged on. Andrastus was already dead, Arnold Napier listed as missing, though no one appeared to be pursuing him. No ID was available for the Chinese national found washed up on the beach a quarter mile west of the point where Andrastus's yacht, the *Aristotle,* had burned and sunk. Beijing, officially, ignored the whole affair, but rumors of a small-scale Party purge in progress were reported by observers in the field to CIA headquarters and the White House.

It was cool inside Yad Vashem's Hall of Names, where some 3.2 million victims of the Nazi Holocaust were memorialized. That still left nearly half of the

Third Reich's Jewish victims unidentified, but the collection of names was ongoing, as it had been since 1955, and would remain in perpetuity. Adjacent to the Hall of Names, another chamber held the Pages of Testimony penned by survivors of those slain, preserved as *mazevoth*—literally "tombstones"—for the dead.

Bolan had toured the Holocaust Museum in Washington and found it moving, but there'd still been something distant about that memorial, built as it was on American soil, so far removed from the scene of the crime. Granted, Jerusalem was nearly as far from the killing fields of Poland, Germany and Russia as the District of Columbia, but Israel itself was a kind of living memorial to the victims of those dark years, lending a greater immediacy to the sacrifice.

"Uncle Yakov visited this place a week before the madness began in Tel Aviv," Mindel told them, speaking barely loud enough for Bolan to make out her words. "He called it the heart of our nation. I never quite thought of it that way before."

McCarter scanned the walls inscribed with names, surrounding an eternal flame that hissed and flickered in the middle of the room. "It's easy to forget," he said.

"Here, too," Mindel admitted. "It's before us always, in our fiction, art and history, of course. But current events always seem to take precedence. Today's victims, and tomorrow's, overshadow the past."

"For what it's worth," Bolan said, "there'll be

fewer victims tomorrow thanks to Katz. Thanks to you.''

"It doesn't matter what I've done," Mindel told him, "but he would be pleased to hear you say that. He was never far from Israel in his heart, I think, even when he was traveling around the world.''

"It makes me wonder, though," McCarter said.

"Wonder?" Mindel asked.

"If we ever really make a difference. All these dead, and some folk say it could've been avoided if Hitler was killed at the start. Somehow, I can't help thinking that some other monster would've come along to take his place. It feels inevitable, somehow, if you follow me.''

"Perhaps it was," she said. "But not again. Never again.''

"I hope you're right," Bolan stated. But at heart, he wasn't sure. The Executioner had seen too much, and there was too much in the morning news each day that spoke of terror, pestilence and genocide. From Rwanda to East Timor, Guatemala to Myanmar, something told him there would always be more killing fields, more predators who cared for nothing and no one except themselves, their boundless appetites.

And while they roamed at large, there would be work to do.

"I need to say kaddish," Mindel told them. "Excuse me, please. I won't be long.''

McCarter looked embarrassed as he answered, "Take your time." Bolan stood silent. What was there to say?

She knelt before a railing near the flame and began to intone the Hebrew prayer for the dead. Bolan didn't understand a word of it, but the recitation still had a visceral power, drawn from Mindel's faith and from her grief. In some small measure, Bolan knew those attributes reflected the soul of a nation besieged, fighting for its life for more than half a century, from the day it was born.

Fighting forever? Endless war?

He knew the feeling, right, from personal experience. The bitter loss and lust for vengeance, tempered into something more enduring than revenge.

The soul of a crusade.

Where would the battle take him after this?

Would he prevail?

Surrounded by the dead, Mack Bolan closed his eyes in homage to a fallen friend. Tomorrow's enemies would come when they were ready.

And the Executioner would be there, waiting for them.

One more battle in the everlasting war.

It was his promise to the dead.

Amen.

James Axler
Outlanders®

MAD GOD'S WRATH

The survivors of the oldest moon colony have been revived from cryostasis and brought to Cerberus Redoubt, leaving behind an enemy in deep, frozen sleep. But betrayal and treachery bring the rebel stronghold under seige by the resurrected demon king of a lost world. With a prize hostage in tow to lure Kane and his fellow warriors, he retreats to the uncharted planet of mystery and impossibility for a final act of madness.

Available February 2004 at your favorite retail outlet.

Or order your copy now by sending your name, address, zip or postal code, along with a check or money order (please do not send cash) for $6.50 for each book ordered ($7.99 in Canada), plus 75¢ postage and handling ($1.00 in Canada), payable to Gold Eagle Books, to:

In the U.S.	In Canada
Gold Eagle Books	Gold Eagle Books
3010 Walden Avenue	P.O. Box 636
P.O. Box 9077	Fort Erie, Ontario
Buffalo, NY 14269-9077	L2A 5X3

Please specify book title with your order.
Canadian residents add applicable federal and provincial taxes.

GOLD EAGLE®

GOUT28